SO-CFI-062

All Q, No A

More Tales of a 10th-Grade SOCIAL CLIMBER

Other Graphia Titles

The Rise and Fall of a Tenth-Grade Social Climber
by Lauren Mechling and Laura Moser

A Certain Slant of Light
by Laura Whitcomb

I Can't Tell You
by Hillary Frank

After Summer
by Nick Earls

The Education of Robert Nifkin
by Daniel Pinkwater

Whatcha Mean, What's a Zine?
by Mark Todd and Esther Pearl Watson

Real Time
by Prina Moed Kass

Check out graphiabooks.com

All Q, No A

More Tales of a

10th-Grade

SOCIAL CLIMBER

by Lauren Mechling
& Laura Moser

An Imprint of Houghton Mifflin Company
Boston 2006

Copyright © 2006 by Lauren Mechling and Laura Moser

All rights reserved. Published in the United States by Graphia,
an imprint of Houghton Mifflin Company,
Boston, Massachusetts. For information about permission
to reproduce selections from this book, write to Permissions,
Houghton Mifflin Company, 214 Park Avenue South,
New York, New York 10003.

Graphia and the Graphia Logo are registered trademarks of Houghton Mifflin Company.

www.houghtonmifflinbooks.com

The text of this book is set in Apollo.

Library of Congress Cataloging-in-Publication Data
Mechling, Lauren.
All Q, no A : more tales of a 10th-grade social climber /
by Lauren Mechling and Laura Moser.
p. cm.
Sequel to: The rise and fall of a tenth-grade social climber.
Summary: Reconciled with her friends and enjoying life with her
father in New York City, fifteen-year-old Mimi hopes for a happier
second term at the progressive Baldwin School but soon finds herself
drawn into complications involving the school's finances, her father's
new girlfriend, and her own romantic entanglements.

ISBN 0-618-66378-9 (pbk. : alk. paper)

[1. High schools—Fiction. 2. Interpersonal relations—Fiction.
3. Fathers and daughters—Fiction. 4. Best friends—Fiction. 5. Friendship—Fiction. 6. Schools—Fiction. 7. New York (N.Y.)—Fiction.]
I. Moser, Laura. II. Title.
PZ7.M51269 All 2006
[Fic]—dc22
2005031527

ISBN-13: 978-0618-66378-1

Printed in the United States of America
HAD 10 9 8 7 6 5 4 3 2 1

To Ben and Anna

All Q, No A

More Tales of a

10th-Grade

SOCIAL CLIMBER

To: Roger Schulman
131 Barrow St., Apt. 1
NY, NY 10014

December 27

Dear Dad,
Hello from Day One of the tenth-grade girls' mystery vacation. We're supposed to keep the location a secret, but the Puerto Plata postmark might give it away. You would TOTALLY approve—we're at Green Amigas, a collective of women who plant community gardens for underprivileged locals. It's run by Ilana Dominguez, née Feldman, a Baldwin alum who married a Dominican financier she met on a vacation down here. Everyone's very hippie-dippy and zenned to the max. It's a wonder I haven't run into the Upstairs Judys yet!
Love and miss you to the moon,
Señorita Mimi Schulman

To: Rachel Lieber
3412 Sunset Blvd.
Houston, TX 77005

December 28

Rach,
I know, I know, you're probably fuming about my bailing on Texas for Christmas—but trust me, it's a long story. Not sure if I updated you on the massive social catastrophe that befell me at the end of last semester (I doubt it, since I was too humiliated to leave my bedroom, much less discuss it long-distance), but anyway, all's well that ends well, and I'm now in the Dominican Republic, vacationing with the friends I almost lost. I'll tell you all about it when we next see each other. Which might be soon, right? What about the promised NYC visit? C'mon, mama, how could you not? Crazy fun guaranteed, what do you think? Hi to everyone at holiday parties, OK? More soon,
Luuuuuuv,
Mimi

To: Ariel Schulman
Littlefield Dormitory Box #406
University of Texas
Austin, TX 78712

December 29

Whaddup, sis?
How's my favorite Kappa Kappa sister? Abs still hard as granite? It's bathing-suit land down here in the D.R., and I've dreamed of trading bodies with you several times. Are we really related? Life is not fair. . . . Weather is blissful and scenery all blue skies and tie-dyed sunsets. We spend most days gardening with earnest middle-aged women—you'd hate it. So how was Xmas? Did Mom get all Christian on you now that her Jewish husband is halfway across the country, or was she as annoyingly Freudian as ever? I realize I should send Mom a postcard but I have no desire to address it to Maurice, too, so please just tell them I'm alive and healthy.
XOXO,
Your tubby-tummied little sis,
Mimi

To: Sam Geckman
231 W. 87 St. Apt. 8A
NY, NY 10025

December 30

Sam,
Hi from the winter vacation I almost missed thanks to a certain on-off-on-off redheaded friend of mine, ahem, ahem. Right, so, um, I've started this postcard seven times already and realize there's no witty way of putting it: Last semester kind of (major understatement) sucked for us, but I really hope the next one is better. We're too cosmically connected to wreck such a special friendship. In other news, this vacation is truly awesome—still top-secret, but let's just say, you'd be way impressed with my "shallow" friends. If you dare so much as hint to anyone where this postcard comes from, you and I are through. All over again. Got it? Hope you're having fun in Florida and see you soon.
XOXO,
Mimi

To: Myrtle Lanchester
2401 Bolsover St.
Houston, TX 77005

December 31

Myrtilian,
Howdy from the Dominican Republic, where I'm planting veg-
etables for world peace. And you thought you knew me inside
out. . . . How's my favorite almost-stepsister holding up?
Please tell Simon he is the most beautiful, intelligent cat in
America—make that the Americas, as I've seen no feline con-
tenders on this island. Congrats on getting all your college
apps in. I so hope you choose a school in New York—the men
of Gotham await! You would love it down here—many kiss-
able botanists. On my next gardening excursion, you're defi-
nitely coming with.
X's and O's,
Mimi

P.S. HI, MOM! I KNOW YOU'RE READING THIS. FIN-
ISHED THE BOOK YOU SENT ABOUT THE MENTALLY
ILL STREET PEOPLE IN BEIRUT. VERY ILLUMINAT-
ING. HOW ABOUT SOMETHING A TAD *LIGHTER NEXT*
TIME?

To: Roger Schulman
131 Barrow St., Apt 1
NY, NY 10014

January 1

El Papá,
Happy New Year! I realize this will reach you long after I do,
but I couldn't resist . . . Como estas? Still surviving in a house-
hold of one? I hope you've remembered to shower and eat.
Apart from my most brutal sunburn ever, everything remains
dreamy, perfect, etc. Have dirt under toenails and know how
to say lettuce *in Spanish. Last night Ilana Dominguez threw*
an elaborate New Year's Eve bash. Picture moonlight, lapping
waves, and a fourteen-piece samba band. Have used all the
Polaroid film you gave me so I'll have plenty of pix. I miss and
love you so much.
XOXOXO,
Mimicita

P.S. Get this: One of my fellow Green Amigas residents was
Upstairs Judy #2's girlfriend "back in the Berkeley days." Did
I not call it?!

The Incredible Flying Goat Show Girl

IMAGINE THE TIME YOU COULD SAVE if you didn't have to say goodbye. Not the word *goodbye,* but the hugs, sniffles, and promises to stay in touch that accompany it. I could've mastered Swahili in the hours I spent bidding *adios* to our forty new best friends at Green Amigas. We were on our way out the door when Ilana Dominguez unveiled our sendoff *tres leches* cake, frosted with purple and white squiggles to resemble a head of cabbage. I thought it rude not to stay for a slice, or three.

By the time my friends and I reached the airport, our flight was already boarding, and lines at the check-in counters snaked outside. Lily, the most organized of the group, immediately started freaking out, but Pia, the daughter of Italian diplomats, rose to the occasion. She unapologetically glided to the front of the line and snapped her fingers for us to follow. When we obeyed, the other tourists revolted. "Get in line like everyone else!" one shouted. "Don't you dare!" another threatened. "We've been here since dawn!" I half sympathized with the people we cut, but not Pia, whose emotional intelligence was still playing catch-up with her sky-high IQ. "When will people understand jealousy is *so* unattractive?" she mused wearily, and handed us our boarding cards. We got to the gate with a minute to spare at a magazine kiosk. "And I mean *one* minute," Pia said. "As in, sixty seconds. I did *not* just make five thousand new enemies so we can miss our flight!"

With that, she disappeared behind a rack of novels in Spanish, leaving the rest of us to browse the newsstand's paltry offerings: inspirational greeting cards, tins of local nuts, and travel-size bottles of mouthwash. Of the several newspapers scattered across the floor, only the *Irish Standard* was in English. It was four pages long and cost more than most annual gym memberships.

"Perfect!" Jess scooped the *Standard* off the dingy floor. Depressed by her boyfriend Preston's long-distance neglect, Jess had spent much of our vacation perusing a gloomy book of Russian short stories, and I was glad to see her moving on to lighter reading material. "I'll get that," Viv said, and tried to take Jess's newspaper.

Jess had allowed our wealthy friends to pay for her week-long vacation, but here she drew the line. She didn't have cash to toss around like our friends did, but she had plenty of pride.

"It's mine," she huffed, "so *I'm* paying for it!"

"They just announced final boarding," Lily said nervously.

"No, seriously, let me buy it," Viv pressed. "It's only money."

"I said NO!" Jess protested. "End of conversation."

"Tick-tock, tick-tock . . . " Lily, genetically anal, was growing more and more impatient.

"C'mon, what part of *final boarding* do you people not get?"

I was admiring two amazing blank notebooks (neither of

which I could justify buying, given the number of unfilled journals I already had at home) when Pia shoved past me with a handful of novels in Spanish. We all watched in awe as Pia snatched both the *Irish Standard*, Viv's package of souvenir lighters, and then, for good measure, the two notebooks I was about to put back on the shelf.

"Does no one listen to poor Lily?" Pia seethed, throwing a stack of Dominican pesos onto the counter. "There's no time for multiple transactions—we have a plane to catch. *Vamos!*"

On the plane, I squeezed into a cramped seat designed to punish lanky 5'11" girls like myself, and waited for the short man in front of me to recline his chair back into my knees. Then, to distract myself, I studied my beautiful new notebooks. The first one—handmade, with a purple cloth cover—brought back fond memories of my bookbinding seminar at The Baldwin School last semester, highlights of which included Ivan Grimalsky's chronicle of his vegetarian Venus flytrap's "fight for life," Arthur Gray's book-burning presentation, and Blowjob Harry's "dinner party cookbook."

My second notebook was flimsy and spiral-bound, with a picture of two goats kissing on the cover and the words THE SANTO DOMINGO NATIONAL SHEEP AND GOAT SHOW. It was high kitsch, and I loved it.

I had special plans for both of my notebooks. To repent for ditching my dad over the holiday, I'd snapped endless pictures with his Polaroid, from shots of the community gardens to the gigantic I MISS YOU, DAD! I'd drawn in the carrot patch. (Dad was a professional photographer, so I knew he'd appreciate my creative use of his favorite camera.) The next day at school, I would paste these photos in the purple cloth notebook and give it to Dad for New Year's. While the flight attendant explained emergency evacuation procedures, I opened the notebook with the kissing goats and felt the rush of looking at the blank page.

Across the aisle, Jess was skimming the expensive Irish newspaper with a bored expression while Pia appeared entranced by her steamy Spanish bodice-ripper. Viv, between them, had strapped on her monster headphones and was listening to a reggaetón CD she'd purchased on the road one day. Next to me, Lily scribbled on a yellow legal pad, brainstorming for the first winter edition of the *Baldwin Bugle,* the school paper where she worked and I played.

I wrote a column called "Texan in Gotham," billed as an examination of Baldwin culture through an outsider's eyes. At first I'd enjoyed this excuse to learn more about my new school, but lately I'd struggled to come up with a new story idea every two weeks. It's hard to keep that outsider's perspective when you're more on the inside every day. Writing about my winter break would prove even more challenging, given the hush-hush nature of our Green Amigas experience. Baldwin had a weird, cultish tradition shrouded in secrecy and intrigue that dated back two decades. Every year, the most popular sophomore girls embarked on a trip to an undisclosed location and the next year elected another group to follow in their footsteps. Speculations about the nature of this trip ran rampant, and most Baldwinites (including, I admit, myself) pictured something five-star, like a cruise to St. Barts or a visit to a royal castle in Tuscany.

Dusty, un-air-conditioned Green Amigas fulfilled none of these fantasies. Its guests slept in bunk beds and peed in outhouses. Even so, no over-the-top celebrity destination could outclass our week. I stared out the window, restless and exhilarated, reliving the amazing experience. On how many vacations can you sunbathe, salsa dance with farmers, binge on deep-fried plantains, harvest cabbage, and win back your best friends? I'd dreamed about this mystery trip from the moment Sam Geckman, my oldest friend, told me about it last September and bet me I couldn't make the cut. Sam believed I'd been in Texas too long to navigate the bewildering world of Baldwin, a school that rejected grades, valedictorians, and even tests with right or wrong answers. Its social traditions were stranger still: girls who in Texas would make prom queen were, by Baldwin's exacting standards, considered too "conformist." Meanwhile, girls who could pass for hobos in most cities, with their sloppily layered outfits and unkempt hair, reigned supreme over their classmates. Talk about disorienting. If only the school had outlined these customs in its welcome packet.

Offended by Sam's lack of faith in my social skills, I had vowed to score an invitation to the popular girls' annual winter trip early last semester. Though I ended up winning the wager, my victory came at a huge cost. In retaliation for a grisly romantic episode, Sam stole my journal and posted its damning contents on the Internet. With one click of the mouse, Sam exposed my unflattering first impressions of the girls and—even worse—

my mercenary scheme to win them over. And just like that, the girls hated me, I hated Sam, and my happy New York existence effectively ended.

When I posted a teary apology on the Internet, I wasn't arrogant or insane enough to expect a response. I was shocked, then, when the girls showed up on my doorstep at the beginning of winter break and invited me to the Dominican Republic—even Viv, though she remained pissed off at me. I knew I didn't deserve the honor, and throughout the trip I kept worrying that my friends' forgiveness was an act, groundwork for the perfect revenge scheme. But our week together was catastrophe-free, unless you count Ilana Dominguez's New Year's party, when the girls encouraged me to wear a white dress and then, in front of hundreds of revelers, hurled me into the pool. So much for vengeance—before I hit the surface, the four of them jumped right in after me. That was when it sunk in: Lily, Jess, Pia, and even Viv really *were* my friends.

Lily Morton, only daughter of the glamorous domestic goddess Margaret Morton, lived in nubby gray sweatshirts and wore her brown hair in a messy ponytail. Though obsessed with success, warm-hearted Lily lacked her mother's cutthroat instincts. Even after getting to know the other girls, I always felt a special attachment to Lily, who was my first actual friend in the group.

Despite her exotic beauty, half-Jewish, half-Filipino Vivian Steinmann had major self-confidence issues. She suffered from a permanent inferiority complex courtesy of her academic torments and lived in the permanent shadow of her supremely cool older sister, Mia, the darling of the Brooklyn art scene. Thin-skinned Viv refused to speak to me for the first half of the trip, and it took a shared near-death experience in the back of a ramshackle Jeep for her to warm up to me. At Ilana's party, after the two of us ran dripping wet into a cabana bathroom, Viv confessed her "sort-of crush" on Sam. Rather than tell Viv that Sam and I had hooked up last semester, I gave her my blessing and even told her about my passion for Max Roth, the smartest and most mysterious member of the tenth-grade class, or humanity.

When she wasn't gardening or reading, boy-crazy Jessica Gillespie mooned over her ultralame boyfriend, Preston, who had ignored every single one of her expensive international phone calls. At first glance, preppy Jess was the blandest of the group, but her perfect exterior was misleading. She was a serious bookworm, and though I'd never seen any of her poems, I'd heard they were heart-stoppingly good. One day while the two of us planted seedlings, Lily told me about the scandalous affair Jess's dad had conducted with her sixth-grade Life Science teacher, Gwendolyn Carroll, four years earlier. Baldwin fired the voluptuous Gwen, and then—in a concession characteristic of the school's ultraliberal philosophy—placed Jess on full scholarship. After her dad, and his income, vanished, Jess was forced to remain at the institution that was indirectly responsible for her parents' breakup. Lily attributed Jess's weirdness about men, namely her do-or-die passion for Preston, to her father's public abandonment.

Pia Pazzolini, another serious piece of work, resembled a cross between Jackie Kennedy and an expensive show pony, and had an even more complicated personality. She was simultaneously nerdy and glamorous, equal parts bossy and loyal, vain and humble. And though Pia had everything any girl could want—credit cards galore, luxurious vacations, a perfect math SAT score in the eighth grade—she was also a chronic shoplifter. From what I could gather, her habit wasn't limited to designer cashmere; she also helped herself to drugstore lipsticks, supermarket cookies, even hard-boiled eggs from the school cafeteria. Because Pia had no material justification for this compulsion, I could only assume deeper psychological issues were to blame.

And then there was me, Mimi Schulman. I had, until recently, grown up in a boringly normal nuclear unit: scatterbrained mother, oblivious father, wannabe-anorexic big sister. Having divided my life between Texas and New York, I felt at home in both places, but I belonged to neither. I loved Dolly Parton, Bette Davis, J. D. Salinger, the Houston Astros, and cats, in no particular order. I should also add that I'd managed to turn fifteen without kissing a boy.

But though I was awkward and inexperienced and uncosmopolitan, the girls liked me, and it worked. I took a pen from my overstuffed backpack and got started on my Goat Show book. It was New Year's Day—what better opportunity to draft a few life-altering resolutions?

1. Be the best friend ever to Pia, Viv, Lily, and Jess. Esp. Viv. You so owe them.
2. Be nicer to Amanda France / a better long-distance friend to Rachel / around more often for Dad's weekly pancake dinners.

3. No more sunburns, sun blisters, or excess freckles. Wear thick muumuu and sun visor on next tropical vacation and slather on moisturizer with SPF every day, even in the dead of winter.

4. Stop slouching. Tall is beautiful.

5. Cultivate mysterious, woman-of-the-world aura to improve chances with mysterious man-of-the-world Max Roth.

6. Think less about boys and more about the grave threats of globalism and other issues raised by kick-ass women at Green Amigas.

7. Take advantage of Baldwin's course offerings and load up on electives. To quote our headmaster, Zora Blanchard: "Learning is a feast. Glutton up!"

8. Speaking of which, try not to eat so repulsively much. In public.

9. No more cramming sessions on subway ride to school, no matter how easy assignments. Do home-work the night before to make time for unassigned (or Mom-assigned) material on commute, thereby developing intellect and, depending on the nature and strangeness of reading material, enhancing mysterious, woman-of-the-world aura (see res. numero 5).

I shut the book. The nuzzling goats on the cover got me thinking about Max, which, I'll admit, might seem a little creepy. But that wasn't why I loved my new notebook. As a memento of our trip, the Goat Show book would bring me luck in the upcoming year,

I felt sure of it. I vowed to carry it with me everywhere—use it as a repository for deep thoughts, amusing ambulatory observations, *Bugle* article ideas, grocery needs—anything, everything, and even a little bit of nothing.

Doo-Dah, Doo-Dah

THE BALDWIN STUDENT BODY came back from winter vacation unrecognizably improved. My classmates had devoted the last two weeks to fine-tuning their wardrobes and redesigning their eyebrows, submitting to scruffings and buffings and blow-dries. I, too, was unrecognizable, but not for the better. On the last day of the trip, our first with no gardening responsibilities, I'd thrown caution to the wind and hit the beach sans SPF. Big mistake, huge. But what do you expect from a girl whose mother had nagged her on this very subject two million times over the course of her life?

When I alighted from the town car Vivian's parents had dispatched to the airport for us and entered our narrow brownstone on Barrow Street, I didn't yet feel sunburned, just woozy, too exhausted to catch up with Dad over a sit-down dinner. Oddly enough, Dad didn't seem to mind the brush-off. He was acting strange and giddy. Too sleepy to investigate his behavior, I grabbed a leftover bowl of what appeared to be homemade baked ziti from the fridge and, without bothering to heat it up, took it down to my room. Dad and I would hang out the next afternoon, after I'd slept and pieced together his gift.

That night, the rash erupted. The next morning, I woke up fried, sunburned on body parts I hadn't known existed: armpits, the insides of my knees, the backs of my ears. My skin was as raw as ground hamburger meat. And the ache—the ache was indescribable. Motion intensified the torture, walking especially. I arrived at school on time, but it took me thirty minutes to reach my locker, by which point first period was more than halfway over. At least it was only World Civ, a gut at Baldwin. Because our snuggly teacher, Stanley, rejected the "hegemony" of taking attendance, I opted to skip the last ten minutes of what would no doubt be another one of his directionless roundtable discussions. My time would be better spent inching toward my new spring semester second-period elective, Indigenous Crafts, which met in Baldwin's "studio space," a dilapidated old brownstone across the street from the main building.

After the pain of crossing Pierrepont Street, I panted and winced up the studio building's narrow staircase, periodically edging toward the rail to let unblistered students lope ahead of me. I'd just perfected a rhythm, hopping up the stairs without bending any joints, when something slammed into me from behind, propelling me into the wall.

"OUCH!" I yelped as another layer of epidermis departed. A skinny girl on her cell phone shoved past me.

"Excuse *you!*" she said bitchily, and flicked her ass-long, peroxided hair. The dyed blond mane struck my body like a thousand tiny whips. I winced in pain.

Indifferent to the five-alarm damage she had inflicted, the girl immediately returned to her conversation. "Yeah, I *know!*"

she said into her tiny cell phone. "How many times do I have to tell you? I read the script, and it sucked, all right? Screw what her agent thinks—I am *not* wasting my time on some straight-to-DVD disaster, do you hear me?" The girl's chicken legs vanished after the next landing, leaving me to grip the banister, weep for my lost skin, and wonder who that demon-girl was. Because I'd been at Baldwin only four discombobulating months, I was still unacquainted with most of my classmates. My friends, though, had surely met this monster diva, with her designer high heels and clingy minidress, and I made a mental note to ask about her.

As I trudged up the final flight of stairs, I wished for the galactic-scale self-esteem of Pia, her enviable ease in the world. Pia—and Lily, too, probably—would've laughed off this creature, but not me. At nine-thirty in the morning I was already feeling completely depressed. The Indigenous Crafts studio soon boosted my spirits, however. The room had been decorated like a Hawaiian hut in an Elvis movie, with potted bamboos and leafy houseplants that cast intriguing shadows on the assembled students' faces. The studio's paint-splattered radio was broadcasting an orchestra of bongo drums at maximum volume. The classroom was surprisingly crowded for Baldwin, the school that boasted the highest teacher-to-student ratio in the city. I spotted Viv in one of her trademark black-on-black outfits right away, and this, too, was surprising. When I'd mentioned signing up for Indigenous Crafts in the D.R., Viv hadn't piped up. Then again, maybe she'd still hated me back then.

Viv was waving me over but I saw no free stools in her vicinity—or, in fact, anywhere else. After a few seconds, I spotted a seat in the distant corner of the studio, directly across from Sam, my oldest friend in the world. Still unsure of how things stood with him, I approached him cautiously, half dreading the encounter. Had Sam received my sappy postcard yet? What had he made of my proposal for a truce? His expression revealed nothing.

But as I drew closer to his worktable, Sam lifted his eyebrows and smirked. "Hey," I said, my voice as friendly and relaxed as I could manage.

"Nice," he said, with a low, construction-worker whistle. "I've been looking for something to match that stoplight out front—I think you'll do just perfectly." My face flushed—even darker, that is. Before Sam's comment, pain management had eclipsed all fashion-related concerns. Now my fleece pants and hooded sweatshirt, the only garments loose enough for my raw, wrecked skin, suddenly filled me with shame. Sam, a pale, freckly redhead, never overdosed on the sun. I knew this because I had known him all my life. Even as a pre-kindergartner at City Sprouts day camp, he'd worn baseball caps and retreated to the shade while I enjoyed my bagged lunch under the scorching midday rays. "You sure you shouldn't be at the emergency room, hotcakes?"

"Shut up." I concentrated on dragging the stool out. But as I levered myself onto the seat, I understood why it had been vacant. The stool was broken, its third leg dangling loosely like the wand of a metronome.

"Really, Mims," Sam said. "*El sol* did quite a number on you."

"Did you not hear me?" I growled. *"Shut up."*

To avoid wobbling over and further disfiguring myself, I planted my feet on the floor and pretended to lean against the stool as Sam continued teasing me, louder and louder, attracting the attention of students at neighboring tables, who started to point and snicker. Arthur Gray, Baldwin's resident wise-ass, shot me a double thumbs-up. To think that I'd poured out my heart to Sam, and on a postcard his parents were likely to intercept! When I next opened my Goat Show book, I'd be sure to strike that suicidal promise to re-befriend my remorseless tormenter.

"Shalo-o-OM, comrades!" yodeled our teacher, Yuri Knutz. He stood at the main worktable with a frayed hardcover book in one hand and a rotten coconut in the other. "Welcome, everyone, to Russian Dissident Fiction!" he said, and banged these two objects together like castanets.

Russian Dissident Fiction? Uh-oh. That made me 0 for 2 for the day.

"I'd also like to welcome everyone here to my Indigenous Crafts seminar," Yuri Knutz went on, and set about theatrically emptying a brown paper bag from Wild Things health food store. "Owing to certain unavoidable last-minute circumstances, we've had to combine the classes."

People starting shifting and murmuring, wondering what was going on.

"Sounds odd, doesn't it?" Yuri said agreeably. "To avoid confusion, we're going to alternate the subjects every other session. Today, we'll focus on crafts, and at our next meeting, we'll read a story. A Russian one, of course. Make sense?"

Arthur Gray spoke on behalf of everyone when he shouted, "NO!"

Last semester, when persuading me to enroll in the Indigenous Crafts elective, Sam had described Yuri Knutz as a one-time "up-and-coming sensation" of the New York art scene. Now in his midforties, Yuri hadn't come up much further than this fourth-floor studio, but he seemed pretty upbeat as he cried, "No use dilly-dallying—let's kick-start Indigenous Crafts right away! For this curriculum, we'll be using found objects and found objects only. In indigenous cultures, remember, there are no twenty-four-hour superstores, no organic delivery services. I just returned from a trip to Peru, where I saw indigenous life *in action*. Natives live off the land down there, making do with whatever they scrounge up—an inspiring philosophy that we'll be applying to art supplies!"

Yuri rubbed his palms together excitedly, then reached under the table for another Wild Things goodies bag. "Our goal," he said, "is to be resourceful with the basic materials of everyday life. Use absolutely anything you'd like."

"What about people?" Arthur Gray asked from beneath the signature baseball cap that obscured ninety percent of his face. Ordinarily, I tuned out Arthur and his nonstop witticisms, just not when he happened to be positioned next to dreamboat extraordinaire Max Roth. Just inches away from Arthur, Max was leaning back on his stool, staring upward, his whole face on display for my marveling pleasure. While Arthur entertained, I stealthily admired the contours of Max's gorgeous profile, giving special attention to his dimpled cheeks.

Perhaps I stared too long because Max turned to look at me—just as I was digging my hand into my sweatshirt to loosen a charbroiled swath of skin caught under my bra. I shot my eyes back to Arthur.

"People can be part of art, right?" he was asking. "Like an arm. Or a butt?"

Yuri mulled Arthur's suggestion with great seriousness before nodding. "Why, yes, that's an excellent suggestion, Arthur—provided, of course, you haven't purchased the people for that express purpose. Human trade is *not* coolness."

"What about kitty litter?" asked Meret Altman, a short guy who played fantasy games in the library and contributed articles on science trends to the *Bugle*.

"There you go!" Yuri Knutz liked this suggestion even more than Arthur's. "Kitty litter would be a real trip—way to think like an indigenous craftsman!"

"Um, excuse me?" Sara Ramos was waving her hand in the air. "Hello?"

Sara was a senior who wore raincoats every day, whatever the weather. Every self-respecting Baldwinite needed a shtick, and poor Sara had simply waited too long to choose hers, when only raincoats and heart-printed shoelaces remained. So it was shiny rain slickers for her, even on the sunniest days.

"Isn't this a jewelry-making elective?" Sara asked. "Aren't we, like, learning to set pendants and shit?"

Yuri shook his head regretfully, unbothered by her classroom cursing. "Not in this class, I'm afraid," he said. "At the department meeting, Michelle did mention a metalworking elective, but that was before the budget doo-dah."

The words "budget doo-dah" got the restless class's attention at last. At Baldwin the word *budget* was used about as often as *winner* or *percent*—i.e., never. Baldwin was among the most elite private schools in the city, and therefore also among the richest. Even if we had no lacrosse field or marching band, no school could beat Baldwin for its supply of NASA-grade telescopes and authentic Broadway costumes. The words "budget doo-dah" rippled through my head. Was this why they'd combined the classes—because the school was going under?

Giving us no chance to ask follow-up questions, Yuri hustled us to the front of the classroom. "Now, believe it or not," he said as we shuffled toward the main drafting table, "I stumbled upon every single one of these gems on my way from the Borough Hall station this morning." He fanned out his arms and let us examine his assortment of indigenous treasures: an opened airmail envelope, a wet sock, a sad-looking Dunkin' Donuts bag.

Nonindigenous materials included glue sticks, crumbly Crayolas, and rusty scissors, but these also technically qualified as "found objects," since Yuri had found them in the classroom.

Midway through this show-and-tell, Sara Ramos took off, her purple rain slicker squeaking as she strutted out the door.

"Ugh, I am *totally* switching to African Drumming before I get scabies," Jasmine Lowenstein muttered, and followed Sara out.

Viv left next. "I'll be back for the Russian Dissident whatever," she said, a note of apology in her voice. She lingered at the door for a few seconds, gazing at Sam and me. Did she expect me to go with her? I wondered. Unable to brave another four flights of stairs, I just smiled wanly in response.

Yuri, meanwhile, took no notice of these defections. After peacefully distributing the materials, he put us to work on our "tribal self-portrait masks."

Back at our worktable, Sam pushed his stool toward me. "Use it," he said. "I work better on my feet."

Too weak to protest, I flung myself down. While eager to ask Sam about the "budget doo-dah," I was still irritated by his sunburn taunts, so I just took his stool with a soft grunt of thanks.

A few minutes later, as Arthur Gray emitted Tarzan sounds, Sam broke our conversational stalemate. "Yuri Knutz here," he said in a funny accent, holding his mask over his face. "Over break, while researching handicapped tortoises in Papua New Guinea, I was abducted by a tribe of man-eating indigenous craftsmen. I was forced to listen to sitar music by day and sleep on a pallet of kitty litter by night. I've only just escaped and must inflict this illuminating experience on my students."

I couldn't help it: I started laughing hysterically. So what if Sam had ruined my life last semester—he remained the only person at Baldwin with any perspective on the place. Pia, Jess, Lily, and Vivian saw nothing bizarre about a school that offered meditation meetings instead of phys. ed., and electives like Victorian Etiquette and Vegan Baking Against Globalization.

"Class!" Yuri Knutz suddenly called us to attention. He was standing behind Max Roth and gesturing for us to join him. "I want everyone to see what a tremendous job Max has done with this project. Talk about indigenous!"

Yuri indicated a Wild Things bag that had been cut into the shape of a potato, with asymmetrical cotton-ball blobs for eyes, a mashed orange peel for a nose, and coconut hair pasted haphazardly along the perimeter. The artwork reminded me of a project a two-year-old might bring home from daycare, but what did I know? Baldwin's faculty unanimously believed Max was fated to become a world-famous artist any day now.

"Can you demystify the process of creation for us a bit?" Yuri implored Max.

"Uh, sure," Max said. He stepped back from his table and assessed his project, while I assessed his shoulders under his thin white T-shirt. "Over break, I was reading about tribal arts in Melanesia, and there was this, um, shrunken sloth head? I wanted to play with forms that are of this world and, like, transcendental?"

Anyone else delivering that speech would have been accused of ass-kissing or insanity, but Max was met only with *oohs* and *aahs* from his audience. He could read the instructions from a nasal-spray bottle and still sound deep and dreamy. Porter Yurnell punctured my reverie with a supersonic burp.

"I got one, too!" he bellowed. "Yo, come check it out!" He displayed a bag with a wad of Raisinets Scotch-taped on it. "It's me if I had only one eye."

"I see." Yuri Knutz nodded encouragingly. "Porter's got it. All it takes is a little imagination and inspiration."

Back at our tables, I felt looser around Sam.

"So, apart from the scorch trauma, you had fun in the sun?" he asked me.

"*Mucho.*"

"That's good—really," Sam said, his voice warm and kind—the old Sam's voice. "I'm really glad you got to go, after everything. Your postcard—" He stopped. "Your postcard was really nice. It, um, made a lot of sense to me."

"Thanks," I said quietly. "It, um, made a lot of sense to me, too."

And then, like little children, we stayed hunched over the worktables, Crayolas and scissors in motion. In our silent cutting and drawing, Sam and I had reached our old understanding at last, and I was overjoyed.

The Multi-Accented Home

On the subway ride from school that afternoon, I looked forward to catching up with Dad almost as much as I looked forward to soothing my raw skin in a lukewarm bath with Epsom salt. I'd finished Dad's photo album in Lance's bio class, and as I walked from the West Fourth station to our brownstone, I pictured Dad poring over the stupendous Polaroids while I babbled about my rad vacation.

I never factored Fenella von Dix into my after-school equation, but when I walked inside the apartment, there she was, charm bracelets jangling and ostrich neck bulging, looking right at home at 131 Barrow Street.

"Mimi, welcome back!" Fenella gurgled in her weird accent, flapping open her bony arms for a hug. I recoiled in horror, but Fenella had already surged forward to trap my throbbing body in her talons. As I tried to extricate myself from her embrace, I remembered first Dad's high spirits the night before, then the unexpected contents of our refrigerator that morning.

Since moving to New York, Dad and I had subsisted on take-out from the celebrated ethnic eateries of Greenwich Village. But that morning, instead of rock-hard pizza crust and week-old

Kung Pao chicken, the shelves contained actual groceries, milk and yogurt and fruit. And suddenly it all made sense: Fenella von Dix, an installation artist by trade, had expertly installed herself in our apartment. And to think I'd only been out of town for a week.

In the kitchen, Dad was whistling and making pancakes— yet another unpleasant jolt, since today was Monday and pancake night was Tuesday. Sure, last semester I'd skipped a few sessions of this holy father-daughter dining tradition, but back then I was frazzled and disoriented, busy assimilating into a new academic environment. Dad was—well, Dad was an adult.

He grinned happily when he saw me. "Hey, Miss Mimikins," he said. "What luck—you're just in time for Pancake Olympics." Screwing up his face, Dad prepared for what he called his "famous flap-flips."

"Here goes." He tossed the oblong pancake in the air and stepped back triumphantly just as the disk splattered the stovetop.

"Try using the pan as a catching mitt," I suggested. "*Or* try waiting until a Tuesday night."

"Why? Is Tuesday the new Saturday or something?" Dad asked playfully. But then he looked at me and his face drooped. "Oh, Mims, I'm sorry," he said. "It's just that Fenella was hungry, and I had nothing else on tap. You know I'm not the craftiest guy in the food department."

"Yeah, right," I said. "Since when does she eat solid food, anyway?"

"Now, now. Be nice," Dad said, adding in a low voice, "She's in the next room."

"Yeah, thanks for the news flash."

"Besides," Dad went on, "she's not to blame for her metabolism—I swear, Mimi, that woman eats almost as much as *you* do."

Oh, right, forgive me for overlooking Fenella's divine perfection. I'm sure in her spare time, she'd also single-handedly saved the whales and the ozone layer. When I'd met Fenella at the Pazzolinis' pre-Thanksgiving dinner party in the Hamptons, I'd happily handed over Dad's number, little suspecting she'd stake her claim this quickly—or ever. Granted, Dad was still vulnerable after Mom dumped him for Maurice the squishy physicist, but Fenella von Dix? The anorexic installation artist with the Saturday-morning-cartoon accent? Was Dad's judgment really that impaired, his desperation that profound?

"I'm making a monster batch," Dad said. "There's enough to go around—what do you say?"

"I'm not the least bit hungry," I lied.

"I'm using those mini–chocolate chips you love."

"I'm. Not. Hungry."

Poor Dad. I was being a tough broad, especially since I'd ditched him over the holidays, not vice versa. Remembering this, I took a step toward him and was about to pull the photo album from my Air India tote bag when—poof! Fenella slithered into the kitchen, my favorite baby-blue crocheted blanket draped over her shoulders like a cape. The tender moment was gone forever.

"Mimi, your dad's going through *quite* the flat-cake phase," she said. "He made ginger-raspberry on Friday, and for Sunday brunch it was—oh, remind me again, Roger?"

"Pistachio-cassis." Dad's voice was sheepish. He turned his back on me to concentrate on the frying pan.

"Oh, of *course*," Fenella said, and with that soupçon of powdered sugar dusted on top—oh, Mimi, talk about ambrosial!"

"So you've been doing this often, then," I said, more a statement than a question, my eyes trained on the nape of Dad's long neck.

"*Mais oui!*" Fenella simpered. "I've never seen anyone so deep into a new hobby. *Some*thing must have gotten into that man!"

Pardon me while I puke. As if Dad had never wielded a spatula before Fenella's scrawny ass! While Dad flipped another pancake, this time elegantly, I scrapped my photo album plans and resigned myself to start work on this week's "Texan in Gotham: Reflections of a Recent Arrival" column for the *Bugle*. It was due the next morning, and I didn't even have a topic yet—the highly classified nature of my Green Amigas sojourn limited what I could write about. If I missed tomorrow's deadline, I could always submit a piece for the next issue in two weeks, so maybe I should first knock out the plant life cycles project my bio teacher, Lance, had assigned: "Get a (Plant) Life." We were supposed to describe the stages of a plant's development in the form of a social calendar. "Be creative," Lance had told us. "Plants can have social obligations, too—coffee dates at the solar café, dinner at the photosynthesis greasy spoon."

Dad and Fenella didn't notice when I excused myself. Once in my bedroom, I was too depressed by their flirtathon to focus on homework and decided to tackle one of my New Year's resolutions: reconnecting with Amanda France. Amanda was the blond, beautiful, fat-free squash fanatic who had befriended me during my first hour at Baldwin. After one seriously lame night at her favorite spoken-word café, I'd pretty much ditched her. In December, when my friends pretty much ditched me, Amanda stood by me. She was even at my house the afternoon that Lily, Jess, Pia, and Viv had shown up to give me a second chance and whisk me off to the Dominican Republic. I wanted to make up for my brisk goodbye to her that day, to prove to her—and to myself—that I wasn't a complete schmuck. I picked up the phone and dialed her number. An older-sounding woman with a voice as bright and energetic as Amanda's answered and informed me that her daughter had gone straight from school to the gym, to "burn off all those stocking stuffers." I left no message, assuring Mrs. France that Amanda and I would catch up at school the next day.

A few minutes later I was staring despondently at a blank computer screen when Dad appeared in the doorway. "I just had an idea," he said. "Why don't we invite Sam over here, get a little back-to-school party going?"

"Uh, uh . . ." I fumbled for an appropriate answer. For reasons I couldn't voice, Dad's generous suggestion made my stomach churn. Last semester, Sam had all but moved into the Schulman residence, spending most weeknights on our couch, but then we ruined the comfy sibling setup by hooking up—not just once, but twice, and semi-extensively. My adorably out-of-it Dad, of course, knew nothing of these exploratory sessions, or of Sam's subsequent betrayal. So despite out provisional truce in Indigenous Crafts, I couldn't invited Sam for dinner yet, not on the first night of school. It seemed too . . . *soon* or something.

Before I'd formulated an excuse, Fenella popped her head into the bedroom. "Oh, yoo-hoo!" she twittered. "For a second there, I thought I'd misplaced you!"

"Fen, have you met Sam, my surrogate son, yet?" Dad, still determinedly jolly, asked the intruder.

"No, Rogey, I don't believe I have," Fenella replied, and it was "Rogey" that did it.

Screw any lingering awkwardness between Sam and me: I needed a buffer ASAP. A half-hour later Dad was folding paper towels into untidy diamonds when the doorbell sounded. I hurtled to let Sam in, crying "Hi!" with such off-the-charts enthusiasm that he staggered backward and gave me a strange look.

"Don't ask," I muttered, and as soon as he laid eyes on Fenella he seemed to understand.

"I love double dining," he said, bounding into the living room. "I just rocked some roast chicken uptown at the Geckman Estate, but I'm equal opportunity." In one motion he shucked off his coat, sneakers, and backpack. Then, on his way to the table, he inspected his surroundings appreciatively. "Hey, I like what you've done in here. It's very—Turkish."

Sam directed the compliment to my dad, but Fenella seized it. "Roger, I like this boy already!" she oozed, plumping the beaded magenta floor pillow at her feet. "I thought this place needed a few personal touches," she told Sam, "so we did a bit of accent shopping last week!"

Sam threw me a what-the-hell glance as, for the first time, I observed the so-called accents—shiny fringed pillows, all in garish shades of marigold and chartreuse and fuchsia, piled in every corner of the room. How had I *possibly* overlooked these hideous home improvements? I was scanning the room for more von Dix territorial markings when Dad summoned us to the table.

Aside from praise for Dad's inventive mesclun-mandarin appetizer and slightly mushy pancakes, conversation faltered. My earlier misgivings about Sam obviously had some basis, because he soon lapsed into quiet nervousness. Oh, if only glittering Quinn would soar into the apartment! Quinn, Dad's favorite student in a photography course he taught at the New School last summer, was a regular on Barrow Street. He helped Dad develop prints in exchange for some cash, twenty-four-hour access to the darkroom, digital cable, frequent takeout dinners, and the singular pleasure of our around-the-clock company. More so even than Sam, Quinn was part of my New York family, and with him on a prolonged visit to his *real* family in Ohio, our dinner was doomed.

After several fruitless attempts to enliven the conversation, Dad, in desperation, mentioned a letter he'd received from Baldwin that morning. "They're hitting everyone up for some development fund," he said. "You can sign up by category— 'friend' is ten grand, and 'family' is twenty-five. Talk about nerve." Dad shook his head. "I was pretty put out by the whole tone of it."

"Yeesh," Sam said. "Talk about desperado—they should introduce a 'prostitute' category for parents who donate their children's organs along with the buildings."

"There might have been one," Dad said. "I stopped reading at 'superhero'—forty grand. Seriously, how could they think that, on top of tuition, I'd want to fork over another small fortune? Mimi, have you been misrepresenting my material success?"

Fenella looked up from her plate, her prominent neck tendons twitching and bulging, and grinned.

"Beats me," I said. "Our art teacher said something about a 'budget doo-dah' this morning, but that's all I know."

Fenella coughed. "Budget doo-dah?" she repeated. "What a *quaint* way of putting it."

"What do you mean?" Dad asked.

"I don't think this information is public domain yet," Fenella said, "but, well, I have this friend, Helen—who has this *fantastic* sense of humor, really irreverent. We're in this wo*ooon*derful nineteenth-century book club together . . . she's the one who got me so *hooked* on Trollope, in fact—"

"What does Trollope have to do with Baldwin?" I couldn't help but cut in rudely.

"Oh, yes, Helen." Fenella brought herself back. "Where was I? Oh, yes, well, Helen *also* happens to be on the board of Baldwin, and apparently one of the trustees made a major investment boo-boo last year."

Now, stocks and bonds aren't exactly my specialty, but I got the basic gist of Fenella's gossip. Apparently, some finance genius transferred part of Baldwin's endowment from a mutual fund to a "risk-free" technology stock. After a few months of gratifying returns, the stock tanked bigtime over Christmas, severely depleting Baldwin's "liquid assets" and constricting the school's operating budget. Until a smarter advisor could "reallocate" its remaining investments, Baldwin had very little ready cash. This much I definitely understood: Baldwin was dead broke.

"So *that's* why we're using kitty litter for art supplies," I said.

"Yeah, and Frank Abrahams told me the tech crew is in charge of hand-making decorations for the spring dance," said Sam. "The only cool thing is that Max Roth—you know him, right, Mimi?"

Eyes on my pancakes, I nodded quickly. "What about him?" Amazingly enough, clueless Sam *still* didn't know about my crush on Max.

"Well, he's this superstar painter," Sam told Dad and Fenella, "and the school has asked him to do a series of thematic paintings to decorate the cafeteria the night of the dance—for free, of course. Compare that to last year, when the theme was 'flower power,' and Zora commissioned the staff of the Brooklyn Botanic Garden to fill the room with orchids and plant Japanese maple trees. They even installed a lily pond in the lobby. It was completely over the top."

While Fenella gasped at the beauty of it all, Dad seemed genuinely troubled by these revelations. "So what does this mean?" he asked. "Should I start looking for tenth-grade openings at other schools?"

"Of *course* not," Fenella said. "Helen said there's been talk of selling the studio building, which is worth a king's ransom, and converting the cafeteria into a makeshift art studio and making the students go out for lunch every day."

"That wouldn't be the worst," I said, thinking of all the delicious and affordable restaurants near Baldwin. A Croatian diner was slated to open any day.

After helping Dad clear the table, I took my Goat Show notebook to the couch, where I planned to give my "Texan in Gotham" column one last stab.

"Don't worry, I'm not going to distract you," Sam said, plopping on the cushion directly next to mine. "I have work to do, too." He took an old *New Yorker* off the coffee table, glanced at a thumbnail restaurant write-up, and flung the magazine back down.

I didn't say anything. Part of me wished Sam would leave, for the sake of our still-delicate reconciliation. Another part of me dreaded being left alone with Dad and Fen-ella again, a third wheel on their accent pillow love-mobile.

Ignoring Sam was a worthless exercise. Before I'd even closed my Goat Show book Sam brought up the "mystery vacation."

"The postmark gave away the location, remember?" he said. "So you might as well spill the rest. Were any satanic rituals involved? Were your friends the most popular human beings ever to grace the poverty-ridden provinces of the Dominican Republic?"

Not this again—already. "Poor Sam," I tutted. "It's highly unbecoming to diss your fan club."

"What do you mean, my fan club?" In roundabout language, I alluded to Viv's "not exactly a crush" on him.

"Viv *Steinmann?*" Sam was openly incredulous. He rubbed

the knees of his jeans. *"She* has a thing for *me?"*

"Yeah, as if you never suspected it."

"No, actually, I didn't," Sam said. His mouth still hung wide open.

"Well, what do you think? Are you interested?" Sure, it was weird to set Sam up, but maybe if he had a girlfriend, things would return to normal between us.

"I don't really feel comfortable discussing this with you," Sam said quickly. "Can we talk about something else?"

"Fine," I said. "But don't think I'm dropping it forever—I like watching you squirm too much. How about *your* winter break then?" I loved that the ultrapretentious Geckmans now wintered in Florida. When Sam and I were little, his parents spent vacations on Himalayan yak treks and "late Byzantium" tours of Istanbul. I guess even the most pompous culture-lovers eventually must eventually cut loose.

"Wacked out in the extreme," Sam said. "The tropical climate did crazy things to my mom. She flirted shamelessly with every hotel employee within a one-mile radius."

"Really? How far did she get?"

"Not very. But she did succeed in getting my dad to pay more attention to her. He took her out to a 'romantic dinner' practically every night, and I stayed at the hotel by myself."

"Must've been pretty boring," I said.

"Hardly." Sam kicked his feet onto the coffee table. "There were, like, a hundred other New York families at our hotel— imagine a six-day house party, but with a bottomless bar and round-the-clock housekeeping. At least that's what it was like in B.P.'s wing."

"B.P.?"

Sam looked incredulous again. "What? Miss Mega-popular is still unacquainted with such a pillar of New York high school high society?"

"Cool it, Geckman, " I warned him.

"B.P. refers to Boris Potasnik," Sam said, "the firstborn son of Alexei Potasnik, the lunatic real estate tycoon who drives low-income housing residents to homeless shelters and gets away with it because he's a self-made Russian émigré who escaped the gulag, or some shit like that."

"And you hung out with this dude? Charming."

"No, dumb-ass. With his *son*. Boris is a total teddy bear—a bon vivant, as my own dad might say. But I feel a little sorry for him. Alexei is always harassing him about not 'applying himself.'" Sam sank back into the couch and chuckled. "One night," he went on, "Boris and I were sitting on the pool deck, just chilling and drinking beers, when his dad appeared out of *no*where and lost it because Boris was drinking. Have you ever heard of a Russian pissed off about *alcohol?* Talk about psycho—he ordered Boris to stand up and do pushups on the ground. Now, Boris is a big guy, like six foot four, but he's no gym rat, so he gave up after a couple of pushups. Alexei lost it, saying he wouldn't leave until Boris had done at least ten more. He was pacing by the pool, mumbling to himself, and suddenly there was this gigantic splash in the water. Boris had rolled right into the pool—it was awesome!"

"Jesus," I said. "Sounds like he'd be better off in Russia."

"Nah, Boris grew up here. He's pretty lazy, and his life is undeniably sweet. He has a trust fund the size of Siberia, hobnobs with every teenage celebrity in the city, and what's more, he's on a first-name basis with the managers of every chi-chi restaurant around. Watching him order dinner is the experience of a lifetime."

"Nice," I said approvingly. I knew a thing or two about gastronomy myself.

"No, no, Schulman," Sam said, "he's not a pig like you. He's *discerning*. This guy actually knows a thing or two about the crap he stuffs in his mouth."

Before I could object, Fenella poked her scarecrow neck into the room. "Oh, kiddos!" she trilled. "Can I offer either of you an espresso?"

Sam and I exchanged bewildered looks. What a space cadet. Did Fenella really know fifteen-year-olds in the habit of drinking digestive espressos? What was she going to offer us next, bifocals? Dad and I needed to have a serious talk, and soon.

Little Mermaids

By the end of our first week back at school, the easing-in period had faded to distant memory. Baldwin's financial dilemma, no longer a secret, had disturbed the institution's fragile ecosystem. Rumored threats of job insecurity transformed even the gentlest teachers into psychopathic taskmasters. This bastion of enlightened progressivism, known for its antigrades, anticompetition, and antijudgment policies, was beginning to resemble a boot camp, or at least a normal high school.

What with my suddenly hefty course load and the demands of sunburn recovery, I was beyond drained by Friday afternoon, determined to chill out at home all night. The girls tried in vain to cajole me into accompanying them to an "epic" house party on the Upper East Side. What I needed was sleep, and lots of it. Dad was out when I got home—where, I had no desire to learn—so I grabbed some granola bars and a carton of orange juice and brought the sugary meal to my bedroom on the bottom floor, slightly below street level. Sometimes I liked just sitting on my bed and watching the bottom half of everyday life pass by my barred window: the parade of high heels clicking down the block, the rattling of baby strollers, the barefoot winos howling obscenities at garbage cans. Our street was slender and residential, but never dull.

That night, as I lay in bed half listening to the hip-hop radio show blaring from a parked car outside, I thought about the recent changes in my situation. A year ago at this time, I lived in Texas with a stable family, or what I'd mistaken for one. In those far-off days, I'd fantasized about getting my learner's permit and taking my then best friend Rachel and cat Simon for a joy ride. If occasionally interesting, my life had never been mysterious. I fell asleep wondering what had become of that world.

Early the next morning, I woke up feeling well rested and renewed. Sam and I had made a daylong appointment to collaborate on our Russian Dissident Fiction project. To launch our "Soviet Diaspora" unit, Yuri Knutz had instructed us to interview an ex-Soviet citizen and compose either a five-minute one-man play or a one-minute five-man play—"dissident's choice"—about our subject's experiences. Sam's friend from Florida, Boris Potasnik, had volunteered to give us a grand tour of a Russian bathhouse, or *banya*, in Brighton Beach, which Sam claimed was the only place to research our assignment. He'd already briefed me on the illustrious history of *banyas* in Brooklyn. In the early 1900s, before most tenement buildings had indoor plumbing, dozens of *banyas* opened all over the borough to service the immigrant population. A century later, the remaining bathhouses—about half a dozen, Sam said—primarily functioned as social clubs for the Russian community, a place for families— infants, teenagers, and grandparents included—to relax over the weekend. "They sound like water parks," I'd commented when we were firming our plans.

"I guess," Sam said. "Except instead of going down scary slides, the point is to sit absolutely still in sweltering heat."

"Stinky." I'd made a face.

"It's not bad, crab apple," Sam assured me. "You'll soon be a convert, just wait."

The morning of our excursion, I was upstairs fixing myself some peanut butter toast when the phone rang. It was Pia, unwilling to waste energy on pleasantries.

"You eat yet?" she barked into the receiver. Despite her fancy diplomatic upbringing, Pia didn't worry much about etiquette, especially on the phone.

"I just made toast," I told her, crunching loudly as evidence.

"Ugh, you animal. I feel like I'm inside your mouth."

"Breakfast is the most important meal of the day," I intoned robotically. "What's up?"

"I stole some ciabatta and prosecco and other fine goodies from my parents," Pia said. "The Mortons have gone AWOL. Their counselor made them go to some all-day silence retreat at a healing arts center, so we're having a little brunch party *chez* Lily—get up here ASAP!"

"No can do," I said with real regret. "Sam and I have to schlep out to a Brighton Beach *banya* for our Russian seminar."

"Seriously? How gross." Pia made a retching sound. "Alessandro took me there once in one of his ill-conceived seduction schemes. The place was totally disease-infested and packed with jiggly-bottomed women in dental-floss thongs."

"Alessandro?" I asked, hoping to redirect Pia's torrential negativity. She'd had many exotic escorts over the years, but I'd only ever heard her mention Giacomo, Giancarlo, and Pasquale. "Do I know about Alessandro?"

"Dad's press secretary before Dad discovered he was taking me on inappropriate field trips and gave him the boot. Poor guy," Pia said without an ounce of emotion. "Anyway, good luck getting there before dusk. I swear to God, Guyana is more accessible by public transportation."

After hanging up with Pia, I found that her graphic warnings had punctured my initial enthusiasm. The remoteness of our destination no longer seemed interesting, just inconvenient. There were plenty of ex-Soviets in the East Village—why did Sam need to drag me all the way into the outer reaches of Brooklyn?

"Why isn't Boris here?" I asked peevishly when the two of us met outside the pet store on Union Square. "I thought he was coming with us."

"He had a family brunch," Sam said. "He's meeting us out there." When I scowled, Sam only laughed. "But c'mon, Mims, aren't I entertainment enough? I learned shitloads of new knock-knock jokes down in West Palm—aren't you just burning to hear them?"

"Not really," I grumbled, following Sam down to the Q-train platform. Though I'd chosen to skip the party last night, I now resented missing this opportunity to hang out with the girls.

Sam made another stab at conviviality on the Manhattan leg of our journey—"Did I tell you that my dad's thinking about turning his study into a karaoke den?"—but he soon gave up and turned to his new favorite zine, *Four-Eyed Gorilla,* which really did appear to be about primate look-alikes in glasses.

As the train crawled into Brooklyn, I took the book Mom sent me about mentally ill street people in Lebanon out of my Air India tote bag, and we spent the rest of the train ride reading.

Approximately ten hours after boarding the train, Sam and I disembarked in a lonely corner of Brooklyn and walked through the cold, empty streets to the bathhouse. From Pia's descriptions, I'd expected a dank grotto teeming with hairy cave dwellers and all their mingled sweat, but the people in the bathhouse lobby seemed attractive and clean-cut, altogether hygienic. The building, too, was airy and inviting, with a light wood-paneled lobby and wide windows facing onto a beach, which was empty except for a small flock of birds poking around a trash can for food.

After yanking her wet hair into a ponytail, the woman behind the counter issued an incomprehensible Russian greeting and collected our twenty-five-dollar entrance fees. In the women's locker room, I debated swimwear options. I preferred the electric blue Farrah Fawcett–era beaded bikini my dad had excavated from a fire sale in Houston, but I decided it was too racy—no reason to provoke Sam—and went for the modest polka-dot tankini. As I stripped, I began to feel vaguely uneasy, worried the in-your-face foreignness of the *banya* might awaken my inner hick. I'd worked so hard to get my bearings in New York, and I was *still* constantly bracing myself for the next big challenge. It got old sometimes, this fast track to cosmopolitanism, but I was too far along the highway to get off.

Wrapped up in towels, Sam and I met outside the locker rooms and walked down the stairs together into the *banya*'s main room, which centered around an ice-cold "plunge pool" with crushed ice flowing down a chute into a vertical coffin of water. Two corridors led from this room, one to a hallway of steam rooms and saunas of varying heat levels, the second to a sunny café. I was tempted to start with a snack, but Sam would have none of it. He pushed me into the first steam room. Although advertised as "moderate," the room was hotter than high noon in the Dominican Republic. Its three benches were crammed with men and women of various shapes and sizes, all in revealing swimwear, all conversing in Russian. A little muscular man was making his way from bench to bench, beating the guests' bodies with a bunch of leaves. The fellow bathers welcomed the little man with squeals of "Da! Da!"

"Birches," Sam told me, "an old tradition. You'll get your turn soon."

While the other women in the room seemed unperturbed by the flesh flopping over their bikini bottoms, I was as self-conscious as ever, and clutched my towel tighter around my tankini. Sam, too, kept tugging at the elastic band of his baggy plaid swimsuit.

Over the next half-hour, we sampled every boiling-hot room, and I soon felt dizzy and drained. "Why don't these people just sit by the fireplace at home?" I asked Sam. "I'm ready to go. Even Boris knew better than to come." Tired of brushing against Sam's exposed flesh, I longed to be back on the subway, bundled in my winter coat, face buried in my notebook.

"*Chill,*" Sam said, his pale skin flushed after the sweat shack. "How many times do I have to tell you he's at brunch? If he tried to slip out early, his dad would go totally Stalin on him—maybe force a few more pushups, who knows? He'll be here, I promise. And need I point out that we haven't met a *single* member of the diaspora yet?" While Sam had a decent point there, in my dehydrated condition I required a cool-down session in the café, so this time I didn't ask, just led him into a room filled with men drinking beer and women munching cubes of watermelon. The beers looked good, but I didn't dare suggest joining the merriment for fear of Sam turning judgmental and self-righteous on me. Last semester, he'd taken my newfound fondness for the occasional refreshing beverage as evidence that I'd "changed."

I sat down and opened the menu, then just as quickly closed it. "I can't read this," I whined of the 100 percent Cyrillic document. "How can I order watermelon if I can't say it? Your reliable friend Boris sure does come in handy."

"Re-*laaax,*" Sam said. "I've got everything under control. Have I ever let you down at a foreign café? Now, what say we stop complaining and start hydrating?"

A moon-faced child-waitress appeared at our table, and before I could order a Coke (a universal word, right?), Sam cleared his throat and uttered the word "*voda.*" The waitress nodded and scuttled off to the kitchen.

"That's Russian for 'water,'" Sam was proud to point out.

"I wanted a Coke," I started to say pissily. But as I spoke, I noticed, in the distance, a bizarrely familiar person walking down the corridor toward us, then another bizarrely familiar person, and then a third. I squinted, looked again, and gasped— could that possibly be? Next to me, Sam's groan confirmed my happy suspicions. In a single-file line, in order of height, Lily, Pia, and Vivian had entered the bathhouse café.

"The socialite spaceship has landed," he snarled. "You are such a traitor!"

I was stunned. "Sam, I swear to God, I did not—" I didn't finish. The girls had already descended: Lily in her usual Speedo-and-oversize-towel combo; Pia, runway ready in her olive green Gucci bandeau, her tawny legs more gazelle-like than ever; Viv, her tiny, curvy body swaddled in a black halter-top bikini, with black makeup smudged all over her eyes, displaying her amazing flair for looking Goth even in a sunny communal bathhouse.

"Salutations, kiddies," Pia said dryly. "Fancy meeting you here! What say we get our party on?" She signaled for our waitress.

"Uh, Pia," I began, "this morning, you said—"

Pia raised her palms like a television evangelist, her favorite silencing motion. "Now, listen, I've sent Guillermo back to Park Slope to pick up Jess," she said. Guillermo was Pia's family limo driver and, of course, another of her former foreign boy toys. "When we swung by earlier, she was mid-crisis."

"I hope she's OK," Lily said.

"I wouldn't lose sleep over it," Viv said. "She can really over-dramatize anything."

"Now tell me," Pia inquired. "Do you think this place can mix a decent white Russian, or is it more of a grain alcohol kind of joint?" It always startled me, Pia's boundless sense of entitlement. She expected to be served alcohol wherever she went, as if she were forty and not fifteen.

"I don't know, aren't you the expert?" I asked her, but Sam talked over me:

"We actually ordered water? Do you guys *do* water, or is it always straight to the chase—or should I say chaser?"

I cringed at Sam's joke. Sometimes he was just so not smooth.

"It *is* a little early to crack out the booze," Viv said uncertainly.

"Oh, so, what were you looking for in your thermos in the limo just now? Was it your *memory*?" Pia demanded. "You sure didn't think it was too early for a mimosa half an hour ago!"

"You know," Viv sputtered, "I always match my alcohol consumption with water. It's so easy to get, you know, dried out and stuff . . ." She looked imploringly at Sam, who crimsoned and coughed.

"Oh, what the hell," Sam said finally. "Why not have a cocktail—when in Seagate, right?"

When our baby-faced waitress returned, Sam ordered a round of the house specialty, Baltika #9 beers. She gave Sam a you've-got-to-be-kidding-me look, whereupon Pia whipped a fifty-dollar bill from her waistband and slid it toward the waitress. "Much better," Pia said after this successful transaction. "That was itching me."

Boundless entitlement, boundlessly rewarded. Of *course* Pia got her way; when didn't she?

As we clinked our frosty brown bottles, Jess blazed into the room, her face smeared with tears and snot. Her dirty-blond hair was tousled and tangled, and her normally sleepy bedroom eyes—a major reason so many guys lusted after her—were puffy and bloodshot.

"Holy cow," I said. "You weren't kidding about her crisis."

"In*tense*," Viv said under her breath.

After collapsing into a chair, Jess emitted a low animal wail that sounded something like, *"Aah-moo-caaan-buuul."* We begged for an explanation, but she was crying too hard to answer. *"Ee-wah-so-wuh-eeeees,"* she howled intermittently as we took turns patting her shoulder and murmuring, "There, there," and "Come, now." Even Sam pushed his beer across the table to Jess, who without looking up took a long, grateful pull.

Ten minutes into this baby gurgling, she collected herself sufficiently to utter a complete, comprehensible sentence: "He was with someone else."

Preston cheated on Jess? That puffy, beer-bellied lout betrayed the hottest girl in the tenth grade? It seemed inconceivable, and Lily was the first to say it.

"Oh, don't be ridiculous!" she scoffed. "You can't believe everything you hear."

"I *can* believe it," Jess moaned. "I have to believe it. I heard it from him."

"What?"

"With who?" Pia lurched forward.

"Jasmine Lowenstein," Jess choked out.

"Jasmine Lowenstein?"

"That skankfest?"

"You can*not* be serious."

"Isn't she, like, officially brain-dead?"

Jasmine Lowenstein, a well-maintained but famously fatuous member of the senior class, had only one passion in life: collecting designer high heels. Every day she came to school in a new pair of spiky slingbacks or four-inch canary yellow patent-leather stilettos, but her personality was blander than a cheeseless, sauceless pizza.

Poor Jessica. Since Preston had publicly professed his undying love for her and lured her into bed last November—her first time—their relationship had deteriorated fast. And Jess, it should be said, hadn't given up her virginity lightly; she'd thought it might bring her and Preston closer together. Instead, he checked out. First he pleaded constant busyness and college application stress, then his phone went permanently on vibrate and he almost never picked up her calls, even when they were from other countries on New Year's Eve.

"I'm sorry, baby," Viv said, squeezing Jess's shoulder. "Jasmine Lowenstein *is* stooping pretty low, even for Preston."

Jess jerked away, aghast. "What do you mean, 'even for Preston'? Are you implying that my boyfriend has no taste?"

"Sorry, did you say your 'boyfriend'?" Lily broke in. "Don't you mean your *ex*-boyfriend? You haven't sent his pathetic ass to the curb yet?"

Jess wiped her face. "I—I—but Lily, you don't understand. It's complicated—he got deferred from Dartmouth! Dartmouth's the goal of his whole existence! And even if his SAT score blew, his dad's an alum, and he gave them so much money, so he thought it was definite! And the thing is," she blubbered on,

"Jasmine got deferred from Princeton on the same day, and they were, like, consoling each other! Neither of them planned it. Nobody's *perfect*—just ask any first lady."

"Wait, you're comparing Preston to a *president?*" I asked.

"I'm sorry," Lily said, "but getting deferred from college does *not* excuse—"

"Wait a minute," Pia cut in. "Can we take a comedy break? Jasmine Lowenstein actually applied to *Princeton?* And she didn't get outright rejected? I'm sorry, but I don't care how rich her dad is. That girl can hardly tie a shoelace without the help of a private tutor."

"Does she even own any shoes with laces?" Viv asked.

"Please"—Jess was whimpering again—"please can we stick to the point?"

"We certainly can," said Lily, her voice hardening. "The point, Jess, is that you're dumping his lame deferred ass, and I mean today. Have a little self-respect, for God's sake!"

"I know, I know," Jess said tremulously, her big blue eyes once again filling with tears. "But these last few weeks have been *so* hard on him. After his dad made those alumni contributions, he just took it for granted that he'd be accepted. Who can blame him for going into a complete tailspin, you know?"

"*I* can," Sam said quietly. Jess started, as if registering his presence for the first time. "Oh, God, I'm *so* sorry," she said. "I'm not always like this, only in the middle of massive nervous breakdowns. You probably don't even know, or care, who Jasmine Lowenstein is."

"Of course I do," Sam said easily. "Who doesn't know Miss Ho-enstein?"

Jess smiled for the first time that day. "Ho-enstein, exactly! Good call!" The presence of a Y chromosome never failed to animate Jess, even in these circumstances. Though she hardly knew him, she clasped Sam's wrist and launched into a catalog of Preston's sins. And, to my growing amazement, as Jess talked, Sam—the same Sam who'd only last month derided the "idiot quartet"—sat listening, glued to his chair, breathless with sympathy and concern. With Jess monopolizing Sam, I turned to Pia.

"You're the last person I ever expected to see at Seagate," I said.

"Why's that?" she asked innocently. "I never miss a good party, unlike *some* people I know"—a reference to the blowout I'd been too sleepy to attend the previous night. Sipping at her Baltika #9, Pia now described this party in hyperbolic language chosen to spark my jealousy.

"It was one of the hottest parties this year," she claimed, "right up there with the Baldwin grad party the seniors throw every year. *Wild*—just ask Lily. She seemed to be having a pretty good time by the end of the night there."

"Pia!" Lily's eyes bulged out. "That's enough out of you."

"What's the problem?" Pia asked, in a syrupy voice. "Lily, there's no shame in sharing a cab with Blowjob Harry. You're part of a proud tradition—you and every other female in the tristate area."

I couldn't help but cry out, *"What?"* Lily Morton, who'd

never kissed a boy in her life, had shared a cab with the infamous Harry Feder? From the rage imprinted on Lily's face, I saw that Pia wasn't lying. And, in a way, it made sense. Mysterious as it seemed to me, very few girls could resist Harry, a human carrot with zero male friends and all the charm of an emory board. But somehow, by his senior year, Harry had achieved legendary status for his superhuman hookup record. First week back in school, and he'd already added chaste Lily Morton to his list of conquests?

"Pia!" Lily looked ready to explode. "Please don't spread nasty rumors just to conceal your own shame! Last night," Lily told me, "Pia hooked up with this super-geeky guy from Stuyvesant. Talk about standards going down the drain!"

"Oh, shut up!" Pia snapped. "Isaac and I were just talking and you know it."

"Who's Isaac?" I asked, but the girls had forgotten I was sitting between them.

"Oh, yeah, right—I'm sure you two 'talked' about all sorts of interesting things," Lily said with a sneer. "I'm sure it was pure coincidence that he just *happened* to show up at a Baldwin party last night. Doesn't he take advanced placement classes at Columbia with you, or is that also a coincidence?"

"Shut up, I said, just *shut up!*" Pia practically screamed.

Across the table, Sam, Jess, and Viv were kicking back like old friends. I heard Sam invite Viv to join our Russian Dissident monologue team, and her happy acceptance: "I was just going to interview our Mexican housekeeper and, like, change the geographical details. But this is a much better idea."

Midway through our second round of Baltika #9s, Boris Potasnik showed up. Although I'd never seen a photo of him before, I recognized him instantly from Sam's descriptions: larger than life, a few inches north of six feet tall, with spiky yellow hair and pale eyebrows. He was handsome—if slightly extraterrestrial-looking. With a flourish, Boris placed two large shopping bags in the center of our table. "Special delivery," he said. "The best knish place in New York is right in the neighborhood, and I'm incapable of coming out to Seagate without paying my respects." From the first bag Boris removed a huge white box and opened it to reveal rows of square-shaped goodies. "Dig in, everyone, please," he said. "We've got broccoli, onion, cheese, strawberry, spinach, and some other special ingredients I don't care to name."

My stomach rumbled approvingly, but Viv declined, claiming, "Beer kills my appetite."

"And I just ate about three tons of prosciutto," Pia said.

"Preston *loved* Jewish food," Jess said, and burst into tears again.

And so the knish-conquering task fell to Sam, Boris, Lily, and me. We quartered them to maximize our sampling possibilities, but even after twelve pieces, or three knishes each, we'd scarcely made a dent. "Wimps," Boris said, and he got up, box in hand, and circulated the café, offering fellow diners our leftovers in what was without a doubt the most impressive display of generosity I'd witnessed since moving to New York, where everyone was either too greedy or too broke to share.

Back at our table, Boris grilled me about life in Texas, barraging me with ultradetailed questions and nodding so attentively that I soon felt more fascinating than Napoleon and Albert Einstein combined. Within half an hour, I'd told him all about my feline obsession Simon, our Mexican butcher's pig bladder specialty, and my all-time favorite food, double-fried funnel cake at the rodeo, among other highlights of life in the Lone Star State. I even talked about Rachel—whom I'd barely mentioned to my Baldwin friends—and wondered aloud if the two of us would ever be as close as we were in ninth grade, before Rachel fell in love with a sailing instructor at Camp Longawanga and I decamped for Manhattan.

"You get to live in Texas and you chose to come *here*?" Boris marveled when I paused for breath. What was Boris doing frittering away his life in high school? He could make a fortune interviewing people professionally. I hadn't talked this much about Texas since moving to New York, and I loved it.

I had to give Sam serious credit for once: Boris was truly special. His presence at the table had boosted Jess's spirits and somehow even defused the Pia-Lily showdown. His cheerful personality was so infectious, in fact, that with no difficulty he persuaded all of us, even Jess, to make another assault on the steam rooms. Our enlarged group chose one of the smaller, hotter rooms, colonizing the entire two lower benches. Sweat was dripping everywhere off my body, but for some reason I became transfixed by one particular droplet. I really, really wanted to wipe that salty globule off my shin but vowed to resist until it hit my ankle. Sometimes I invent pointless little challenges for myself, like holding my breath whenever I pass a cemetery in a car or hopping from the kitchen to the bathroom on one foot. This time, though, I never got the chance to test my discipline. Boris must have noticed me staring at the bead of sweat, because when it was a few inches above my anklebone, he flicked it off. For all our efforts to inhale the steam in respectful silence, we kept dissolving into pointless giggles. Once, when a pair of intense locals on the upper bench shushed us, Boris made some witticism in Russian and the men cracked up.

The lively exchange reminded me why we'd come to Brighton Beach in the first place: the diaspora stories. Finally ready to start gathering material, I leaned over and nudged Sam.

"Hey, Sam, what say we try to—"

The words froze on my tongue. Sam was bent over Viv, who had peeled down her bikini bottom to display the fish skeleton tattoo in the small of her back. I watched as Sam extended his hand and touched the tattoo, his fingers lingering on Viv's skin for a long moment. As if he could feel my eyes boring into his hand, he jerked around and looked up.

"*What?*" he asked me.

"N-nothing," I said. "I'm just dizzy from the heat." And I was, suddenly. I gripped the wooden bench and hoisted myself up.

Boris stood up right after me. "Let's get some bottled water. I can never stay in one of these things for more than five minutes, myself," he said, "which my father calls an insult to my Russian heritage."

"Speaking of your Russian heritage," I said, "how about

helping me out with a little project?" I opened the steam room door, instantly steadied by a swoosh of cool air.

"I've already been debriefed," Boris said on our way back to the café, where we were soon slugging cool water with an old man named Grigory Mikhailovich, who with little prompting, recounted his life story, insisted Boris and I attend his son's wedding the following weekend, and invited us to examine his ingrown toenail. Yuri Knutz would be ecstatic.

Nightmare on Pierrepont Street

THE BELL RANG, signaling the start of World Civ and the end of my good mood. Last semester, World Civ had been a veritable fun ward of learning, ranking among my favorite classes at Baldwin. That, of course, was before our beloved teacher Stanley had galloped off to the Eastern Hemisphere. While we'd never taken his spirited rejection of "uncivilized confinement" and "indentured identities" all seriously, over winter break our gentle teacher hitchhiked to JFK, hopped the first plane to Bhutan, and sent Zora Blanchard his resignation letter from an Internet café in Thimphu.

What a void he left! Stanley's unique teaching style had hinged on "open-ended discourse," which meant no cold calling and no right answers, only "right paths." Stanley believed in understanding cultures through their cuisines, so a week exploring "revolutionary Thai perspectives" meant a week feasting on satay skewers, and our unit on aboriginal Mexican civics brought with it many a mole sauce–tasting extravaganza. Sometimes Stanley spent entire class periods playing us his old Calypso records. Other days, he encouraged historical reenactments, which he felt facilitated the essential process of "internalizing the past." On one especially entertaining morning, Arthur Gray, our class's comic relief, donned a fake beard and writhed on the carpet in his role as a street hobo in Jack the Ripper—era East London.

With Stanley, I aced tests after studying during a single downtown subway ride. I drifted through class drooling over Max Roth, or formulating plans with Lily and Viv, who sat on either side of me in Stanley's "parliamentary" semicircle of desks, or just relaxing. And so, when my sunburn prevented me from attending the first class of second semester, I hadn't worried about it. I'd assumed Stanley was still with us and I knew that he viewed school as a voluntary activity.

Even after Lily warned me that Stanley had been replaced by a "turbo-bitch"—a woman who took roll and insisted students call her "Ms." Singer, an unheard-of formality at Baldwin—I didn't freak. After six years in Texas, I could handle addressing teachers by their last names.

I scarcely expected, on the second day of school, to find Room 10-S so completely transformed: Stanley's haphazard half-moon of desks was now arranged in orderly military rows, and his beloved travel agency posters of Machu Picchu and Ulan Batur had been replaced by metal filing cabinets and racks of color-coded hanging folders. At the blackboard stood a gray-haired woman dressed in a suit appropriate for a corporate takeover. "How pleasant of you to join us, Miss Schulman," she said in a clipped tone. Before I could figure out how she knew my name, she pointed to a desk in the front row. "I'm sure you have a perfectly sound excuse for cutting the first class of the semester."

"Oh, I didn't cut," I started to explain. "See, I got sun—"

"Ahem!" Baldwin's newest teacher rapped a ruler against the blackboard. "I look forward to reading about it in a signed note from your parent or guardian."

Three rows over, Amanda France rolled her eyes at me in a comradely gesture of support. By the beginning of class the following Monday, we all knew who was boss. Even bright sunshiny Amanda darted to her seat like a squirrel about to be shot. Me, I kept a low profile and endured Ms. Singer's tedious Mary, Queen of Scots lecture by counting down until the bell. With two minutes to go, I slid my notebook into my bag and fastened the first pearlized button of the vintage football letter cardigan my father had given me for Christmas-Hanukkah.

"And so to wrap things up . . . " Ms. Singer abruptly stopped pacing in front of the blackboard. Then, with ferocious, hungry eyes, she scanned the desks until her eyes rested on yours truly. "Miss Schulman," she said, "you seem ready to wrap things up. Why don't you help me out here?"

My hands, which had been disentangling a button from my prized saddle pendant necklace, dropped to my lap.

"Sure thing," I said.

"Have I left anything out?"

"Where to begin?" I said, doing my best to sound confident. "There's *so* much left to discuss."

Ms. Singer frowned as if I'd just farted inside the Oval Office. "No need to go over everything," she said. "Just the biggest highlight, or lowlight, you'd like to toss out there."

There *was* something I'd like to toss out there—out the window, that is. Here's a hint: it had two arms, two legs, gray hair, and a briefcase. Instead I smiled phonily and waited for a brilliant idea to strike. Within seconds it hit me, pure genius. "She was an avid golfer, Ms. Singer." I almost high-fived myself—take that, embittered spinster!

Ms. Singer didn't blink. "That's very interesting, Miss Schulman, but what about a major event? Something—conclusive, perhaps?" As she spoke, the bell of heaven chimed. With immense relief, I started to stand up, but like a drill sergeant Ms. Singer rapped out, "Don't anyone move!" The entire class watched me wriggle back into my seat. I glanced imploringly at Lily, but she was about the only one there who wasn't staring at me. Was it my fault that Jess had called us to her house at nine p.m. for another Preston powwow? My fault that he'd cried and begged her to take him back and forced us to intervene? I'd done my stupid Mary, Queen of Scots reading, just not the last two pages.

Down the row, Max Roth caught my eye and—rather meanly, I thought—slid his finger along his neck, indicating mine was about to be sliced. Next to him, Amanda tugged theatrically at her pearl choker. But I could no longer think straight. I felt feverish, stomach-sick, and wished I could melt into my desk. I hadn't been this humiliated since sixth grade, when Rachel's older brother hid behind the shower curtain and photographed me stuffing my training bra with toilet paper. In the end, Ms. Singer did what she always did, just as Stanley had done before her. She called on Max Roth, or "Mr. Roth," as she called him. "Care to educate your benighted classmate?"

Max stretched. "Uh, yeah," he said softly. "She was beheaded."

"Bravo! *Finally*." Ms. Singer gave me a snide look. "Class, you may go now. But thank you, Miss Schulman, for the golfing tidbit." My throat went dry, and I blinked back tears. Please, please, please do *not* cry, do *not* give that wrinkled old prune the satisfaction, I prayed as I jumped up and ran into the hall. Too scarred to risk facing Baldwin's star pupil, Max Roth, again, I decided to lick my wounds in the privacy of the *Bugle* office. Lily had this period free, and I could count on my *Bugle*-obsessed friend to show up and console me.

I arrived there dry-eyed, and Jon Loman, the sports editor, held the door open for me on his way out. Once inside, I was dismayed to see my least favorite member of the newspaper staff, our humorless editor in chief, Ulla Lippman, mouth breathing and fiddling with her orthodontia at the main drafting table. As I tried to cross behind her, Ulla removed her white-noise headphones and bleated, "Boys are from Vancouver, girls are from Tokyo! What's your gut reaction to that, Schulman? I'm testing out headlines for the foreign exchange student article." My gut reaction was nausea, thanks to Ms. Singer, but because Ulla never waited for replies I just lifted my shoulders and settled onto the windowsill, where I tried to absorb the contents of my *Great Ideas of Western Civilization* textbook by osmosis. Several minutes later, Lily burst into the room.

"Oh, thank *God!*" I cried, catapulting off the windowsill. "Can you *believe* that woman hung me up to dry like that? Why not just superglue a dunce cap to my head?"

"Mmph." Lily nodded distractedly and wound a strand of

sandy blond hair that had fallen from her ponytail around her index finger. "It's too bad you never got around to writing that column last week," she said.

"I'm sorry," I told her, not for the first time. "But the only thing I could think to write about was our vacation, which was obviously off-limits."

"Right," Lily said tonelessly. As the sophomore editor of the *Bugle*, she took her responsibilities within these walls extremely seriously, treating her position more as a full-time job than an extracurricular.

"Maybe I should write about how evil Ms. Singer is," I suggested wryly. "Give a blow-by-blow account of my public humiliation."

"Can we talk about this later?" Lily asked. "I'm pretty stressed about newspaper stuff right now. We have a meeting tonight and almost no story ideas. Plus, Vikram Mohini contracted chronic eye fatigue over Christmas, and he's not allowed to spend more than an hour a day in front of the computer. An hour a day! How's he supposed to lay out an entire newspaper in an hour a day?"

"Well, find a freelancer, then," I grumbled, determined to appear as unsympathetic to Lily's problems as she was to mine.

"Yeah, right," Lily said, "we really have the budget for freelancers. This morning Zora told us that unless we generate advertising revenue the *Bugle* will be going monthly. Apparently Baldwin no longer has the money to put out a newspaper every two weeks."

At this revelation, Ulla left the drafting table and tromped over to us.

"Just watch them cancel the whole paper and give all the money to the pathetic *Poetry Review*!" she brayed.

Ulla loved dissing the *Poetry Review*. According to Jess, who was on the magazine's editorial board, this was because over the past three years Ulla had submitted twenty-three epic narrative poems about prisoner-of-war camps and Third World dictatorships and the *Poetry Review* board had rejected every single one of them. That morning, as Ulla railed against that "overfunded, wannabe edgy, pseudo-angsty rag," I grinned knowingly at Lily, but she was too busy glaring at the *Great Ideas* textbook in my hand to notice.

"This really isn't the place for homework, Mimi," she said. "Maybe you'd like to help us troubleshoot, instead of always just standing around."

Something in her voice prickled, and I took a step back.

"What does *that* mean?"

Lily had been so grumpy this past week! I suspected that her bad mood related either to her mom's return from rehab or to the cab ride with Harry Feder, but Lily hadn't confided in me and I wasn't one to pry, especially since I didn't exactly volunteer confidences about my own familial or romantic dysfunctions. Still, I missed her. In the few months that we'd known each other, Lily and I had grown extremely tight. In addition to collaborating on article ideas, we also shared a rare medical condition known as terminal sexual inexperience. And so I dropped my defensive tone and agreed to join the brainstorming session at the drafting table.

"We totally blew it on the fiscal crisis," Lily said, flipping open her legal pad. "We should've played that story *much* bigger. Instead, what did we push on the cover? That silly how-to-survive-your-parents-over-vacation puff piece."

I'd loved that piece but refrained from broadcasting that fact.

"What we need are some solid ideas," Lily went on. "We have to stop hiding from the big stories."

"Hey, how about I write a behind-the-scenes feature about the school dance next month?" I said. "I could hang out with the planning committee and get an insider scoop on the theme or maybe profile the DJ or—"

"See what I mean?" Lily said wearily to Ulla. "Pure fluff."

"Absolutely right—fluff in a nutshell." Ulla popped a rubber band on her left incisor. "You know, Mimi," she said, "it's good you're here, because Lily and I have been discussing ways to boost your input."

"What, you've been talking about me behind my back?" I accused Lily, but she kept her eyes on the drafting table.

"Your last article was perfectly fine, Mimi," Ulla droned on, "but as usual, it fell short of your full potential."

"My full potential?" I asked in a wavering voice. Ms. Singer's tar-and-feathering session had left me unusually sensitive, vulnerable to criticism. "S-so neither of you likes my school dance idea? But—but Baldwin only holds one a year!"

Lily pried her chin off her neck. "The dance idea is fine, Mimi," she said. "We just thought maybe you could try something more ambitious for a change."

Right then, the door of the *Bugle* office opened and our headmaster, Zora Blanchard, poked her head inside.

"Ulla, may I speak with you outside?" she asked, gesturing with her coffee mug. Less than a minute later, Ulla returned, brimming with excitement, her face bloated with self-importance.

"What was that all about?" Lily gratified our editor in chief by asking.

"Let's just say, I think I have Mimi's next big story idea," Ulla replied cryptically. She cleared her throat and drew in a moist breath, trying to prolong the moment.

"Your attention, please! Baldwin just had some news—some very good, very major news. Our next cover story promises to be *huge*." Ulla paused to pick at a rubber band. "Now, I would ordinarily be the obvious choice to cover this plum assignment, but because I got into the Northwestern journalism program over break, I've decided to take a bit of a breather from the front lines for a while. Besides, with my editorial responsibilities, I couldn't *possibly* find the time to report such a huge story like this—"

"C'mon, Ulla, just tell us what it is!" Lily tapped her foot impatiently. Slowly, Ulla looked from me to Lily, ensuring that we hung on her every word.

"As you know," she proceeded grandly, puffing up her chest, "Baldwin's been financially challenged lately. Some foul play in the bull market, and now we're all paying the piper."

What a perfect comment to fall from the blistered lips of Ulla Lippman, daughter of Jim Lippman, the deposed—and recently incarcerated—CEO of ToyBoy Inc. Since Lippman Senior's international money-laundering scheme hit the front pages of every newspaper in the country, the Lippman family finances had taken a huge plunge. After spending her childhood in a swank apartment on the Museum Mile, Ulla now commuted to Baldwin from her grandparents' house in Jersey City.

"Are you guys ready for this?" she was asking now. "Serge Ziff has just given Baldwin a sizable chunk of change. Sizable enough to save this paper."

"That's great!" Lily exclaimed.

"Does that mean we can hire a page designer?"

"Who's Serge Ziff?" I asked, causing both Lily and Ulla to stare at me in amazement.

"Who's Serge Ziff?" Lily echoed. "Only the most famous art dealer in Lower Manhattan!"

"Yeah, and his daughter, Nikola, is far and away the most sophisticated member of the senior class," Ulla sighed, then plucked another saliva-soaked rubber band.

"So here's the deal. We *need* some of that money at the *Bugle*, so we've gotta milk this story for all it's worth. I'm thinking a multipage spread, glossy, high-res photo montage, a timeline of his life, and most important of all . . . an intimate, sizzling interview with the donor! Now, as I said before," Ulla went on, "I'd normally be the one to take this assignment, but I think my energies would be better spent working on the layout. As for you, Lily, I'd been wanting to promote you to deputy editor, and this would be a great chance for me to prep you for next year's responsibilities."

Lily nodded, clearly thrilled.

"So, guess which undermotivated *Bugle* reporter has just landed the assignment of her life?" Ulla gave me a big juicy wink and then immediately clapped her white-noise headphones back on to begin devising headlines for the big story.

I stood there, reviewing the conversation that had just taken place and mentally forming objections to the donor-article Ulla had somehow just assigned me.

"She's crazy," I said to Lily.

"Are you kidding?" Lily returned. "That was Ulla's best idea *ever*. Mimi, you *have* to do it. If he likes the story, maybe Serge will give the *Bugle* the lion's share of the donation." And then her face hardened as she said, "Really, Mimi, I've been selling you so hard to Ulla. You could at *least* give it a shot."

"I still can't believe you didn't like my 'Texas in Gotham' columns," I said, walking over to the air-conditioning vent to collect my books.

Did Lily expect me to be flattered and grateful? Because I wasn't; I was actually pretty hurt. Lily had basically pegged me as a lightweight, trivial and silly and even lazy.

Feeling exiled and misunderstood, and still with half an hour to kill before third period, I sloped off to the lobby in search of peer distractions. The school's trench-coated theater kids usually convened there to practice unicycle tricks, but that morning the lobby was dark and creepy, and completely abandoned. The light from the preposterously gigantic chandelier overhead flickered occasionally, shuddered, and dimmed.

I sat on the bottom stair and rested against the banister. My eyes fluttered shut, and I was half dozing when the sudden foghorn blare of Zora Blanchard's voice roused me. She was standing directly over me, flailing her arms and shouting orders to Elvis, Baldwin's all-purpose custodian and elevator operator.

"What's the story on this lighting?" Zora roared, the contents of her coffee mug sloshing precariously above my head. "Teen suicides are on the rise these days. What are we trying to do, encourage the trend?"

Elvis naively tried to reason with the crazed administrator.

"We're waiting for a new shipment of bulbs," he said. "There was a problem with the billing, but the accounting office is taking care of it."

Zora, however, had no patience for explanations. She wanted the lights on now, end of story. "I can't *see* anything in here!" she cried. "Are you standing there, Elvis? I can't see you. Is that Mimi Schulman underneath me? I can't see her." For added effect, she raised her thermos and missed her mouth by an inch.

"Mrs. Blanchard," Elvis pleaded, "we're taking care of it. Our account got frozen, but it's all cleared up now."

"Now isn't good enough! I want it cleared up yesterday. *Yesterday!* Now go! Run and save my kiddies from the darkness!"

Once Elvis had shuffled away, Zora squatted next to me on the staircase. After emptying her coffee mug in one glug, she began rubbing the top of my head as if I were a genie. I'd seen her do this to other kids before, and, unsure of the protocol, I sat still as she messed up my bangs.

"Let there be light," she said. "Let us bask in light."

This was the closest to religion I'd ever experienced at Baldwin, and, I must say, it freaked me out. Zora was still reciting her mantra when a loud click reverberated above us, and just as she released my skull, a bright fluorescent glare illuminated the lobby.

Pleased to Almost Meet You

It snowed that afternoon, and the streets were so quiet, I could hear the crunch of my footsteps in the ice as I walked back from school. Once home, I pried off my wet cowboy boots in the hallway we shared with the Judys, a couple of documentary filmmakers who were remarkably cheerful despite having spent their lives interviewing various oppressed minorities. I hadn't seen the Judys—or their adopted daughter, Gilda—since returning from the Dominican Republic and could only assume they were holed up in some Third World nation with a film crew. When I let myself into the apartment, I saw a Joe's Pizza menu propped up on the entryway table, with seven messages scrawled on it, each one increasing in urgency and handwriting size. The first one, "Mom in search of Mimi," built up to "Mimi: Call Mommie Dearest ASAP," and finally "Mimi, if I have to take one more message for you, I'm getting a slutty secretary outfit and charging you for it!"

"Hooray!" I pounded down the stairs, shouting Quinn's name at every step. I'd begun to fear he'd forsaken his screwball second family for good, but there he stood, silhouetted by the darkroom and stinking of fixer solution, looking gorgeous in stiff jeans and a tight gray T-shirt. I shivered in spite of myself. Gay or straight, Quinn was still the hottest.

He wiped off his hands and spun me around while I reveled in the long-overdue completion of our family unit. A few minutes later, when we went upstairs, Quinn asked me about Dad's new design scheme. "All these knickknacks and tassels! What's next—Roger gets a fez and a magic carpet?"

I agreed that the décor had taken a turn for the worse, but rather than discuss the visionary responsible for these curios, I sat Quinn down and hurriedly updated him on my life, from my glorious trip to the D.R. to Baldwin's budget crisis and Ms. Singer's vendetta against me.

"She's totally out to get me, I swear," I said. "She only calls on me when I *don't* know the answer."

Quinn listened to my complaints with more amusement than pity.

"Maybe she's secretly in love with you and desperate to conceal her burning passion?" he offered. "All the signs point to that."

"Yeah, or maybe she just hates me," I said. "She also has the worst taste *ever*, and wears her hair in these retro tortoiseshell combs that—" I broke off, realizing I'd completely monopolized the conversation. Overstimulation often turns me into a self-absorbed bore, what can I say? "But what about you?" I asked Quinn. "How're tricks in the Midwest? Did you just get in to town today or what?"

"Last night," he said. "Today I had to meet with this scary business titan who might want me to take portraits of his company's employees. The money would be phenomenal, but I seriously doubt I'll get the job."

"Yeah, right. How could *anyone* refuse the fabulous Quinn?"

"Maybe when the fabulous Quinn gets off a plane and goes out partying until six in the morning, with barely enough time to shave and deodorize before his interview?"

I laughed—I really *had* missed this man. "Wow, you must really be starving right now," I said. "And as luck would have it, so am I. What say we rock some triple cheese pizza?"

"No. No!" Quinn said, pointing at his abdomen. "We are not eating or talking about food until I trash this seasonal addition once and for all!"

"Are you joking? You look *exactly* the same," I said truthfully. "And trust me, I pay attention to these matters."

Quinn smiled at this reference to my recent crush on him. "Speaking of hopeless passions," he said, "when I was home I ran into my old friend Robert McCarter, the high school quarterback who also happened to be my senior-year paramour."

"The quarterback of your high school was gay? Who knew you lived in such a progressive corner of Ohio?"

"Robert McCarter *was* gay, ragingly so," Quinn said with a somber expression. "Still is, gay as the Easter parade. But *out*? Not in a million years. In high school, our trysts were of a strictly behind-the-bleachers nature, and now . . . " Quinn shrugged. "Let's just say Robert McCarter is a pillar of the Bowling Green community, with a pert young wife and the most fetching little children. He was the love of my life—and now he sells car insurance."

The love of his life? My dad's free-spirited darkroom assistant didn't even strike me as a love-of-the-week type. But before I could learn more, Quinn's cell phone rang, and though he declined the call, the interruption shattered his reverie enough to remind him of the numerous messages Mom had left me. He picked the cordless off the floor and pressed it into my hand.

"Now, Mimi, for the love of God, call the woman whose birth canal spat you out fifteen years ago. She was getting hysterical there."

"OK, OK," I said. "But what's she doing calling me seven times during the school day? Does she think I've enrolled part-time or something?"

"Be nice," Quinn scolded me. "I don't care what she did—she's your *mother*, and the poor woman claims she hasn't heard from you since before your trip. She kept going on and on about cult rituals and bounty hunters, and I didn't know *how* to calm her."

If only Mom had been so concerned about my well-being eight months earlier when she'd traded Dad for her doughy Rice University colleague Maurice, America's biggest hypochondriac. For all her psychobabble self-justifications, I'd never forgive her for ruining my precious father's life like that—never. Then again, I'd been home an entire week, and at times Mom had an overactive imagination. It was with theatrical reluctance that I dialed the phone number that had once been my own.

My mother picked up on the second ring. "Oh, hey there, dumplet," she said, evidently underwhelmed by the sound of my voice. "Playing hard to get, are we, chicken wing? I was just taking a straw poll over when you'd call."

"What can I do for you, Mom?" I asked warily, my defenses raised by Mom's stupid terms of endearment. "Dumplet" and "chicken wing" only entered her vocabulary in association with unpleasant surprises. On the day she threw Dad to the curb, for example, she'd called me "bonbon," "llama girl," and "peanut butter cup" in the space of five minutes.

"What can you do for me?" she purred. "Why, not a thing in the world, daffodil. I just wanted to make sure you were still alive and see how your semester's going. And have you gotten a chance to read that devastating memoir I sent you, the one by the widow of an asbestos-poisoned railroad engineer? Such *terrible* suffering that woman endured . . ."

I stoically endured Mom's monologue about the "entrancing" American bison exhibition she and Maurice had seen at Houston's Natural History Museum last weekend. Mom didn't seem to notice how little I chimed in, but that was the pattern these days. Since our relationship no longer felt natural, our conversations had grown strained and one-sided. Rather than ask me about my new life, she preferred to pretend it didn't exist, a trick that left me feeling lonely and detached whenever we talked. At least as Mom segued to Maurice's latest respiratory ailment, I overcame my initial bombshell anxieties. Maybe she really had missed me over Christmas and now just wanted to talk.

"Oh, and on the subject of Maurice," she said, "the two of us are planning a little New York getaway over Presidents' Day weekend, so pencil us in! His coccyx has been killing him lately, and he deserves an out-of-town treat, like, say, heading up the Hudson for some R&R at a little B&B. I was going to call up the

Audubon Society and see what migrations we can catch. Whaddya think?"

Bang. There it was. Pia had already mentioned a Presidents' Day party in the Hamptons, and in a recent e-mail Rachel had proposed visiting New York that same weekend. Because I knew my best friend in Houston would love the Hamptons, I'd already encouraged Rachel to buy her plane ticket. So of *course* my mom would choose that weekend for her bird-watching expedition to Rhinebeck. I died a thousand little deaths, but I kept my agony to myself. Mom always got whatever she wanted or, as in the case of Dad, got *rid* of whatever she no longer wanted.

"You in, unicorn?" she chirped. "How does a long weekend of bird watching sound?"

"Super," I managed to reply.

"Marv! Then we'll talk soon, 'K?" And with that, she dropped me like a video in the after-hours slot at Blockbuster. At some point during my phone conversation, Quinn had flipped on the television and found an *I Love Lucy* marathon on cable. When I tried to steer him back to Robert McCarter, the love of his life, Quinn was already too mesmerized by Lucy and Desi to respond.

"All right, then," I said loudly, getting off the couch. "I was asked to do a huge assignment for the paper, so I'd better get cracking." Much to my disappointment, Quinn made no effort to detain me.

Downstairs, I e-mailed Rachel about the Presidents' Day bird-watching disaster, suggesting she plan an even longer trip up here over spring break instead. Then, to avoid dwelling on the Mom-Maurice situation, I decided to conduct some preliminary fact-finding on Serge Ziff. I wanted to dig up a few morsels—maybe his gallery's Web site and some random society pics, if there were any—just to get a taste of him.

Boy, did my out-of-the-loop ass underestimate Serge Ziff's standing. Once I Googled him, I couldn't escape the man—he was almost as popular as Viagra. The first picture I located, on *Empire* magazine's Web site, appeared under the heading "Bully Waters's Twenty-Fifth Birthday Extravaganza" and it showed my interview subject posing with a young man in a fedora, a white T-shirt, and suspenders—probably Bully Waters. Serge, who had big fish lips, shiny platinum hair, and an eerily creaseless face, was staring straight into the lens, neither smiling nor frowning. It was weird. Though Serge Ziff's name and face graced everything from charity-dinner photo collages to German architecture chat rooms, I unearthed almost no biographical information about him. Adjectives like "brilliant" and "innovative" abounded, but no interviews or FAQs or descriptive paragraphs. Oh well, I thought, at least Serge seemed fun, more interesting than your typical private-school-parent bore. I opened my Instant Message box and wrote Lily.

Mimicita85: Yo. W. U.?

GildedLils: At Bugle. Things nuts over here . . . Ulla screaming at sports ed.

Mimicita85: Y?

GildedLils: He didn't know Baldwin had a bsktbl team.

Mimicita85: We do?

GildedLils: Shut up.

Mimicita85: Ha ha . . . I'm IMing you in official reporter capacity. The Serge Ziff profile. I'll take it.

GildedLils: UR a freak. I already assigned it to u 5 hours ago. OMG . . . BRB.

Mimicita85: What?!

GildedLils: Jon Loman just threw his tape recorder at color printer. Ulla v v v pissed. Your piece is due Tuesday. Got2go.

Mimicita85: Sounds scary. Be safe.

USER GILDEDLILS IS NOT CURRENTLY SIGNED ON.

An hour later, I bopped back upstairs with a brighter outlook on the Serge Ziff profile. I became still more chipper when I learned that Quinn and our upstairs neighbors, Judy #1 and Judy #2, would be replacing the vampiric Fenella von Dix at dinner that night.

While Dad showered off the grime of an afternoon spent shooting abandoned shipyards in the Red Hook section of Brooklyn, an assignment for an Australian fashion magazine, Quinn and I consulted our delivery menus.

"It's a conspiracy against my tush," Quinn kept whining as he discarded menu after menu. "There's nothing here I can eat—Indian is just spices and clarified butter, and tapas is pure lard . . ."

We were still deliberating when the Judys—with their adopted toddler, Gilda, in tow—tumbled into the apartment, jubilant because that day Gilda had finally learned to distinguish between Judy #1's title, "Ma-ma," and Judy #2's, "Ma-mee."

"Talk about precocious!" #1 raved. "She already recognizes how special her family is!"

"I know what," Quinn said, throwing down the menus. "I'm going to call Empire Szechuan and get steamed veggies for myself, and then I'll call Awash and get Ethiopian for the rest of you. I love how Ethiopian smells, and for now scratch-and-sniff is all I'm allowed."

Judy #2 thunderously approved the plan: "Gilda *adores* injera!"

"Most parents wait far too long to introduce their children to the varied cuisines of African cultures," #2 added.

"We almost did a PBS video project on the Oromo Liberation Front," #1 said. "We would've brought Gildy along if not for safety concerns."

"Speaking of the forgotten continent, we *did* find Gildy the neatest little trinket!" #2 said brightly. From her straw satchel she pulled out a colorful cloth toy shaped like an elongated strawberry. "Her very own stuffed Africa! Isn't it the plushest thing?"

I hoped I still lived on Barrow Street when Gilda grew to fall in love with Barbie dolls and fun-size ovens. Only time would tell.

After placing the food order, Quinn was about to switch off the TV when what he described as the "best episode EVER!" came on.

My dad, with wet hair and a shaving nick on his chin,

entered the living room at roughly the same moment, and he, too, was psyched. "Pardon us, ladies," he said, "but the candy factory episode's a classic."

The mashed foodstuffs and soggy steamed greens arrived conveniently during a commercial and as soon as we'd piled our plates with food, Dad and Quinn returned to *Lucy,* leaving me to entertain our guests.

Straight off, the Judys wanted to discuss what #1 dubbed the "Baldwin imbroglio," an issue of concern because, though Gilda was not yet two years old, her ambitious mothers had already placed her on the waitlist of several elite private schools. Being an Emerald City of progressivism, Baldwin's recent (and by now well-publicized) budget problems troubled the Judys.

"Our dream school's starting to sound like Nicaragua under the Sandinistas," said #2. "Do we trust precious Gildy to such an unstable institution?"

"Then again, she might thrive in an environment of hardship," mused #1. "After all, there's no finer teacher than first-hand experience. Mimi, what's your personal perspective on this scandal?"

"Oh, Jude!" #2 bopped her partner's arm. "She says that to every single refugee we've *ever* interviewed."

"Actually," I said, once my neighbors' giggling had subsided, "I'm afraid Gilda won't be finding much hardship at Baldwin. There's been no official announcement yet, but someone's super-rich dad just pledged a ginormous sum of cash to the school."

"Exactly how ginormous?" #1 wanted to know. "And what's the benefactor's name?"

"Serge Ziff?" I said.

"Serge Ziff," Quinn repeated, momentarily forgetting both Lucy and the tasteless broccoli he'd been nibbling. "*The* Serge Ziff?"

"I guess so," I said. "He owns an art gal—"

"Honey, I have a pulse, don't I? I *know*."

"Well, I'd never heard of him," I said, "and now I'm doing this big interview with him for the school paper."

"You're meeting Serge Ziff?" Quinn simply couldn't get over it.

"Yep, sometime next week, I think." Not that I'd arranged the interview yet, but whatever.

"In that case," Quinn said, "save your Saturday for me. We're going to make a little field trip to Ziffland. I'll take you to Chelsea and acquaint you with the New York art world. Serge Ziff is a famous snob, so he'd probably appreciate some familiarity with his terrain."

"Wow, thanks!" I welcomed the prospect of hanging out with Quinn for an extended time period, and outside the apartment, too. I could also definitely stand to learn some art world basics, both for my interview *and* for my Max Roth seduction scheme. Familiarity with contemporary art would definitely bolster my mysterious, woman-of-the-world aura.

Energized by the good news, Judy #1 scooped up the plush Africa and thrust it in Gilda's face. Gilda swatted the stuffed continent away, then erupted into deafening wails.

"So vocal!" #2 rhapsodized. "How could *any* admissions committee resist this free spirit?"

Caged Vanity

Quinn WRAPPED UP HIS CONVERSATION with his personal trainer and clicked his phone shut. "How did I just get talked into a boot camp session tomorrow at six in the morning?" he moaned.

"I believe I overheard you threaten to oink out at McDonald's if he didn't squeeze you in," I told him.

"Did I? All this extra flesh must be blocking the blood flow to my brain. Remind me why I want to wake up at the crack of dawn to do pushups, would you?"

"Your nonexistent flab will be gone long before I could ever begin to understand," I said, and landed a kick on Quinn's butt. When my friends complained about being overweight, I felt irritated—you can't diet away height, after all—or in the case of itty-bitty Viv, genuinely concerned. Quinn's complaints, though, were too melodramatic to be taken at all seriously.

It was Saturday morning, the beginning of my Chelsea gallery tour, and Quinn and I were walking down West Twenty-Second Street, so close to the Hudson River that we could feel the wind blowing in from New Jersey. The street was wide and bleak, empty but for several inappropriately underdressed women who stood outside the galleries, sucking down cigarettes.

Even as the freezing January wind whipped over their skeletal forms, the women didn't shiver or blink.

"They're all so perfect," I said of these expressionless stick figures. "Like fashion models."

"Oh, you're one to talk!" Quinn scoffed. "*I'm* the one they'll float over the Rose Bowl if I don't watch it!"

But I wasn't joking. In my knee-length parka and goofy, ironic pompom hat, I looked like a fluffy feather pillow next to these women, definitely an undeserving companion to Quinn, who was debonair in his long tweedy trench coat and Russian fur cap.

"Hello, Tamara? You here?" he called out in the first gallery we entered, a building roughly the size of the Houston Astrodome that was empty except for one white blobby sculpture near the doorway. The explanatory plaque read only, "Woman Untitled IV (or: Belief, Blue, Bra)."

A malnourished woman clicked toward us. "Quinn—I'm absolutely over*come* to see you," she said. But she didn't look overcome. In fact, not a single muscle of Tamara's face moved as she spoke. She obligingly led us to the sculpture, which she proceeded to analyze in the context of woman's ongoing struggle for equality.

"Arresting, isn't it?" Tamara murmured. "You should see some women's reactions. The other day, a lady kneeled over and wept. Just *wept*."

I examined the sculpture closely, searching for marks of tragedy.

"No, you need to look here," Quinn said, and pointed behind the sculpture, where a video monitor showed a wooden chicken head spinning on a record playing "Heartbreak Hotel."

"Pop quiz. What would we say about this to Mr. Ziff?" Quinn inquired after Tamara left us.

"Um . . . it powerfully evokes the oppression of an inedible rotisserie chicken?"

"Mimi, I'm serious here," Quinn said. "Say you're in his office and he shows you this work. You just put your hand on your hip, cock your head, and say, 'What an absolute *triumph* of poststructuralism.'"

"Huh?"

"Oh—and try to throw in the word 'utopian,' too," Quinn advised me. "That's always effective. He'll be blown away by your advanced taste, trust me."

"But what does any of that *mean*?"

"It doesn't matter. Just try it out."

"Right. So you want me to say this sculpture is fallopian?"

"You're terrible," Quinn said, and started for the door. "Ta-ta, dahling," he called to Tamara, who waved listlessly in response.

The whole outing stuck to this format: Quinn and I would enter a large warehouse with a suspiciously low inventory, he'd exchange double cheek kisses with an emaciated receptionist, who would then recite a garbled lecture about Space and Identity, or Effervescence and Immortality, or Submission and Formlessness.

Only at our fifth gallery, White + Dutch, did the gaunt hostess fail to guide us in this fashion. She was in the back corner of the gallery, laughing with an older man who was conservatively dressed but for the rainbow clown wig on his head. Quinn studied the architectural drawings on display—geometric smudges almost too faint to discern—before pursing his lips and remarking, "We're in *quite* a cage of narcissism, don't you agree?"

I fished for a clever rejoinder, but all that came out was "Sorry, but I've never had to pee so badly in my life." Quinn forced me to admire about ten more framed smudges before directing me to the bathroom. When I stepped inside, I was pleased to find the facilities more festive than the rest of White + Dutch, with bright murals covering the walls and oversize pieces of foam fruit suspended from the ceiling. En route to the toilet, I stopped to examine my troubled T-zone in the mirror.

"We're in a page of narcissism," I said, using my two index fingers to attack a monster pimple at my hairline. "Don't you find it so, Dieter?" I turned to address the humongous foam banana hanging behind me. "Just a *terrible* page of narcissism."

"A cage," the banana corrected me. "If I heard your friend correctly, he said 'cage.'"

"Oh, yeah, right," I said. "A *cage* of narcissism."

Wait a minute—was I losing it, or had I just accepted an art tip from a foam banana? To answer my question, a woman stepped from behind the fruit sculpture. She was meatier than the other gallery types, with a pretty, round face and glossy red lips. She was older, too, around sixty, and wearing tight black leather pants.

"You're a quick study," she said in a hoarse smoker's voice. "I couldn't hold my own in the narcissistic cage category until I was in my midthirties. What's your excuse for beating me to it?"

"Long story," I muttered uneasily.

"I've got time," the woman told me. She pushed the banana back into the corner, and it gave off a cloud of dust. "My old friend Richard seems to have forgotten that he's the one who invited *me* here and not the other way around. He's so busy hitting on Miss It Girl out there that he didn't even see me slip away—and besides, that stupid rainbow hairpiece he's taken to wearing since his mid-life crisis really obscures the view. I find it physically painful to watch him prey on these infants." She touched her hair, which was coated in banana dust, and gave it a shake.

"He can't take a hint?" I asked.

"If only he'd *get* a hint!" she hooted. "They absolutely *adore* him. Can't get enough. I don't mean to knock him—he's a very good friend, but he should know how to behave a bit better at his age." The woman walked to the door and opened it a crack, just enough for us to see the clown-head man clap the gallery girl on the shoulder.

"Ew," I said, out of solidarity for the banana woman.

"Quite," she said and reshut the door. "So, please, I have *hours* to kill. Won't you take pity and entertain me?"

I hesitated, reluctant to spill my soul to a stranger in the ladies' room of White + Dutch, but then decided, screw it. It's not every day a foam banana befriends me in a public restroom. Besides, I liked this woman, who seemed open but not annoyingly so.

I tried to give her the abridged version. "I was assigned to write an article about this guy Serge Ziff, and I didn't want to sound stupid when I interviewed him, so my dad's darkroom assistant offered to bring me up to speed on the art scene."

"Serge Ziff, you said?" The woman arched her eyebrows.

"You know him?" I asked, for what felt like the hundredth time.

"Honey, *everyone* knows him," she told me. "Now who'd you say you're writing the piece for again?"

Embarrassed, I told her about the *Bugle*. "Our circulation grows with every issue," I added apologetically.

"Hmm," she said. "Mighty interesting, that. Serge Ziff is an *extremely* colorful character."

Before I could ask for her definition of "colorful," the woman reopened the bathroom door. "I should go check on Richard now, to make sure he hasn't been arrested," she said, "but let me know how your article goes—I'd love to read it. Here." She dug into her pocket and handed me a square card with the name Harriet Yates on it. "I don't normally encourage strangers to get in touch, but those boots of yours are really exceptional." She smiled, indicating my lucky red cowboy antiques.

Afterward, Quinn and I were seated in the booth of a trendy Mexican restaurant on Ninth Avenue. "You did fine today," he told me. "With some practice, you'll be bullshitting your way through Chelsea like a pro. I mean, you're only in, what, eleventh grade?"

"Tenth."

"Even better. Enjoy your metabolism while you can."

Quinn ordered the *siempre hambre* special, consisting of a spoonful of black beans and four grains of rice. As I plowed into my Swiss chard burrito, I rehearsed my new vocabulary. *Abstract gargantuan. Being and believing. Mini art. Mart art. Me art.*

Artspeak really was a mind-bender. The more people talked, the less they said.

"Oh, I meant to tell you," I said. "I met this really cool woman in the bathroom—Harriet something or other." I took the square card from my coat pocket and showed it to him.

Quinn put down his fork and grabbed the card. "What? *You* met H. W. Yates? She was there? Honeybunch, I don't know how you do it, but you sure are *some* starfucker."

"Why, is she famous or something?"

"Squirt, H. W. Yates was the leader of It Girls before It Girls even *existed*! She also happens to be a brilliant critic, and a pretty decent artist, too."

Quinn spent the rest of our meal rattling off Harriet's accomplishments until I knew there was no way I'd ever dare phone such a wonder woman. After my cinnamon sorbet, I ducked into the bathroom and returned to find Quinn studying the check.

"Give that to me!" I protested. It wasn't right for Quinn to pay, especially since I was the only one who ate. Also, knowing Dad's financial cluelessness, I'm sure he paid Quinn Industrial Revolution–era wages.

But Quinn only pulled out a credit card and signaled for the waiter. "None of that," he said. "You'll get it next time, when you're rich and famous."

Shrink Wrap

AFTER SCHOOL ON THURSDAY, a large group of Baldwinites congregated on the sidewalk outside the main building. In the center of the large circle stood Sara Ramos in a black patent raincoat, emoting at full volume:

"*Sweet red blood,*
Ketchup, candy,
Blood-red, wine-dark,
Driving and crying to Daddy
Into the milky bloody dawn . . . "

Jess sat at the edge of the circle, as usual a silent participant in the "workshop readings" the *Poetry Review* had started holding, part of a schoolwide effort to "bring literature to life." Jess loved editing the *Review,* but she would never publish her own work, much less declaim it for all of Brooklyn Heights to hear. Her life was rich in material, so I could only guess what she chose to write about: her debt-ridden mother, or her deadbeat dad with his new life (and family) in Pennsylvania, or maybe just her seriously stupid relationships with seriously stupid guys.

Julia, an English teacher once cast as a nurse on *Guiding Light,* was pumping her fist in rhythm with Sara's words. Julia was the *Poetry Review*'s faculty advisor and had been campaigning for me to join since my first *Bugle* column ran, which was why I ducked my head and scurried toward The Wall, where my other friends were waiting.

Though some dismissed it as a mere slab of concrete, to me, Baldwin's Wall was as daunting as Berlin's. Among the cruel unwritten laws governing my progressive school, one stipulated that only twelfth-graders could hang out at The Wall without serious repercussions. My girls, of course, bucked every rule, but I hadn't yet achieved their high-level immunity and so I approached it with a little quiver of fear.

That afternoon, Pia, Lily, and Viv were sharing The Wall with a posse of punk senior girls who were debating the cultural status of naval piercings.

"But how exactly does a navel get 'spontaneously pierced'?" one mohawked girl asked doubtfully.

Her purple-haired comrade shrugged. "If you have to ask, you probably don't have to worry."

When she saw me, Pia hopped off The Wall. "It's time to leave this fascinating conversation," she announced, pausing only to smooth her empire-waist dress and give her black leather riding boots a tug. "Let's hit it, shall we?"

We stopped by the *Poetry Review* circle for Jess just in time to see Amanda France scoot into the circle. What a funny addition to this black turtleneck society, I thought, as Amanda shut her eyes, the better to appreciate Sara's poem.

"He told me he'd be back,
back when we touched in France,

When French music do I hear,

I think but 'Au revoir, my dear'—"

I then remembered Amanda's enthusiasm for open-mike night at the Gray Dog, and with it my Goat Show book vow to spend time with her. Granted, we'd exchanged many a sympathetic eyeroll during World Civ, but socializing outside of school was a different matter altogether.

Jess gathered her books and joined us at the edge of the circle. "So what are we all waiting for?" she asked with marked impatience, as if she regularly skipped afterschool *Poetry Review* events. She was clearly excited that the girls were heading out to her Park Slope apartment that afternoon, a rare treat. Of our group of friends, Jess and I lived in by far the most modest circumstances. With no rooftop pools or indoor greenhouses to lure visitors, the two of us had learned to be resourceful. I depended on Dad's kooky salt and pepper shaker collection and DVD library, Jess on her bottomless stash of eye shadows and shimmer wands and lip glosses. The girls usually visited "Primp Central" before extra-special occasions, and that afternoon definitely qualified.

In a few hours, Pia's chauffeur was going to drive the girls to rural Massachusetts to visit Nona Del Nino at "Promises Farm," a boarding school for kids in recovery and (as the name suggested) also a farm. In addition to homework and group AA meetings, Promises Farm believed in recovery through milking cows, cleaning stables, and harvesting crops. Though I didn't exactly understand the need to dress up for a bunch of sheep and teenage drug addicts, I refused to dwell on the possible outcomes of the girls' long weekend in the country. I had more pressing concerns.

That night, I was meeting Serge Ziff at his gallery, where he was having an opening reception for a German engraver. Serge's assistant, Michael (who, I should probably mention, was a woman), had told me to arrive an hour before the festivities got under way.

At Jess's, we went straight to her bedroom. From her closet, Jess retrieved a bottle of her mom's red wine and untwisted the cap. "I love twist-offs," she said. "The only reason they still make cork bottles is so waiters can make a big production of opening them at fancy restaurants."

"My mom once did a segment called 'Twist-off Elegance,'" Lily said with a snort. "She just *loves* connecting with her core fan base."

"Speaking of moms, isn't yours going to notice?" Viv asked. "No offense, but she doesn't exactly have the Pazzolini wine cellar."

Whoa. If I were Jess, I'd be insulted by these comments, but our hostess appeared unfazed. "It's cool," she said, filling a large coffee mug with wine. "I hid this one a long time ago when my mom bought a whole case, so I'm pretty sure she lost track."

"I wonder if we're going to meet any of the people Nona's written about," Pia said as Jess passed her a mug. "I'd *pay* to see the Naked Doctor."

Viv giggled. "Yeah, or what about Parachute Girl? The one who—"

"Kept trying to fly over the salad bar in the cafeteria!" Pia finished for her.

Jess passed a mug of wine to Viv and then to Lily. When

pouring the fourth mug, though, she emptied the bottle. "Whoops," she said, looking uncertainly from the mug to me, then to the empty mug next to her. "Mimi, do you mind if we split this—?" she asked. "I'm not so experienced a bartender yet, I guess."

I shook my head. "No, no, don't worry about it," I said. "I probably shouldn't drink before my big interview, anyway."

Jess accepted my excuse with a shrug, and the girls began slurping with obvious enjoyment, and continued to talk about Nona Del Nino. I should've just gone straight home, I thought bitterly, where no one else offered to share the wine, either. I couldn't fault them for wanting to spend the weekend with one of their best friends in the world, but I'd be lying if I said it didn't make me the slightest bit uncomfortable. Jealous, even. Jess was rummaging through her closet, auditioning possible outfits, while Viv was at the vanity mirror, piling on the liquid eyeliner. Lily, sprawled on the bed, was flipping through one of Jess's fashion magazines. "Do you think we'll really have to do group therapy, like Nona threatened?" she asked. "After all the therapy I've gone through with my parents these days, I'm not sure I can deal."

"Shrinks *suck*," Viv said with conviction. "The way they trace every single thing you say back to your family. . . . I'm sorry, but hating school is *not* the same as hating my dad."

Unlike every single other resident of the New York metropolitan area, I'd never seen a shrink, probably because Mom had fed me with enough academic psychobabble to last a century. "Shrinks rub me the wrong way, too," I said in a last-ditch bid to join the conversation.

"But you've never had one, have you?" Lily asked.

"Well, no, not officially," I said. "But my mom's a psych professor, which is pretty much the same thing."

"It is, is it?" an unimpressed Pia asked.

"Take pride in your sanity," Jess told me. "When my parents split up, Baldwin recommended that I go see this gross shrink on Livingston Street. I called him Dr. Doo-Doo because the only color he ever wore was brown."

"I might need his number," I said. "I've actually been thinking of seeing a shrink to dissect my anxieties about not having a shrink." No one laughed. The girls were silent, and through the paper-thin walls, we could hear her next-door neighbors arguing. First a woman's voice: "If your plans are so important, then bring Aunt Sabrina with you. She is not coming all this way to be ignored by her nephew!"

"Well, I didn't invite her, did I!" an adolescent boy yelled back.

A dog yelped. Jess lobbed a sneaker at the wall.

The girls were staying at Promises Farm until late Sunday, and however much I dreaded a friendless weekend, I felt even lonelier in their company right then. I wanted to leave, and I would have, if not for the research I had to conduct. "I need your help. Can you tell me everything you know about Serge's daughter Nikola?" And just like that, the mood changed. Babbling and laughing and interrupting, the girls competed for the best description of Nikola Ziff, the prima donna of Baldwin's senior class.

"You'd know her if you saw her," Viv said, after describing

Nikola's hair, which was platinum blond like her father's, and fell past her waist.

"She's one of those pretty people who are actually butt ugly up close. Guys love her."

"She's *never* at school," Lily said. "She's too busy with Fashion Week in Paris or some royal wedding in Monaco or whatever. I took African dance with her last year and she came a grand total of once. Her dad probably only forked over all that cash to ensure that she'd graduate."

"Yeah, and she *claims* she wants to be an actress," Pia chimed in, "but she's never performed in a single school play in all her years at Baldwin."

"Ooh, and here's a good one!" Jess clapped her hands. "Last year, she went to Mexico when her dad was filming that movie about Cuba, and she hooked up with *both* male leads."

"How did *you* hear that?" Pia asked, annoyed because she hadn't.

"Nona told me," Jess said. "Her dad was one of the leads."

Everyone agreed that this was disgusting.

"Oh, and by the way, Little Miss Journalist," Pia said, wagging her finger, "that is strictly off the record, OK? Kinda like Lily's hookup with Harry Feder."

"Pia!" Lily's face blazed red. "At least I'm not dating a nerdy Stuyvesant math whiz."

"I am *not* dating Isaac," Pia said, "but forgive me for having a new friend. He brings a new perspective to the table. We talk on the phone, that is it."

"Mm, sounds like l-u-r-v," Viv teased.

"No, more like m-a-t-h," Pia said decisively. "But what about you?" she said, turning to me. "Still pining for Deep Painter Boy, Max Roth? Apparently he has *quite* a project planned for the dance."

I sighed. "God, he's cute, isn't he? *So* depressingly out of my league."

"I wouldn't go that far," Pia said—another opaque comment that could be interpreted as either a compliment or an insult. "I mean, sure, Max is easy on the eyes, but he's not as talented as everyone, particularly himself, seems to think."

"I guess it's natural you'd resent the only other genius in the tenth grade."

"Yeah, what*ever*," Pia said. "Frankly, I think you'd be better off with Monsieur Potasnik. He's cute, smart, and correct me if I'm wrong, but did I or did I not detect a little spark between you two at the *banya* that day?"

"What are you talking about?" I asked with genuine per-plexity. "Who's Monsieur Potas—"

Pia puckered her lips. "*Boris,* dumbo. Tell me I'm not the only one who saw something."

"I did, I did!" Jess called from the closet, though obviously this wasn't true, given the tears that had been obscuring her vision that day.

"No way," I said. Sure, I'd had fun with Boris at the bath-house, but I'd never thought of him *that* way. Pia just loved making trouble and I was about to tell her as much when I glanced at the clock on Jess's windowsill.

"What?" How had a full ninety minutes passed? I was now

in serious danger of missing my appointment with Serge Ziff. "I've gotta bolt," I said just as Jess emerged from her closet in a bright yellow Polo minidress over black fishnet tights and brown leather ankle boots. The slutty tights brilliantly offset the prissiness of the boots and the little horse decal. Perfect for rural Massachusetts. "Business calls."

"I *love* the combo," Pia said, complimenting Jess.

"Me, too, totally!" Viv exclaimed.

When I slipped out of Jess's bedroom and into the hallway outside her apartment, only the yelping dog next door commented on my exit.

All Q, No A

As THE CAB PASSED MY USUAL EXIT on the West Side Highway, I removed my compact from my purse to make a few last-minute corrections. I then checked my outfit, baggy pinstripe pants with a supertight T-shirt. Normally, I dressed to conceal my undeveloped figure, but the female gallery assistants I'd met on Saturday seemed to flaunt their flat silhouettes, so I went with it.

Outside Serge's gallery, I paid the driver and—to avoid calling attention to my youth and general ineptitude—tucked my pompom hat into my jacket pocket. The tall, braided steel door of Ziff Projects might have easily been mistaken for the entrance to a medieval torture chamber, but I pushed it open confidently, breathing a silent thank-you to Quinn as I entered. Without his tutorial, I might be quaking with fear right now; instead I was yawning. Well, at least pretending to. I'd spoken to the woman at the reception desk, Michael, several times to arrange the meeting, but her Fenella-esque, mid-Atlantic accent hadn't prepared me for the ghoul who sat before me. Her skin was chalky and dry, her thin lips creased into a frown. Some of my resolve evaporated as she drawled, "Mimi Sch*uuuu*lman, I presume?"

remind me, how can I help you again?" his forehead asked. "You're a friend of Nikola's?"

I outlined my mission, neglecting only to mention that his daughter was a complete stranger to me. Not a lie, mind you—a simple omission. Then I took my brand-new mini-cassette recorder out of my tote bag. "Do you mind if I tape you?" I asked Serge supercasually, as if I dropped this request on a daily basis.

There was a pause while Serge's fingers pressed a remote control that soundlessly elevated him to eye level. "I'd prefer not, in fact," he said coldly. "I don't believe in recording devices. If you're not equipped to write down my answers, then I'm afraid I'm not equipped to deliver them."

Pop! went my fragile self-assurance. "Um . . . OK," I said. "Um, that's totally fine. I can just, like, write down all of your, um, answers." I stuffed the cassette player back into my bag and fished for my trusty reporter's notebook.

"I guess . . . uh, yeah. I guess we should start by talking about Baldwin and your, uh, relationship with it," I said, sounding unauthoritative and apologetic and about eight years old. "Then we can move to other areas? I promise I won't take up too much of your time."

"That's lucky," Serge said, "because Gunther Lollendorp's first solo show in the Western Hemisphere is opening here in approximately three minutes."

"Right." I swallowed. "So we'll just jump right into it then? Great. Um, so . . ." I glanced desperately at my notebook. "Oh, yeah, here we go. When was the first time you visited The Baldwin School, and what was your first impression?"

"Ah . . ." Serge breathed in, evidently liking the softball question. "Probably when Nik was about four," he began, "so it must've been—"

Michael chose this moment to rat-a-tat-tat on the window and motion for Serge to get up. A group of important-looking people had gathered behind her.

"Duty calls," Serge said, standing up. "Back in a jiffy. Make yourself at home—read a magazine, make some international calls, knock yourself out."

Instead, I responsibly jotted down observations on Serge's outfit (handsome charcoal gray suit over a ribbed black T-shirt), hair (just as blindingly platinum as in the Web photographs), and office décor (with special attention given to the aerodynamic office chair). Too bad I had no friends in Sierra Leone, I kept thinking, as the party sounds increased in volume and Serge still didn't reappear. At least not for another half-hour, and when at last he did breeze back into the office, he made no reference to the duration of his absence.

"Now, where were we?" he asked casually. "Run that last question by me again?"

I was repeating the question about his first Baldwin experience when the rat-a-tat-tat on the window recommenced. Michael was pressing her forehead into the glass and signaling at the businessman behind her. Once again, Serge hopped right up. "I'm terribly sorry about this," he said. "But Gunther's show is proving a bit sensational, so I can't really help you out much more tonight. You're welcome to stay, mix and mingle—our sushi chef's the best."

"B-b-but," I stammered, "my deadline's Tuesday, see, and it's already Thurs . . ." But I'd already risen, and was shadowing Serge into the gallery.

"I'll tell you what," Serge said. "Why don't you swing by my place Saturday, and we'll have brunch? How does eleven-thirty suit you? The whole scene will be much more relaxed, I promise. Michael, you got that, right? Saturday at eleven-thirty? You'll remind me?" Michael responded with a nod so brittle, I feared her neck would crack.

Saturday was only two days away, which meant I could still meet my deadline. I was nodding gratefully when Serge vanished into the crowd, leaving me alone in the center of the room. One look at my surroundings and I decided to bail. I had no place here, amid these cultured people with their sparkly jewelry and nasal accents. But I'd hardly pulled on my hat and jacket when some idiot knocked the pompom hat off my head. I spun around angrily, only to see Max Roth wearing my favorite winter accessory. "Well, if it isn't Miss Texas," he said.

"Hey!" He looked adorable, rosy-cheeked and winter-kissed.

"I had a hat just like this in second grade," Max said. "It had a robot on it and came with matching underwear. My mom and I fought over the underpants because I wanted to wear them every day and I didn't understand why she wouldn't let me."

"Well, why didn't she?" I asked playfully, dare I say, *flirtatiously*.

"I'm not sure, come to think of it," Max said. "Thanks for reminding me. I'll ask her the second I get home about stealing my robot under—" He broke off as a petite girl floated up with a diamond tiara on her head and a cup of wine in each hand. Without speaking, she passed one to Max, then stood there evaluating me with open disdain. And no wonder. She was minuscule, this girl, a fraction of my size, with wavy strawberry-blond hair and floaty layers of couture clothing. I felt enormous next to her, like a giraffe or rental clown or female wrestler.

"So, what's your verdict?" Max asked me with an odd formality.

I had no idea what he was talking about, but still. That was no excuse for answering as I did, and for as long as I live I will regret the words that burst from my mouth right then: "I think robot underwear *never* goes out of style. In fact, if you find them, let me know—maybe I could borrow them!"

Max blanched and the tiara girl exploded in laughter.

"I was actually asking about the art," Max said. "The Gunther Lollendorp etchings?"

"Oh, of course! The drawings!" My stomach dropped through the floor. The drawings! What brilliant, mind-blowing, or at least vaguely normal-sounding comment could I come up with about the drawings? But the tiara girl was already tugging at Max's wrist.

"Come *on*, Max," she whined. "I thought you were here to *network!*" She pulled him away, and Max tossed the pompom hat over his shoulder at me and glanced back as a way of saying goodbye. As I galloped to the gallery exit, I'm certain I heard the word "freak."

Outside, the wind was blowing hard, and I yanked the childish hat over my ears. What a dreary, terrible evening. I'd composed three worthless sentences about Serge Ziff's outfit and discussed soiled underwear with the hottest guy in school and his celestially perfect consort. Not only that, but my friends were off milking cows with recovering addicts for three days, and I was actually *jealous*. When would this stupid New York life *ever* start to feel normal?

Several feet from the gallery, I thought I heard someone calling my name but I kept walking. Running into Max was coincidence enough; I couldn't possibly know *two* people in this up-market crowd. But then I heard it again, this time distinctly, "MI-MI!"

When I turned around I recognized the woman instantly, less from our brief encounter at the gallery bathroom than from the subsequent Web searches I'd conducted. "It's Harriet Yates without her banana!" I exclaimed. I was amazed that such a living legend remember the name of a human termite like me. Somehow, Harriet wasn't that intimidating, at least not after She-Michael and Serge and the tiara girl. That night, Harriet was wearing a crocheted beret and a frown, which combined to make her look older than she had in the bathroom, and she was accompanied by the same guy I'd seen in the gallery that day, still in his unmistakable rainbow afro wig, but with a different rail-thin girl coiled around his waist. "Where are you going?" Harriet asked me.

"Home," I told her.

When she volunteered to escort me, I nodded happily, too flattered to second-guess her. "I live downtown," I told her, to which she replied: "Of course you do. No one with those cowboy boots could *possibly* live above Fourteenth Street."

At the corner of Tenth Avenue, where we veered south, I asked Harriet if her friends were going to worry. "Oh, Richard always manages just fine, and I can't even remember the name of his latest female accessory," Harriet said. "These days, I feel more like a novelty item than a guest. Mind you, my male friends don't have this problem, or at least not on the nights they commit statutory rape, but my situation is thornier. Or, not thorny, but . . . what's the word I'm looking for? . . . Celibate?"

I laughed even as the embarrassing Max Roth underwear exchange replayed in my head.

"In that case, my situation's pretty thorny, too."

"A styling thing like you?" Harriet asked. "I don't believe it. The last time I got dragged to one of these openings, a beautiful young woman who'd just moved here from Tennessee asked me if I'd work for her as an advisor. Guess what for."

"An art magazine?" I ventured.

"That's what I'd thought, too. But no. She had a costume party coming up and wanted to go as me." Harriet paused. "Me *thirty* years ago. She wanted costume suggestions. Can you believe the nerve? After that, I vowed never to go to one of those things again, and if I hadn't seen you, I might've broken my word. But what about you?" she asked. "What's your excuse for being there?"

As we turned on West Eleventh Street, I told her I'd just interviewed Serge.

"Ah-*ha*. Of course. So was it everything you'd hoped it would be and more?"

"Try much, much less," I said. As I detailed my miserable

visit to Ziff Projects, Harriet bobbed her head sympathetically. My account lasted for most of our journey through the zigzagging streets of the West Village. Even as we stopped to look in a few store windows, Harriet let me vent.

"What's your gut impression of him now?" she asked at one point.

"I'm not sure," I said. "He seemed fine, except when I took out my tape recorder. But his assistant, that Michael woman, was seriously dire. I'm going to brunch at his house Saturday, so maybe he'll be nicer without her hovering around."

"I'm sure the brunch will be sublime," Harriet said, "but take a little advice from an old hand. When you're writing about somebody, you don't necessarily have to spend a lot of time with him."

I remembered this comment only later—too late for it to do me any good, because Harriet uttered it on Barrow Street just as my house came into view.

"This is where I get off," I said, and then invited Harriet in for a cup of tea. She and my dad, I suspected, would love each other.

Harriet, however, declined the invitation. "You've cheered me up as much as possible, but right now, I just need to go home and stare at the television."

I assured her she'd redeemed my night, too, and with that we said good night. Inside, I consulted the glowing green numbers on the microwave clock, pleased that it was only 10:28. With some discipline, I could still knock off my World Civ take-home essay, which until that moment had slipped my mind entirely. When Ms. Singer had introduced the assignment that afternoon—on the rise of the bourgeoisie in eighteenth-century France—she'd specified a two-hour limit.

"If you use more than the allotted time, I'll find out," she'd warned us ominously, "so don't even try." All eyes in the class zoomed on Frank Abrahams, brown-noser extraordinaire, who sometimes gave himself extra-credit assignments for fun.

By the time I'd devoured some cold sesame noodles and caught the finale of a runway modeling reality program, I was in no danger of exceeding Ms. Singer's two-hour limit. It was almost midnight when I turned off the TV and opened the blue exam booklet. I yawned, too exhausted to contemplate the unhappy peasantry of eighteenth-century France, the steep price of grapes (or grain?), the fatso kings and powdered courtesans, and the expression on Max Roth's face when I'd asked to borrow his robot underwear.I woke to the sound of my father's wake-up call.

"Up! Up! Up! Up! Up!" Dad was standing in the middle of the living room, pounding on his chest like a tribesman on public television. Winter light was breaking through the curtains: shit, shit, and double shit. I ran to the kitchen, where the microwave clock read 7:46. World Civ essay or not, I'd still be late for school.

"Dad, there's no time to chitchat," I said when he followed me downstairs to the bathroom. "I have to get ready and write about Enlightenment and Napoleon and industry!" I slammed the door in Dad's face. I took off my clothes, stepped into the shower, and turned the knob to my favorite position.

"Well, what about a quick sit-down breakfast?" Dad tried through the door. "They say proper digestion is critical to—"

His voice was lost in the spray of water.

Sweet Charity

A HALF-HOUR LATER, as I hurtled out of the train station, a great wave of hunger hit me. I could make it to World Civ, but only if I skipped the bagel shop. Having just seen a local news segment about malnourished fifth-graders looting a deli in Queens, I went for the veggie cream cheese bagel. Because I was now ten minutes late for class, I decided to skip and finish my assignment. I knew Ms. Singer would be mad, but this way I had time to formulate a good excuse, and by taking the essay to her office, I'd deny her the pleasure of tormenting me in public.

Though it was still cold outside, I was wearing about twelve layers of clothing, so I headed for the Brooklyn Bridge. It might be nice to take in the views without all the German tourists who usually crowded the walkways. I walked close to the rail, and slowly, to keep from slipping on the occasional patches of ice. It was quite an effort, so I took a seat on the first available bench, which some intrepid pedestrian had already scraped clean of ice and snow. There, still on the Brooklyn side of the bridge, I turned to the essay. With no noise but the steady whir of traffic below, I had no trouble concentrating. I had just finished my conclud-ing paragraph when I felt a tap on my shoulder. I assumed it was a lost tourist, in which case I wouldn't be much help, until I heard the word, "Texas." Was it possible? Two random run-ins in twenty-four hours? Sure enough, there stood Max Roth, his broad shoulders framed by Manhattan's skyscrapers. He was wearing a knit hat and holding on to a black spiral-bound sketchpad.

"Hey, what are *you* doing here?" I asked, rolling up my exam book. "Aren't you supposed to be in World Civ right now?"

"Just what I was about to ask you."

"I'm finishing the World Civ take-home. And you?"

"I turned it in yesterday," Max said. "Ms. Singer gave me today off to work on my art project. The dance is only a few weeks away, and I'm supposed to mount a whole one-man exhibition."

"Ms. Singer let you skip class?" I asked in amazement. "I mean, you shouldn't get stressed about the dance—I'm sure whatever you do will be awesome." Then, with no idea where I found the courage, I added, "If there's one Baldwinite who can pull of a solo show, it's Max Roth." And I meant it. Even after resolving its budget crisis, Baldwin still wanted Max to supply the decorations. And with good reason, too. Everything about him was perfect. My eyes moved from his chapped lips down to the jagged hole in his left sneaker.

"I hope so," he said, and took a seat next to me on the bench. OK, so maybe "next to me" is a slight exaggeration. In fact, Max positioned himself at the farthest edge, but still, after my underwear blunder the previous night, he was generous to acknowledge me at all. "The theme of the dance is prison chic," he was saying now, "so I'm supposed to make a 'thematic' contribution, but I have no clue where to search for inspiration."

Was that a hint, and, if so, what kind? But as Max sighed and gazed into the distance, I remembered the frosty tiara girl and vowed to keep quiet. I just sat still and kept staring at his shoes and did my best not to implode. A few minutes into this exercise, a couple with their hands in each other's butt pockets stopped by our bench to look out over the choppy water. Stirred by this urban panorama, the guy twined his arms around the girl's neck and kissed her lightly, then less lightly. Max was still angled in the other direction, toward Brooklyn, which was lucky. I didn't want him to notice the lovebirds and read the perverted hopes their PDA was awakening in me.

Much to my relief, they disentangled just as Max directed my attention to the huge digital clock on the Watchtower, the Jehovah's Witness world headquarters next to the Brooklyn Bridge. "Class starts in ten minutes," he said, and got to his feet. "Shall we?"

I can only offer one explanation for what happened next: I am a naturally clumsy person, all arms and legs and awkwardness, doubly so when nervous or self-conscious. When I stood up after Max, I tried to shave an inch off my gargantuan height by bending my knees and slumping my shoulders, but the choreography was too elaborate, especially with my cowboy boots slick on the ice. I lost my balance and wobbled forward, windmilling my arms uselessly in the bitter cold air, until—oh, God—until I fell ass-first onto the icy wood-planked walkway of the Brooklyn Bridge. And that wasn't all. As I tumbled over, my World Civ assignment slipped from my grasp and sailed high into the air. I watched in disbelief as a gust of wind carried my tidy, incisive paragraphs off the bridge's walkway and over three lanes of traffic. I was bruised and wet and freezing and wanted nothing more than to wail, but I couldn't, because Max Roth was still standing there, his face crinkled into an unreadable grin.

"Man, Texas," he said, "you sure are one messed-up chick. Let's at least get you back to school—maybe you'll be safe there." Max stooped over to pull me up, but I was in no condition to appreciate this thrilling physical contact.

After thanking him, I went straight to Ms. Singer, sopping wet and shivering from the cold, and related the airborne fate of my take-home exam. She listened in silence, her lips pressed together as tight as a whip. When I was done, she said only, "And pray tell, what was your take-home exam doing on the Brooklyn Bridge?"—to which I had no immediate reply. She "suggested" I spend lunch that afternoon drafting an essay on the Tennis Court Oath in the seventh-floor Humanities Department office. Even though my usual lunch companions had ditched me for Nona Del Nino that day, I still dreaded a meal with Ms. Singer, who probably spent her free periods marking papers with her psycho four-color pen. When I dragged into the Humanities office a few hours later, I was ecstatic to find another student in the dunce corner. Ecstatic, then very confused.

"You?" I gaped at preppy, perfect Amanda France, a guaranteed straight-A student if only Baldwin believed in grades. "What are you doing here?"

"No talking!" Ms. Singer barked before Amanda could

answer. "Since you were both too busy to turn in your assignment in a timely fashion, you must now do me the courtesy of spending this hour in thoughtful silence. I've chosen a new topic that I trust you will both find challenging."

Amanda France had flubbed an assignment? From Ms. Singer? Ms. Singer passed me and Amanda two sheets of paper with different topics on them—"in case either of you gets any *ideas*"—and then she perched behind her desk, glowering at us. After a few minutes, she got up and crossed her arms over her chest. "Now, if you'll excuse me," she said, "you have only forty minutes to complete a two-hour essay, so I trust I can leave you with the knowledge that you'll not abuse my good faith."

"So what'd you do?" I whispered approximately three seconds after Ms. Singer left me and Amanda alone together.

"Absolutely nothing!" Amanda countered venomously, and at full volume. "It's squash season, so I'm totally busy to begin with, and last night I got carried away with this creative writing project for Kim's class and I ran out of time. I thought stupid Ms. Singer would understand—Stanley would've—but oh, no. Pardon me for forgetting that World Civ is the single most important thing in the universe!"

I put down my pen and asked, "What are you doing tonight?" Hanging out with Amanda when the girls were gone felt dishonest somehow, but I wasn't motivated by convenience right then. When Amanda was railing against Ms. Singer, her face shed its usual blinding brightness, and she actually seemed like a normal person—a person I might actually enjoy spending time with.

But alas, Amanda was busy that evening—busy, she said, for the next three weekends. "I can't even go to open-mike night at the Gray Dog," she said, "and you know how much I live for that." Did I ever. But I merely nodded as Amanda gushed about that weekend's squash tournament, which kicked off at nine the following morning in a remote corner of Connecticut. "The roads are super rough after the snow," she said, "so we're leaving tonight. Courtney's mom is driving the whole team, and we're staying in this really cute inn that my Dad's golf buddy told him about—there's a bathtub in every room. It's going to be rad."

I agreed that it sounded like a promising weekend and briefly wondered how I was going to spend mine.

Twice Shy

I WENT HOME AFTER SCHOOL to unload my overladen backpack and then walked over to Shine, a salon on Grove Street, for a long-overdue trim. Resigned to a low-key Friday, I little expected the chaos that engulfed me when I got there. An Australian TV crew had packed the salon to document the top-to-toes transformation of Luella, a sales analyst from Perth who'd won a national makeover competition, and I nearly tripped over the tangle of wires and extension cords that carpeted the floor.

Because my chair was about two inches from Luella's, a procession of makeup artists and colorists—all men in belly shirts—kept jostling me and shouting over my head. Oddly, I found myself enjoying the crazy atmosphere—maybe I was starting to develop a taste for the pandemonium of my adopted home. As I strolled out of the salon two hours later, my hair short and shaggy, I throbbed with love for New York—the manic characters on the street, the eruptions on every corner—and devised another vow to add to my Goat Show book. It was time I got reacquainted with this lunatic city, to explore the world beyond Baldwin. I wasn't thinking about the Statue of Liberty or the Museum of Modern Art gift shop, but the musty chess stores on Thompson Street, the Belmont Park racetrack, the two-acre Indian spice shop in Jackson Heights that Vikram Mohini's aunt and uncle ran.

When I woke up late the next morning, I spontaneously decided I would ride the 7 train out to Jackson Heights. Once back home, I'd download a recipe and cook a steaming vegetable curry for dinner for Dad and Quinn. Maybe I'd even invite Harriet Yates to join us. But then, as I opened my blinds and the sharp wintry daylight blasted into my room, I remembered my brunch interview with Serge Ziff at eleven-thirty, just an hour away. Ugh, I'd evidently slept too long and too hard—how could I possibly have let that slip from my consciousness, even for a moment?

Upstairs, I opened the refrigerator and took out the one semi-edible item, a raspberry yogurt. I was peeling off the top when I heard a throat clearing behind me.

"What do you think you're doing?" It was Quinn, bleary-eyed after staying up to watch the Fashion Police Final Countdown in the living room. Though he lived nearby, in the East Village, our superior cable package often stranded him here until late at night. Sometimes he even passed out here, after particularly vigorous evenings of after-hours programming.

"I'm going to Serge's in an hour," I said, "and I know the food will rule, but I need a little something to tide me over."

Quinn snatched the yogurt from me and clutched it to his chest. "I don't care if you're brunching with the Queen of England—hands off the fat-free dairy products!"

"Excuse me?"

"Honey, right now I'm in the zone, and if I don't start my day right my whole system goes haywire and people will continue to think I'm carrying quadruplets in this pooch!"

"Cut me some slack," I said, giving his six-pack a poke. "I have a sketchy brunch date with some dude I hardly know. It's stressful."

Quinn took a spoon out of the dish rack and began inhaling the yogurt. "Honey, if a catered brunch at a world-famous art dealer's megamansion is the sketchiest Saturday-morning scenario you can think of, you need to get out more. Try waking up in bed next to a man reading L. Ron Hubbard with a highlighter. Then we'll talk about sketchy."

Laughing, I pulled a box of chocolate chip cookies from the pantry, but once again Quinn slapped my hand reproachfully. "Mimi, can you not? It takes a village for a diet to work, it really does, and right now I'd really appreciate your support."

"Quinn, I totally support you, I swear—I just need a snack. Besides, I'm saving you from eating these cookies, aren't I?"

But Quinn had already dragged me from the kitchen to drill me on art terms, and when I flagged down a cab half an hour later, there was nothing in my stomach but toothpaste residue.

Serge Ziff's outrageous estate on West Twenty-Ninth Street took up the better part of the block. It was a huge silvery structure with porthole windows and smoked glass balconies on all four levels. I rang the bell uncertainly. A housekeeper opened the door and led me through a tall, glassed-in terrace and into a room where a teenage girl with cascading blond hair lay sprawled over a spider chair. She was flipping through a stack of papers and smoking a substance with a moldy smell that I recognized from my embarrassing marijuana initiation in Williamsburg last semester. With a start, I realized that this girl was the one who'd slammed me into the studio building staircase on our first day back at school. Nikola Ziff. Of course. Who else would be wearing a white fur-trimmed robe and openly smoking a joint at eleven-thirty on a Saturday morning?

Tentatively, I said hello to her. "Hi, I'm Mimi. You, um, go to Baldwin right? I'm a sophomore there."

Nikola took a long pull from her joint and looked up at me blankly. "So?" she said. "I'm a senior there—does that entitle me to barge into your house at the crack of dawn?"

"It's actually almost noon," I pointed out. "And, uh, actually, I was invited here by your dad. For the *Bugle*?"

Nikola exhaled, still bathing me in contemptuous blankness. "My dad? Oh, sorry—he's not home, but if you want, I can double-check that for you."

I thanked her profusely, but Nikola didn't budge. A few minutes into this excruciating stalemate, Serge Ziff came into the room wearing tennis whites, with white terrycloth sweatbands around every potential perspiration point—elbows, forehead, wrists, knees, and ankles. He looked like John McEnroe after a very serious car wreck.

Without acknowledging his daughter's flagrant disrespect for the law, Serge eyed me with perplexity. "What are *you* doing here?" he asked.

Was he serious? "I thought we had a meeting—didn't Michael remind you?"

"Damn it, she was supposed to call you and reschedule. We had a huge sale yesterday, and I have to run over to the gallery to oversee the shipment."

"In tennis clothes?" I asked without thinking.

Serge didn't react as he strode to the door. "Call Michael on Monday, will you, and explain what you need." Then, to his daughter, he added, "And Nik, for God's sake, use an ashtray."

"I'd offer you a cup of coffee," Nikola said once her dad had left. "But frankly I'm not in all that hospitable a mood." She flicked more ash onto the polished marble.

I left the house unaided, too defeated to execute my Jackson Heights spice shop plan. Right now what I needed was a friend. Two blocks from the Ziffs', I stopped at a pay phone and called Sam's cell. He was just sitting down to lunch at Boris Potasnik's.

"Just come over," Sam told me. "Boris always buys *way* too much food, even by Miss Piglet's standards."

Though I'd wanted a private sympathy fest, with my other friends off milking cows in Massachusetts, I accepted Sam's offer. I hailed another cab and rode it to the address he had given me. Then, after disembarking at a prewar building on the Upper West Side, I entered a lobby with swirled marble banisters and intricate designs carved into its mahogany ceilings. It was no joke, and neither was the Potasnik pad on the fifteenth floor.

I hadn't seen Boris since our *banya* expedition, but he greeted me warmly, leading me into a room of ice-skating rink proportions, with wall-size windows and priceless urns on pedestals and paintings with their own lights. "Whoa," I said. As Boris hung my shabby coat on a gleaming antelopelike object, I tried to cover my hillbilly awe and told him that his doorman requested leftovers.

"From what I remember of your consumption talents," Boris responded, "I doubt there'll be much to go around."

We were walking down a long hall cluttered with bright plastic toys, property of Boris's toddler half-brother, Constantine. "The brat's in my bedroom," Boris explained. "My parents don't let him watch cartoons, so whenever I babysit, I help him catch up with his playmates."

"My dad read the parenting manual upside down," I said, "so I have the opposite problem. I've seen every episode of every television show ever made, including those that came out before I was born."

"God, I'll trade you," Boris said as we turned into a room as huge as the first.

"By the way, sorry to gate-crash like this," I remembered to say. "It's just that—"

"Sam told me," Boris cut in. "I was sorry to hear the Ziff interview was such crap."

"More like nonexistent, but yeah, 'crap' also works."

"*I* know," Boris said. "Why don't *I* write a check to Baldwin? Then you can interview me instead. Here's your headline: 'Baldwin saved! Tenth-grade slob spends allowance on printer cartridge.'"

"You can do better than that, big man," Sam's voice called from another room. (This place went on for*ever!*) "With your allowance, you could at least donate a new water fountain."

Sam was sitting at the black lacquer dining room table before a huge spread of delicacies. At his elbow, leaning over a notebook, was Viv Steinmann. "Viv!" I cried, taken aback. "What happened? I thought you were in Massachusetts until Sunday!"

"We came back early," Viv said with studied nonchalance. "Turns out Pia's allergic to manure."

"You missed a very hot review session this morning," Sam said. "I'm helping Viv out with her seminar—she signed up late after ditching Yuri's funny farm, so it's been tough catching up."

"Women in Islam," Viv said.

"Survey says: Don't be one," Boris wisecracked.

"I didn't even realize you were taking Women in Islam," I said to Sam. "That's a lot of multiculturalism for one semester."

"I'm not *taking* it," he said with an unexpected defensive edge to his voice. "I'm merely drawing on my bank of knowledge. The Atlantic Avenue days are finally coming in handy."

I looked at him doubtfully. Sam frequently hung out at the Yemenite café on Atlantic Avenue, but since when did drinking tea and watching Arabic music videos during lunch periods qualify him as an academic expert on Islam?

"I'll take any help I can get," Viv said, reading the skepticism on my face. "We already have a five-page essay. Fucking brutality—I'm seriously considering withdrawing."

"Better luck last semester," Sam said. "Have you forgotten Zora's new antiwithdrawal policy? We can't change classes after the first week. She says we need work on our 'commitment issues.'"

Boris, who'd slipped out during this exchange, suddenly reappeared bearing a huge silver platter piled high with little trays of food. "I got carried away at Fairway this morning," he said. "There's starfruit salad, scrambled eggs, fennel sausages, blue potato salad, blinis, and sour cream and caviar to go with them. And bagels with the works in the kitchen."

After applauding the spread, I busied myself scooping potato salad onto my plate, until Viv made an unsettling comment. "Oh, guess what," she said. "Nona might be coming back to Baldwin. Not this semester, but if her good behavior continues, she'll be back for junior year."

"Excellent," I said with ineptly feigned enthusiasm. In all honesty, I dreaded Nona's inevitable homecoming, for I sensed the girls' posse was too small for us both. Luckily, Boris spared me the necessity of another insincere reply when he passed me a side plate of expertly assembled blinis. "Eat those first," he advised. "They cool fast." I obeyed right away, and for a moment, Boris's supremely scrumptious blinis—the first food I'd eaten that day—succeeded in taking my mind off cocoa-skinned Nona Del Nino, and the consequences of her return. For the next half-hour, Boris and I concentrated on eating, while Sam and Viv playfully debated Smokey Robinson's contribution to the soul music canon. Islam, as far as I remember, never came up.

The two of them seemed comfortable together, familiar with each other's quirks, and I wondered how long this "tutoring" had been going on. *Weird,* I thought. First Pia and now Viv—was tutoring the *only* way to meet guys in this city?

Boris and I were still working on some seriously delicious chocolate babka when Viv got up to leave. She was off to meet her dad at Lincoln Center for an afternoon tribute to Nina Simone—

"the main reason *I* wanted to come back from Massachusetts early." Viv seldom advertised these cultural excursions in front of the girls, but Sam evidently admired her nontrendy musical side.

"So, 'fess up," I prodded Sam the instant she left.

"I believe everybody has a right to excel academically," Sam said, absolutely poker-faced.

"Funny," Boris said, "I've never seen you tutoring ugly members of the tenth grade."

Sam still wouldn't crack. "What can I say? My services are too in demand." It was no fun to tease someone so unresponsive, so I switched to the three-minute version of my trip to the Ziffs'.

"Boris has spent a good deal of time in that manse, haven't you, big guy?" Sam said.

Boris reddened. "Yeah, whatever," he said. "Nikola and I were friends a long time ago."

"How weird," I said. "You mean, like when you were little kids?"

"Yeah," Sam said, laughing, "they used to play doctor together all the time!"

Boris turned even brighter red and suddenly I put two and two together. Boris and Nikola Ziff had a romantic past. I was sure there had been stranger couplings in the history of the universe, but I couldn't think of a single one.

Yakkety Yak

I CALLED ZIFF PROJECTS DURING my first free period on Monday and left a message for Michael. The next morning, I did the same thing, and ditto for the morning after that, but at no point did Michael deign to get back to me. I'd missed my Tuesday deadline and by late Sunday afternoon, I'd pretty much given up on ever getting a story together. "I've called her seven times," I griped to Lily on the phone. "Seven times. I'm starting to feel like a total stalker."

"Sounds pretty frustrating," Lily said.

"Try *extremely*." I was in a foul mood and had declined Dad's invitation to join him and Quinn for a late brunch. Instead, after a brief walk to the Union Square farmers' market, I'd gone home and spent the remainder of the unusually sunny day on the phone, putting off my World Civ assignment and eating Farmer Fred's organic gingersnaps. "I mean—" I paused to crunch into a cookie—"it's not like I'm trying to do a hit job on him, just a fluffy profile."

"Not *too* fluffy," Lily reminded me.

"You know what I mean. I'm trying to write a *positive* piece, so why the constant brushoff? What am I supposed to do, hold him at gunpoint?"

"Maybe you could just research him online and do a profile without any direct quotes," Lily suggested. "You know, like find some old articles and rewrite them so it sounds fresh? You wouldn't be the first desperate journalist to go that route."

Fat chance of that. Despite thousands of references to him, hours of Internet research had yielded only one concrete insight into Serge Ziff: his favorite flavor of martini, a fresh-squeezed tangerine Tropicana.

"Mimi!" Quinn hollered from upstairs.

"I'm on the phone!" I shouted back.

"Ouch!" Lily objected. "Have you ever heard of putting the phone down before screaming at the top of your lungs?"

Right then the phone clicked and Quinn came on the line. "Honey, did you not see the message for you on the refrigerator?" he asked breathlessly.

"No, what message?"

"Good Lord, I thought that was the first place you'd look! Doll, you just scored an invitation to a party Serge Ziff is throwing on Bravura Island! You must've made *quite* the impression—I hope you kept your clothes on!"

"Quinn!" I cried. "Don't be dirty! What if I were on the phone with my math teacher?"

"Now *that* would be dirty," Quinn snorted.

"Hey, Mimi," Lily broke in, "this sounds like very good news. So let's stop moping, shall we, and check in later tonight?

I need to run now—I'm supposed to go out to dinner with my folks."

"Margaret Morton's not cooking Sunday night dinner herself?" I asked, echoed by Quinn's gasp of "Sacrilege!"

"Hello, has my mother *ever* cooked dinner in her entire life?" Lily scoffed. "No, her therapist recommended we start a 'family ritual' of dining out together, so from now on, it's egg rolls every Sunday."

"You'd really think a food show star would steer clear of the deep-fried items," Quinn reflected, "but to each domestic diva her own. Now, Mimi, haul your booty up here!"

After saying goodbye to Lily, I headed upstairs and read the message Quinn waved in my face. "Michael called. U R invited to the Presidents' Day weekend bonanza! Buzz back 2 confirm!"

"What's wrong with you?" I asked as Quinn grabbed my arms and shook them.

"Mimi, this is huge. We're talking about the most exclusive party in the New York art world! Every Presidents' Day, Serge Ziff charters a private jet and flies everyone-who's-anyone down to his Caribbean Xanadu. Do you have *any* idea how lucky you are?"

"Too bad Dad would never in a million years let me go," I said. "He doesn't know any of these people, and neither do I, come to think of it."

"Oh, Mimi," Quinn tutted, "we both know Roger's a major league pushover. I'm *sure* he can be talked into it, especially since we have so much time to strategize! Fenella met us at the restaurant earlier and dragged him to the Film Forum for a noir double feature, so he won't be back for a few hours." I shuddered at the fleeting image of Dad's and Fenella's hands brushing in a sea of salty popcorn.

"But Dad's not the only problem, Quinn," I said. "Presidents' Day is three weeks from now, and my deadline was Tuesday. My editors are forgiving, but only to a point. Lily's getting anxious."

"Screw your deadline," Quinn said, growing impatient with my boring pragmatism. "Honey, no offense, but it's a school newspaper—stop acting like you're breaking Watergate! Now, c'mon, what are you waiting for?" He popped open his phone, dialed the number he'd written down, and pushed the little handset against my ear.

"Roooiiight," Michael drawled when I identified myself. "Yaahs, Mr. Ziff wanted to include you in his salon on the sand," she said, pronouncing *salon* the French way. "It will be held on Bravura Island from February 17. Shall I mark you down?"

"What exactly is it?" I asked her, knowing Dad would want details.

"Well . . . " Michael issued a pained sigh. "It started out as an intimate weekend getaway, but over the years the guest list has grown to about thirty. Because space on the plane is limited, it's *critical* to reserve your spot straightaway." She breathed out noisily again. "I'd be much obliged if you faxed me a copy of your passport tonight—February 17 is *roight* around the corner."

This whole plan was proceeding way too fast. One minute, the guy's ignoring my phone calls, and now he wanted to cart me off to some exotic island?

February 17, February 17, why did that date ring a bell? Then it hit me: February 17 was the day my mother and Maurice were arriving for their bird-watching expedition. Quinn, still eavesdropping, frantically signaled for me to answer Michael. The best I could do was ask if I could get back to her.

"You're saying you don't *have* a passport?"

"Actually, no, that's not what I'm saying. Look, I'll call you back tomorrow. I need to figure some stuff out."

"I wouldn't dawdle if I were you," Michael said, and hung up.

The idea of being on an island with strangers stressed me out, so I went downstairs to tackle my World Civ homework. As soon as I opened my *Great Ideas* textbook, however, Quinn rapped on the door with an urgent question: "Your vintage stuff is cute, Mimi, but there's a time and place for everything. *Pray* tell me you own a bikini that didn't previously belong to a housewife during the Eisenhower administration? Because if not, we *must*—" The phone rang. I picked it up gratefully as I glared at Quinn. I was surprised to hear Lily's voice on the line.

"Back so quick?" I asked. "I thought Margaret Morton was a four-course kind of woman."

"Try zero," Lily laughed bitterly. "The place was packed, and they lost our reservation. What's worse, no one there had any idea who my mom was, so of course she totally lost it. She kept screaming 'We have a party of three for MORTON' over and over, as if she said 'Morton' loud enough, someone might recognize her."

"Really no one knew who she was?" I thought of the Barnes and Noble I'd passed in Union Square that morning. The window display featured at least fifty high-resolution Margaret Mortons smiling from the cover of her new *Country Quiches* cookbook.

"Has the entire staff been living under a rock or something?"

"You sound like my mom," Lily said dourly. "Not *everybody* knows Margaret Morton. Maybe people who work at a Chinese restaurant watch Chinese TV? I tried to explain this to her, but she was too busy screaming to listen."

"Uh-oh. So what happened?"

"She told them she wasn't so sure she was still going to film the wok episode there, nobody seemed to care, and then we left, came straight home, and locked ourselves in our rooms. Another warm, loving Morton family dinner."

"Oh, you *poor* thing," I said. At Baldwin, Lily was the no-nonsense newspaper editor, respected and admired by all. At home, though, she was Margaret Morton's daughter, downtrodden and ignored. She almost never talked about her family, except in crisis situations like this, and even then she was quick to retract her confidences.

"What*ever*," she said brusquely. "There are worse things than having Captain Crunch for dinner. Again."

Sensing Lily's discomfort, I tried to lighten the mood. "If it makes you feel any better, my mother pulls far more mortifying stunts all the time. She interrogates the waiters and busboys about their days, like they're long lost best friends or something. It's the worst."

"Yeah." Lily's voice was flat.

"Not only that," I went on, "but she's *obsessed* with free refill policies. Her life is a contest to score the most possible beverages in one meal—every time the waiter walks by, she holds up her glass and rattles it." But Lily had already shut down. The subject of mothers was officially closed, off-limits.

"So," she said, her tone businesslike again, "what was the whole Serge Ziff message about? Might the great profile be saved? Any chance you're going to make me a happy girl on Tuesday?"

"Not *next* Tuesday, but there's a distinct possibility you'll get something next month," I said, and described Serge's "salon." "Insane, right? A bunch of Chelsea scenesters lounging under palm trees, sipping margaritas and sketching abstract renditions of the sunset." Then, when Lily said it sounded like fun, I told her about my parental issues. "It's one thing staying out all night while Dad thinks I'm studying biology," I said, "but I highly doubt he'll just let me jet off to some Caribbean island that probably isn't even in an atlas."

"Oh, but you *have* to go," Lily said. "You'll have the *best* time and even if your article's a month late, it'd be worth it."

"But honestly, I don't even understand why Serge invited me. He's never expressed any interest in me, and he obviously feels no obligation to Baldwin."

"Maybe Nikola really liked you?"

"Yeah, right, as if she could pick me out of a three-person lineup."

After hanging up with Lily, I flopped across my bed to contemplate my dilemma—tropical paradise and major *Bugle* brownie points versus a big-city weekend with Mom and Maurice. The last time I'd gone out to dinner with them, over Thanksgiving in Houston, Mom had boisterously praised Maurice's new padded walking socks and when I asked her to lower her voice, she talked even louder: "What's wrong with speaking up so people can hear you, Miss Mumble Much? Maurice has chronic eardrum pain, so I'm trying to ENUNCIATE!" Enough. Time to face my fears. I reached for the phone and called Mom.

"Well, la-dee-dah!" she squawked. "If it isn't my disappearing daughter! We're *so* geared up for our trip, Mimi—Maurice has purchased an inflatable neck pillow to ensure that his spine remains straight for the duration of the flight. And oh, I have another surprise for you!"

I took this opportunity to interrupt. "Speaking of surprises," I said, "that's kind of why I'm calling." First I set the stage, reminding her of my passion for journalism and the necessity of "finding my voice" in the Baldwin paper. Then, with maximum casualness, brought up the Bravura Island invitation. "Don't you think it's impossible to refuse such an honor?" I asked before *really* tugging at the heartstrings: "Just think of the frequent-flier miles I'll rack up!" I stopped, bracing myself for the usual cycles of rage and accusation. But then my mother did something unbelievable. She went for it.

"Well, *what* an honor! Our own little international correspondent, how about that?"

"Really? So you'd let me go?"

"Well, doodlebug, of *course*. Go on and nourish that super-ego—who am *I* to stop the march of fame? I can't speak for Ariel, though; I'm afraid she'll be *extremely* disappointed."

"Ariel? What does Ariel have to do with anything?"

"Well, she was planning on coming up with us, and for the express purpose of spending time with her precious little sister."

"Who, *me*? Mom, is Ariel doing OK?" Surely not, or why

would she voluntarily take a trip with Mom and Maurice?

"Sorority life isn't all Ariel dreamed it would be," Mom said, "particularly since Kappa and her beau don't see eye to eye on everything. The sorority president made some crack about Decibel's spoken-word raps sounding like a broken CB radio broadcast, and Ariel got *completely* bent out of shape."

"Wait a minute," I cut in, "who's Decibel? And what about the Vanilla Gorilla—"

Mom laughed. "It's certainly heartening to know that I'm not the *only* neglected Schulman out there. Mimi, the Vanilla Gorilla is ancient history. Decibel has been Ariel's only interest in life for at least the past month. Maybe you should call her, get the scoop for yourself. She said she hadn't heard from you since early December, and I told her to join the club."

"Yeah, well, I haven't heard from *her* since the early nineties," I said.

Though Mom could be annoying, after talking to her, I felt much more optimistic about my chances to attend the Bravura Island extravaganza. Persuading Dad to let me fly south with Serge did still pose a challenge, but Quinn was right—the man *was* a pushover. I was pacing my room restlessly, stacking papers and scheming, when, underneath some books, I caught sight of the purple-cloth photo album I'd made for Dad after the Dominican Republic. I'd never given it to him. For once, my idiocy would come in handy, and how. When Dad came home two hours later, he found me sitting on the couch like a perfect angel, batting my eyelashes and holding out a heartbreakingly thoughtful home-made gift. Dad loved the photo album, but after admiring it at some length, he cast a suspicious glance at me. "Mimi," he said, "why are you being such a sweetheart? If my memory serves, you were breathing fire when I left this morning."

"Oh, Daddy!" I gushed, but Quinn had already appeared in the doorway, so I figured I might as well get it over with. I told him about the Bravura Island invitation, describing the weekend as an educational experience. "I'll be working the whole time," I said, "and it's a private island so it's not like I can get in any trouble."

Dad listened skeptically, chewing on his lower lip. "Oh, please, Daddy, can't I go?" Quinn begged, too. "Pretty please? If you say no, I swear I'll have to quit in protest of your immoral parenting."

"It's totally above board," I assured Dad. "Serge Ziff is a highly respected entreprener *and* a Baldwin parent."

"But Mimi," Dad said, "didn't you just get back from the Dominican Republic?" He gestured at the photo album in his lap. "I don't know—it just doesn't feel right, letting you jet off to the four corners of the earth. What about school?"

"Dad, it's *Baldwin*. And besides, it's a long weekend, Presidents' Day. Oh, and did I tell you? *Mom* thought it was a great idea."

Dad looked at me incredulously. "She did not."

"She did," I told him. And already I knew the battle was won. A few minutes later, I called She-Michael to confirm my spot on the plane. "I was hoping you could have given me an *ansah* by earlier in the evening. It's already past midnight in London," she said. "Well, I suppose we can do some re-orchestrating and get you a seat."

Then, with Michael out of the way, I dialed Ariel's number at the Kappa Kappa Gamma house at the University of Texas.

"Well, how lovely to hear from you," Ariel greeted me in a chilly voice.

"Yeah, sorry it's been so long," I said. "It sounds like you've been going through a lot lately. Mom said you broke up with Vanny?"

"Vanny who? I haven't thought about that loser in *years*."

"But over Thanksgiving, you—"

"Thanksgiving was *last year*, Mimi," Ariel pointed out. "I knew *nothing* about love then."

"Right, wow. So your new boyfriend—Mom was just telling me about him."

"Decibel's completely gifted," Ariel said, "but it's not the kind of thing you can capture on the phone. Listen, Mimi, I can't talk now. Myrtle's visiting this week, and our committee meeting is starting in, like, two minutes."

"Myrtle's in Austin?" What was my groovy stepsister-to-be doing at the Kappa Kappa Kappa house? Tutoring? "With you?"

Myrtle's husky voice came on the line, and she answered me herself. "I hit campus for a biochemistry symposium and thought I'd check in on our homegirl."

"Yeah, right. How much is mom paying you to babysit?"

"We're having fun here," Myrtle said over a din of coeds squealing "Oh, my God!" over and over.

"Do I even want to know what's going on over there?"

"Negative," she said. "But listen, have I got a hot scoop for you! It looks like my dad and your mom are thinking about shacking up in Berlin—and not just for the summer either, but for the entire year! Your mom just landed this research gig at some hoity-toity institute over there."

"Are you serious?" Funny, Mom hadn't mentioned this development on the phone just now. Was *that* why she'd approved the Bravura Island trip so quickly?

"What about our house? Who'll live there?"

"Sublet city, baby."

"But isn't this sort of sudden? They hardly know each other! And, no offense to your dad, but there's no *way* those two could hack it in a foreign country."

"Double affirmative," Myrtle said. "But think of all the comic possibilities. Ariel, for one, is superpsyched to go to Ibiza. She's not totally clear on it being in a different country than Germany, and I saw no reason to disillusion her."

I laughed, my heart surging with sisterly affection. "Hey, will you put her back on the phone? I need to talk her into sticking around New York a little longer than planned."

Now that Dad had green-lighted my trip to Bravura, I didn't want to miss out on Ariel altogether.

"No prob," Myrtle said. "I was about to go watch the spring fling planning committee in action. They're debating whether the theme should be 'Waikiki Murder Mystery' or 'Love-in at Wimbledon.'"

After persuading Ariel to extend her visit, I ran upstairs to Quinn. "So, are we going bikini shopping or what?"

It Island

IN THE WEEKS LEADING UP TO MY TRIP TO BRAVURA, I became too swept away by the glamour of Serge's invitation to factor in the potential downside. Only when I walked down the aisle of Serge's puddle jumper, my back stooped to avoid the ceiling, did the misgivings arise. What was I doing there, anyway? As I searched the rows for my seat, I recognized several fellow passengers from the New York society Web sites I had combed while researching Serge. First I saw the stubble-faced indie actor Orzo Scott chatting with the pregnant model whose image was emblazoned on a huge billboard on lower Broadway.

But the guest I was most surprised—and disheartened—to see there was a small strawberry-blond girl sitting in the aisle opposite me. She was roughly my age but exponentially better dressed in an elegant black dress. In her wavy hair the girl wore—I'd done a double take—a pink rhinestone tiara. Ugh, of *course* I'd be spending the weekend with the girl who'd dragged Max away from me at Serge's gallery opening, the one who'd sized me up with horror and all but laughed in my face and called me "freak." At least she didn't seem to recognize me; that was something.

Almost everyone on that plane was straining hard to stand out. One swarthy man had dyed his eyebrows snow white. One woman took her fashion inspiration from a domino, with three diagonal moles drawn on each of her cheeks, while another had a half-dozen chopsticks sticking out of her beehive. According to Quinn, Serge Ziff invited people once, and only once, to the Presidents' Day bash on Bravura. By next February, this year's luminaries would either be forgotten or just too "overexposed" to merit a second invitation. It was true, I thought. These people practically had "flash in the pan" tattooed on their foreheads. Granted, I was in no position to judge, for of all the guests, I alone had no fame potential, no fabulousness, no chance at over-exposure. Among the city's recently anointed It Boys and Girls, I stuck out like the pope at Yom Kippur services.

I was seated next to Xander Robards, a tobacco-scented land-scape architect and proprietor of an underwear boutique down-town. On our walk home from Serge's opening, Harriet had pointed out his store's bonsai and origami window display and told me about Xander, who'd trained with a gardener in Paris and, later, with a special-effects team in Los Angeles. The trees and paper in the store window had been trimmed and folded to resemble garter belts, with awesome results. But Xander never gave me the chance to compliment his design, for he was busy thumbing his Parisian interiors magazine and energetically ignor-ing my existence. Clearly annoyed he'd landed next to such a bumpkin, after about an hour in the air Xander tossed aside his magazine and craned his neck to inspect me. "Now who are we again?" he inquired with tired condescension. When I coyly identified myself as "a journalist," Xander brightened. "Ah! And we're in the employ of *which* publication?" Here I hit a wall. "Uh, the *Baldwin Bugle*," I said, meekly adding that it was a high school paper.

At the mention of high school, Xander snatched up his magazine with impressive speed, and devoted his attention to a spread on nineteenth-century chandeliers.

How I wished I were with my friends in New York. After my scheduled interview with Serge that evening, I planned to spend the remainder of the weekend holed up in my room, finishing the article so that I could hang out with the girls when I got back. A good thing, too, since I was beginning to feel seriously out of the loop. The only one I still saw regularly was Lily, but mostly in the *Bugle* office, where she was often too busy to joke around with me. Honest to goodness get-togethers, the kind where we went through several bags of junk food and could laugh at the same joke for half an hour, were becoming few and far between. My knowledge of my friends' lives was shrinking to cover basic facts. I knew that Sam continued to "tutor" Viv; that Jess had spent a miserable weekend with her father and his pregnant wife in Pennsylvania; that Pia was still doing algorithms with Isaac from Stuyvesant. But that was it. I had none of the best part, the reconstructed conversations or any of the telling details. We were barely a hundred miles in the air, and I was already homesick for my friends.

Three hours after takeoff, the plane skidded down on a dusty landing pad in a climate completely unlike the one we had left. I grabbed my overhead belongings and hurried down the aisle, glad to leave Xander's eau de cigarette butt behind. The air outside was wet and warm, the temperature of Houston in my favorite season, late spring. My fellow passengers were likewise buoyed by the tropical breezes. Once on the tarmac, they began chatting and laughing like old friends. Given how blasé they'd all been acting on the plane, this sudden boisterousness seemed odd. Over one of our Arabic iced tea sessions, Sam had told me New Yorkers tended to choose the same vacation destinations, going out of their way to be stuck with the same people they stared past in day-to-day interactions in the city. At the West Palm Beach resort where his family had spent Christmas, for example, ninety percent of the guests hailed from the same three zip codes. For New Yorkers, it seemed, the love-thy-neighbor law mattered only several hundred miles from home.

Outside the dusty, one-room airport, Serge's staff of man-boys corralled us in small groups on golf carts. I boarded one with four other guests, including the tiara girl. Everyone went about introducing themselves in the same peculiar way, giving first their names, then their Manhattan addresses. The tiara girl was named Tinsel Mulchgarten and lived on East Eighty-first Street and Park Avenue.

Ruben, a sculptor from Gramercy Park, liked that I lived on Barrow Street. "How'd you score a place there?" he asked me. "I had people on the case," I replied enigmatically. (I was getting good at this!) "But the Village is so grimy!" Tinsel said with a shiver. To change the subject, Ruben politely asked Tinsel where she went to school, a question she processed with considerable confusion. "School? Um, I'm a *fund*raiser—school was cutting into my work!" Ruben gave up trying to make small talk with Tinsel and stared out at the scenery. We were bumping down a palm tree–lined road, under a dazzling blue sky dotted with cotton ball clouds. Bright birds flew above us, some swooping low enough to brush the palm leaves. The air smelled of honeydew and sea salt. As the cart rolled onto a sandy stretch of road, Ruben started raving about a Japanese cream puff factory that had just opened on his block. He said nothing about the salty tang of the air or the cawing seagulls overhead, or the sandy path that brought us right up to the beach—a breathtaking panorama of turquoise water and powdery white sand.

There were very few trees on the beach, and I could see all the way down the shore to where the island melted back into the ocean. Serge's personal palace, a flat white structure, took up a great portion of the shoreline. Down the beach were a half-moon of thatched huts, separated from the main house by an expansive play area—our man-boy explained there were tennis courts, an indoor gym, and a swimming pool with an art deco diving board. I had to hand it to Serge: the place was perfect. Out of control, but amazing.

The only blot on the scene was She-Michael, who stood by the guest huts in a black pantsuit, her high heels sinking into the sand. "Let me help you," she offered vaguely, without moving a muscle, then assigned me to a hut called "Sandpiper." After throwing my bag into the smallest, least desirable bedroom, I went back outside to ask Michael what the plans were.

"Plaaaaahns?"

"You know, like anywhere I'm supposed to be and when? For the interview tonight?"

"Ah, the *interview.*" Michael put on her world-weary face. "Serge won't be in until quite late tonight, I'm afraid, so I'd prefer to work it out tomorrow."

"But—but I thought it was tonight. I thought you'd already set it up."

"I'm sure everything will work out just peachy," Michael said, already moving toward the next golf cart of guests. Back in my austere white chamber, I opened my suitcase and pulled out the society magazines Quinn had given me for research purposes. I brought them to the bed and stretched across it, faint from heat and social anxiety.

I woke up in a deserted Sandpiper, with my face plastered to a "Young Patrons of Covenant House" photomontage. At the window, the sky was blurring a hazy salmon color, and I had to remind myself where exactly I was—at a famous art dealer's private island in the Caribbean. Life was bizarre, no question. After splashing water on my face, I threw on an "effortless casual" ensemble Quinn had coordinated (spaghetti strap tank top, soft cotton skirt, striped espadrilles) and went onto the beach, where Ruben and a few other guests sat huddled on the sand, smoking cigarettes and drinking multihued concoctions.

"Hey, Miss Barrow Street," Ruben called out. "C'mon over and meet my friends."

When I squatted down and introduced myself, one of the new arrivals, a ballerina named Regina, crooned in baby-talk, "Isn't she just the *cutest*?"

Sensing my discomfort, Ruben pulled me into a discussion about one of the few subjects I slightly understand: photography. Turned out we both preferred street to studio photography and we were both looking forward to the upcoming Lee Friedlander show at the Museum of Modern Art. I was just starting to unwind when a golf cart chortled up with Nikola Ziff behind the wheel. She looped around us several times before cutting the engine, and although it was evening and growing chilly out, Nikola wore nothing but a butter-yellow bikini. Her long white hair cascaded over her shoulders, flapping in the nighttime breeze.

Nikola angled her exposed torso out of the cart and waved at me. "Well, *there* you are," she said. "I've been looking for you everywhere—get in!"

"Me?" My tone incredulous, idiotic. Nikola bore down on the golf cart's high-pitched horn.

"Yes, *obviously*. So hurry up, will you?" Awestruck, I clambered into the cart, and without a word Nikola gunned the engine and drove us toward the main house. Perhaps Serge had shown up early for our interview—good thing I'd stashed a handy reporter's notebook in my purse.

But once inside the house, Nikola clarified the reason for her summons. Serge wasn't itching for his interview and Nikola wasn't dying to befriend me. Nope, Nikola had invited scruffy indie-wonder Orzo Scott and his friend Ricky to "hang out" before dinner, and she needed a wingman. She administered my instructions with all the monotonous gravity of a government employee. "Start by asking Orzo a million questions, so it seems like *you're* the one sweating him, right?" With a haughty toss of her hair, Nikola clamped her jaw together and bared her teeth. "I had half a poppy seed bagel for breakfast this morning, and those nasty seeds stay in my teeth for *days* afterward. Can you see any left?"

I assured her she looked perfect but privately wondered if she was planning to wear more than a bikini to dinner. "Just pretend everything's chill and we're good friends and go along with whatever I say," she said, and got up to walk over to the full-length mirror. "He's a good guy. I've known him for ages."

"So are you two, like, going out?" I asked hesitantly.

"Of course not!" Nikola was aghast. "It's more of a *situation*. But let's save it for later. I'd *die* if he walked in here now and overheard us." She turned to look at me critically. "Sorry," she said, "but can you *please* get into a position that looks more comfortable? I don't want them thinking you're nervous. It'd kind of defeat the whole purpose of your being here."

I slouched dutifully, seized with the desire to win Nikola over, to break through her ice queen exterior and unlock the vulnerable child within. We were still seated like that, aggressively relaxed, when the dinner gong sounded. "Crap!" Nikola cried, for Orzo and Ricky had yet to arrive.

As guests began filing into the house, Nikola stomped over to the table with no further directions for me. To her extreme consternation, Orzo was the last to show, by which point the seats next to her had been taken, to her left by Rod Palmer-Guittierez, a ceramics artist, and to her right by Marion Foose, a shrewish middle-aged crime writer with a major Picasso collection. Nikola, now wearing a transparent tunic over her bikini, sprawled between them, glaring. I sat between the pregnant model and Xander, who'd accepted me as Nikola's "associate" and was now regaling me with a story about his recent real-estate dilemma.

"With the market such a mess, I was really torn," he confided. "I couldn't figure out if I wanted to rent or buy, and it took me *years* to strike a decent compromise. I bought my apartment and am now renting it out to myself."

The crowd laughed smugly. I wished Sam were around to appreciate the absurdity of this scene. Across the table, Orzo Scott's friend Ricky was making small talk with the noxious Tinsel Mulchgarten. Not only was Ricky television-actor handsome—with dark skin, penetrating black eyes, and pointy jug ears that only added to his charm—but he displayed admirable patience during Tinsel's drawn-out account of her decision to drop out of Dalton after her sophomore year and "become a full-time hostess." Later, in conjunction with an anecdote about an Egyptian-themed charity gala she'd recently co-chaired, Tinsel inclined her torso over Ricky and, in a sultry voice, announced that Orzo looked "*just* like the Pharoah."

"I can't believe that tramp!" Nikola hissed across the table at me when Orzo winked in acknowledgment of the compliment. "My dad must've been out of his mind to invite her!"

The object of Nikola's passion, Orzo Scott, was certainly an unusual leading man—scrawny and bowlegged, with a bright red beard growth that clashed with his greasy brown hair. As she obsessed over this unlikely matinee idol, ignoring our multicultural three-course dinner of trout terrine, mahi-mahi fajitas, and pan-seared seaweed, I sat there wondering when Serge would show up.

For dessert, Serge's manservant, Rambool, brought out lychee ice cream spring rolls, which I had no idea how to eat. As far as I could tell, there were no chopsticks on hand. Rather than wait to see how everyone else handled the delicacies, I crunched into mine like a regular egg roll. Tinsel, better versed in obscure, ultrafancy sweets, picked up a dessert spoon and shot me a disgusted look. I was wiping lychee goo onto my napkin when Nikola got up and crossed over to my side of the table. "Hey," she said from behind me. "Go get ready and meet me back here in five. We're going out now."

"Out?" I asked. "Where to? I thought this was a private island?"

"Out on the boat, with Orzo and Ricky. Hello?"

"A boat ride? Isn't it a little dark out?"

"Well, yeah it's dark out! That's exactly the point!" When Nikola raised her voice, mousy Marion Foose, the crime writer, jerked forward to eavesdrop—unnecessary, given the volume of Nikola's reaction to my feeble apology. "But I have to wait for your dad. I'm interviewing him tonight."

"Sorry, Barbara Walters, but I know for a scientific *fact* that he's not getting in for another three hours, and we'll be back in an hour, I swear to God. Or at least *you* will be!" Then Nikola resorted to pleading: "Please? We don't even have to take the boat out, how's that? We can just sit on it, OK?" She raised her pinky finger. "I promise."

When Nikola had referred to "the boat," I'd pictured a grand yacht, Aristotle Onassis swank, not a small motorboat with empty bleach jugs tied to its sides. We crawled in gingerly, one at a time, careful not to topple the unstable dinghy. A light shone from the dock, and bright stars splattered the sky. The winds had picked up since dinner, and I tried to stay warm by covering my legs with life vests. While Nikola and Orzo snuggled, Ricky and I got acquainted. At first, I resented our supervisory role, but Ricky turned out to be quite an interesting guy, despite using the words "depressing," "depressed," or "depression" in almost every sentence. Ricky was mourning his boyfriend, Myron, who had recently left Ricky for a rabbinical student at Yeshiva University. Within a month, Myron had converted to Orthodox Judaism and committed to a raw kosher diet.

"Myron doesn't sound very balanced," I remarked.

"I know," Ricky sighed. "He's a total loon. That's what I loved about him."

As Nikola and Orzo's kissy noises grew into loud, wet slurps, lovesick Ricky lapsed into a melancholy silence, leaving me to muffle the amorous noises with disjointed monologues. "You'd *never* guess we were sisters," I found myself saying. "Or even born on the same planet. To Ariel, 'hitting bottom' means only working out once a day."

Then came the plunk of two people falling onto the boat floor. "You were supposed to catch me, idiot!" Nikola cried. "I thought you wanted me to join you," Orzo answered, and on went the slurping.

"Hey," I whispered to Ricky, "do you think they'd mind if we left?"

"He usually doesn't—I say we go for it."

Ricky and I crept slowly toward the edge of the dinghy and then jumped overboard, thumping down onto the sand. Afterward, on the peaceful walk back to Serge's compound, I managed to coax a few laughs out of Ricky. We said goodbye at the pool, where Ricky resolved to swim laps and "sweat off his sorrow." Back at Sandpiper, I sat down on the porch, feeling almost satisfied with my first night in paradise, when, suddenly, a circle of light landed on my face. The light whizzed upward, tracing a parabola over the huts and palm trees before stopping to illuminate the person holding the flashlight: Michael.

"Well, well, well, you at last," she said. "Serge has been searching *everywhere* for you. Where have you *been*?"

"But I was just gone for an hour! Nikola said Serge wasn't getting here for at least three!"

"Hmm, sounds like Nikola might not be the expert on her father's movements now, doesn't it? Serge arrived just as the *digéstifs* were being poured."

"You mean during dinner? Oh, but Nikola said . . . I thought we were supposed to . . . well, can I just run over and talk to him now?"

Michael cackled. "You know what they say about lost opportunities, don't you, Mimi?"

It sounded like a trick question, but I went for it. "What?"

"That they're lost." Michael laughed before switching off the
flashlight and disappearing into the pitch black of the night.

Eureka

By MY LAST MORNING IN THE TROPICS, I'd learned enough about Ricky to pen his biography. I knew about his lonely childhood in a suburb of Boise, the bulk of which was spent sitting alone on the bleachers of the high school stadium. I knew about his fundamentalist Mormon family, his timid mother and bigamist father. I knew about his years as a teenage runaway, camping with other nomads around the beaches of Santa Monica, experimenting with drugs and strumming folk songs for pocket money. I knew about his savior, a benevolent older man who one day rescued Ricky by putting down a year's rent on a little apartment in the Silver Lake section of Los Angeles and setting him up with his casting agent. I knew about his first big break on daytime TV as the third member of a love triangle with a blond tennis pro and her senator husband.

All this, and I still didn't know one iota about Serge Ziff. My no-show at our first appointment had given my host the idea that he was free to dodge all subsequent makeup efforts. Whenever I tried to corner him, Serge blew me off with lines like "I'm in the middle of a conversation" or "Try me later." And though it was his party, he kept a conspicuously low profile all weekend. He graced the table every night at dinner, but otherwise expected his guests to entertain themselves.

A few performance artists mustered the energy to go snorkeling or play tennis, but most people lazed in beach chairs all day, reading trashy novels and drinking colorful cocktails. Tinsel Mulchgarten occupied a foldout chair a few yards away from this group and spent long stretches staring blankly out at the ocean. Serge's friends were evidently less interesting than the fundraisers on East Eighty-first Street. I found it all a bit dreary, and missed my friends even more than I'd expected.

By Sunday night I'd pretty much given up on interviewing Serge, and redirected my journalistic ambitions to Ricky, who obliged me with lurid accounts of his past lives, all of which I recorded in the Goat Show book. Writing down his stories allowed me to feel industrious and pretend my weekend hadn't been a waste of time. Ricky and I were the first ones up Monday morning, well before breakfast.

As we lay lounging on the beach, a few feet from the water, Ricky talking and me transcribing, Serge Ziff strolled outside. The guests' plane wasn't due to take off until noon, but Serge seemed to be slipping off early. Dressed in a dark gabardine suit, he stood watching as Rambool loaded his suitcases onto the golf cart.

Ricky had been outlining the autobiographical television show he wanted to develop. "Say, Mimi," he'd said, "do you have any contacts in the TV biz?"

"Hold that thought," I said, and catapulted off my towel. Though wearing only my electric blue beaded Farrah Fawcett bathing suit and a pair of cutoff jean shorts, I had to answer the call of duty. "Mr. Ziff!" I shouted, tripping over the sand as I raced toward the elusive gallery-owner. "What about our interview?"

"Well, I was supposed to . . ." Serge started to say. But then he stopped, looked at his wristwatch, and seemed to reconsider. "Nikola said such nice things about you last night," he said. "You've been a very good friend to her."

"I have?"

"She says you've been inseparable all weekend, and you know, Nikola's always had trouble making friends her own age, especially girls. She's never had a mother, and she grew up surrounded by"—Serge gestured deprecatingly at the guest huts— "*these* people."

"She's really great," I said, half believing it. Rah, rah, Nikola! In truth, I'd hardly exchanged five words with her since that memorable joust on the boat bottom. She'd spent the weekend making out with Orzo while Ricky shared his sordid secrets with me. But so what? Thanks to Nikola, Serge was patting an empty seat in the golf cart and telling me to "climb aboard." "We can do the interview on the way to the airport," he said. "Rambool will take you back when we're done."

"Excellent!" I couldn't have been happier if Max had asked me to slow dance, and, thank God, I was already equipped with notebook and pen. I jumped into the golf cart next to Serge, whipped out my trusty notebook, and for the next fifteen minutes, scribbled as Serge talked. Quick and scatterbrained, he rambled about art and aesthetics, about his relationship with New

York, his disdain for "McMuseums." He decried real estate development in Chelsea and lamented the sorry state of the New York art world (his verdict: "dead, with some tendencies to necrophilia").

I periodically tried to insert the questions I'd painstakingly prepared: Why do you think Baldwin is such a special school? What other institutions do you support? What was your high school like? Did Baldwin solicit the contribution, or was it your idea? What kind of improvements do you hope to see at the school? Serge talked over every single one of these questions, but I scarcely noticed. I was too preoccupied with taking legible notes inside the lurching vehicle and not getting carsick. Back at Sandpiper, I hugged my notebook and felt lightheaded, psyched, even empowered. I had done it! At last.

Our plane landed in New York at five-fifteen that afternoon, which meant that if I worked nonstop until midnight, I could probably get the story to Lily by Tuesday morning. It was only after boarding the plane that the bubble popped. I reviewed my extensive notes once, twice, then a third time before realizing that Serge had talked and talked and talked, but he hadn't made a single comment relevant to my article. Yet again, I'd been screwed over by Mr. Ziff.

Serge had praised his Estonian grandmother, but said nothing about his life between the ages of five and twenty-five—nothing about where he was born, or in what decade. He'd alluded to "family money" but clammed up when I asked where that money came from. He'd talked about studying "art" in school without telling me the name of the school or the type of art. He didn't say a word about Baldwin—nothing about how much he'd pledged, or where he wanted the money to go. Only a genius could build a decent story from this Swiss cheese research. By the time the cab dropped me off on Barrow Street, I was flipping out. How could I possibly face Ulla and Lily, who'd waited so patiently for my article—would they accept whatever drivel I managed to churn out? Oh, well, I thought, letting myself into the house, at least I wasn't sunburned. It was nearing six-thirty. Maybe I could spend a pleasant hour or two with Dad before chaining myself to my laptop downstairs. That might put my stress in perspective a bit.

But when I walked into the living room, I balked to see Mom and Dad shoulder to shoulder on the couch, holding mugs and studying a large photo album. My suitcase clunked to the floor. "Mimi!" my parents—my parents who had not been in the same room since their split eight months ago—cried in unison. "You're back!"

Uh, yeah. But more relevantly: *they* were back. When I opened my mouth to speak, nothing came out. I'm not sure how long I stood there, frozen, before I found the words to react to the scene in front of me. Well, not *words*, exactly. "Aaaaaaah!"

For most of my life, I'd regarded my parents as a single inseparable unit, two halves of a whole. But ever since my mother called it quits and my father moved 1,500 miles away from her, I'd had many opportunities to dissect their differences—and wonder what brought them together in the first place. Take that evening as an example. My lanky father was slouched over the photo album, his expression joyful but calm, while Mom sat bolt upright, grinning hungrily at me. Their outfits, too, implied irreconcilable world views. Since moving to New York, Dad had spruced up his style. He was wearing army green wool pants, and a loose off-white pullover, as well as the geek-chic transparent glasses Fenella had helped him select at the Chelsea flea market. Mom, on the other hand, was dressed like a spinster substitute teacher. To set off her new choirboy bowl cut, she was wearing a bulky calamine-pink sweater adorned with three-dimensional appliqué butterflies.

In case they hadn't heard me, I spoke again, this time more along the lines of "AAAAAAAAAAAH!"

Mom's lips opened into a smile, revealing her marshmallow-size front teeth. "Well, hello, yourself, Miss Jet Set. Now, come on over here and check out the great snaps we took in bird-watching country. Maurice even climbed up an oak tree for these close-ups!" She turned confidingly to my father: "He'll do *anything* for a blackburnian warbler."

Poor sweet Daddy continued flipping attentively through the album, as if he gave a rat's ass about blackburnian warblers' migration habits. I stumbled protectively toward him, still shocked that he and Mom were in the same room—*our* room—but was intercepted en route. "My own flesh and blood," Mom crooned, suffocating me in her embrace. Drawing away, she pressed her palm to the fake fur collar of my awesome 1960s burgundy coat. "What's this? Don't tell me you lost the parka we got you. From the Turkey Day sale at TJ?" Instead of screaming that we'd bought that ugly parka when I was in sixth grade and the sleeves now met my elbows, I assured Mom that my "favorite coat" was safe at the dry cleaner's.

"It's highway robbery what these dry cleaners are charging," Mom observed, and reached for her own coat, a teal Windbreaker that folded into a weather-resistant pouch. "OK, ready for some great news?" she asked me. "Maurice and I have booked a later flight at no additional charge—we're leaving bright and early tomorrow morning, so we can have one last supper together. I didn't care how late you got back—I couldn't come this far without seeing my Mimikins! Maurice is at the Sharper Image, testing their neck supports, but he'll be back in time for dinner. Now, your father recommended a cute little French place around the corner," Mom went on. "The Paris Table—do you know it? After all my bird watching, I have a *most* politically incorrect craving for coq au vin!"

"It's actually Pilar's Table," I said softly. "And it's *Peruvian*."

"Peruvian?" Mom whooped. "Holy moly, eating is quite the avant-garde enterprise here these days! Now c'mon, Mims, let's take this mother-daughter bonding show on the road! We'll call Maurice and tell him to meet us there. Roger, do you want—"

"I have plans," Dad cut her off.

If only I could be so lucky, I thought, then told Mom to wait while I freshened up downstairs.

"Why don't you just go as is?" Dad cut in quickly, the first time he'd spoken to me since his initial greeting. "You look lovely."

"He's right," Mom twittered. "You always look fresh to me, bluebird! I should get a shot of you."

Mom walked over to the reading chair, where her purse lay. "Mimi, wait! Don't—" Dad called after me, but I was already halfway down the stairs. In the bathroom, I slapped on some hot pink blush and a thick coat of aquamarine eyeliner, mostly to annoy my mom, who was so opposed to makeup she wouldn't let me wear cherry Chapstick when I was little. After brushing my teeth, I tore into my room to unearth a semiclean top. Finding my bureau empty except for a few unpaired socks, I decided to recycle a gently worn item from the hamper in my closet. But when I tugged at the closet door, it pulled inward, as if caught. In my packing frenzy, I'd probably closed the door on a boot or a duffel bag. I yanked harder, and this time the door opened briefly, then snapped shut like a rubber band. "What the . . . !"

"Oh, it's *you*," a voice inside the closet said. "What a relief." The door swung open to reveal Fenella von Dix wedged between the hamper and my wire shelving unit. In one hand, the middle-aged waif held last month's *Teen Vogue;* my miniature flashlight was in the other. Fenella had on a lacy white camisole and, I couldn't help noticing, my Rice University sweatpants, which hung looser on her than on me. "Forgive the intrusion," she whispered, "but this has been a *most* trying afternoon! Roger and I were about to whip up an asparagus quiche when your mother rang the doorbell, utterly unannounced! Roger panicked, so I hightailed it down here to your room. Who knew she'd stay the afternoon?" I nodded slowly, adding it up. No wonder Dad had tried to prevent my going downstairs.

"Don't worry about it," I told Fenella. "But if you could close your eyes for just one sec." She did, and I took off the shirt I was wearing and threw on a low-cut black tank top and a lace minidress in canary yellow over my jeans. I consulted the full-length mirror to gauge how much Mom was going to hate my outfit. A ton.

"You're developing *such* an exciting fashion sense, Mimi," Fenella said after I'd authorized her to reopen her eyes. She exited the closet with my magazine. "Look at this," she said. "This girl's almost two years older than you, richer than the day is long, and she *still* doesn't get it. Some girls think designer clothes make the woman, but you and I know better, don't we?"

I looked where Fenella indicated, and there in *Teen Vogue* was a photo spread of Tinsel Mulchgarten, the snobby princess who'd mocked me in front of Max and then behaved like a lobotomy patient on Bravura Island. The glossy photos chronicled Tinsel's recent trip to Paris, which she spent eating fresh apricots and ordering clothes for the Young Friends of Napoleon Haute Couture Ball, an event she happened to be co-chairing.

"She thinks she's so cheeky, wearing motorcycle boots to a gown fitting," Fenella grumbled. "Who do you think she paid to scuff them up like that?"

"This is *so* crazy because—" I was about to describe my run-ins with this underage socialite when my mother's bray reverberated down the stairs.

"Crap!" Fenella ducked back into the closet. "COMING!" I shouted loud enough to mask any suspicious sounds. On my way up the stairs I thought about my closet conference with Fenella. Maybe Dad's new friend wasn't so awful after all. She was less demanding than my mother and she deserved props for scorning the vile Tinsel Mulchgarten. "We made a rezzie, sugar bear—let's get going!" Mom boomed at me. "My, my, my," she said when I came into view. "A dress *and* jeans. I see we're exploring our creative id through clothing again, aren't we?"

"Hey, where's Ariel?" I asked. "I thought you said she was coming."

"Oh, Ariel," Mom said wearily. "She certainly did come up to New York, and so did her lovely new escort Decibel, of course. They both declined to attend our bird-watching expedition. Your dad's been putting them up, but I haven't laid eyes on her since baggage claim."

Dad, coming in from the kitchen, glanced nervously at me and then, sensing his secret was safe, said, "Well, I have, and it's been most enjoyable. We went to the Chelsea flea markets to look for a vintage eight-ball jacket for Decibel. I don't know where they are now," he went on, "probably out getting a late-afternoon breakfast or something. Those two keep the strangest hours! This morning, I came upstairs at six a.m. to find Decibel polishing off a cheeseburger."

"Will they be at dinner?" I asked Mom.

"Who can say?" she said, throwing up her arms. "Decibel thinks restaurants are 'ghetto' and prefers feasting on food from corner delis. I left a message on Ariel's cell phone, so maybe they'll show up."

I prayed for the best, but when we entered Pilar's Table, I saw only one familiar face: Maurice, the most extensively padded physicist on earth.

"Hiya, Miriam," Maurice said as I sat down across from him.

Maurice was the only person in the world who called me Miriam, yet another reason I disliked him. Unlike his daughter Myrtle, Maurice's geeky exterior concealed no reservoirs of coolness. My mother's attachment to him totally baffled me, despite her many justifications, among them "eminence in his field," "brilliant position papers," and, most repulsively, her "subconscious animal attraction" to him. Maurice sat propped against two pillows, one between his shoulders and the other at the small of his back. To my questioning look, he explained: "I threw out my back this morning—it was out of this world! I was just leaning down to snap a few last shots of some short-eared owls by the riverbank, when CRUNCH! It snapped just like a chopstick." Maurice wheezed contentedly. "The pain is absolutely excruciating."

Hoping to change the subject, I asked after his daughter. "Myrtle and I had a great time when she came last semester to visit schools in New York," I said. "Has she heard from anywhere yet?"

"Oh, sure," Maurice said, "she's racked up some acceptances, but strangely enough, she doesn't seem too concerned about college right now. She's been missing a lot of school lately to work on a research project with some Rice oceanographers. She's in Costa Rica this week, gathering samples from the Turrialba Volcano. I don't see what volcanic lava has to do with engineering, but you know Myrtle—she's really attached to her mentor."

"Who's that?" I asked innocently.

"A graduate student, some fellow from Montreal named Jean-Claude—"

"Jean-Philippe," Mom interjected. "She calls him 'J.P.,' but I call him 'P.B. and J.'" Mom and I laughed, but not at the same punch line. Myrtle was quite the fox. Until she'd visited me in New York, I'd mistaken her for another mega nerdazoid, but it hadn't taken long to gather she was much less interested in engineering than human anatomy.

Dinner proceeded exactly as expected. Mom's request for a free refill met with little success. "But you're welcome to order as many sodas as you like," the waitress said.

"Well, I never!" Mom said after the waitress traipsed away. "As if it's so extraordinary to get what you pay for!"

Maurice, meanwhile, was debating whether to try scoring an emergency x-ray appointment that night, or waiting until they returned to Houston the following morning. "I just don't know *how* I'll survive four hours in one of those plane seats. These airlines need to wake up, they really do. How hard can it be to install ergonomic spine supports in those chairs? They could still cram us in like sardines and charge for headsets."

"Why don't you write them a letter?" I asked, trying to sound concerned.

"Been there, done that." Maurice shook his head. "Bags of 'em."

"While we're on the subject of flights, corn dog," my mother said to me, "how 'bout drawing up some summer blueprints? As I believe Myrtle told you, I have a summer fellowship at the Teichen Institute in Berlin. They're world-renowned for their work with monkeys, and they're making great breakthroughs regarding the spatial-memory gender gap."

I grunted, and crunched an ice cube between my teeth.

Although I understood the tradeoff perfectly—the school year with Dad for summers with Mom—I did not feel like talking about it. "Oh, we'll have so much fun—*Ich bin ein Berliner* and all that jazz! Anyhoo," Mom went on, "Maurice and I are flying to Berlin on the first of June, but your father tells me your school doesn't let out until the twelfth. I've done a little travel research, and it looks like unless we want to pay through the nose, you need to leave on the afternoon of the twelfth and join us the next morning.

What?! Mom couldn't do this to me. The graduation party was held the night of the last day of school. Everyone at Baldwin attended, including the freaks and misanthropes; it was the one occasion where freshmen and seniors mingled as equals.

"Mom, I have to fly out the next day, on the thirteenth," I told her. "There's a huge event on the twelfth that I couldn't possibly miss."

"Now, blueberry, the thirteenth is a blackout day. The flights cost three times as much!"

"But Mom, think about if Ariel had missed prom!"

"Ha!" Mom slapped the table. "Talk about World War Three! Lucky you're not like Ariel," she said, reaching over her plate of roasted chicken to take my hand. "Now, honey, listen. Sometimes it's best to dive right into new experiences. Think of it as a leap of faith!"

The argument never escalated, for at that moment, like an angel from heaven, my sister Ariel breezed into the restaurant, followed by a huge white man wearing aviator sunglasses and a double-breasted suit made of what looked like tinfoil. He bore an eerie resemblance to the Vanilla Gorilla, Ariel's last true love. Over the remainder of the meal, I tried to get to know Decibel. Although his brass knuckles and terrycloth wristbands implied to the contrary, Decibel came from an academic family just like ours. His dad taught Latin American literature at the University of Texas, from which Decibel had dropped out after half a semester. He lived in his parents' garage. Unlike most denizens of the large university town, who favored steel guitar solos, Ariel's beau aspired to be "a hip-hop producer like" and planned to spend his week in New York "recruiting hot acts."

"What are you recruiting them for? The Marines?" Maurice joshed.

"I got me a thunderbolt of a sound system," Decibel replied earnestly, "and me and my boy Rez be in the formulation process of the label and, you know, what it stands for. Like, is we best to think about cross-marketing opportunities, or is we keeping it real focusing on the beats, like?"

"*Totally,*" Ariel affirmed, spearing a small red potato from my plate. Forever on a diet, my sister had a policy against ordering her own meal at a restaurant. "We went talent-scouting in Brooklyn last night. We just walked up to random people who looked cool and asked if they wanted a record deal, you know, hypothetically. Everybody just said yes, just like that. It was inspiring, seriously." Then Ariel said, "Mimi, you should totally check out Brooklyn some time—it's awesome."

"Um," I said, "I kind of go there every day."

"You do? Why?"

"My *school's* in Brooklyn."

"Oh, yeah," Ariel said. "That's so wild. I know you live here and everything, but I never picture you, like, *doing* stuff. All I ever imagine is . . ." Ariel giggled as Decibel emitted a sequence of human beat box sounds. "Well, not much, actually. Sorry."

"No worries," I said. Big news flash that Ariel wasn't interested in my life. I'd once perused one of Mom's books on pathological narcissism, called *Who Cares About You? What About Me?* and it had supplied lifelong insights into my sibling relationship. I tried not to blame her. "Hate the sickness, not the sick," the book had counseled. When the check came, Mom tossed some balled-up bills onto the table without noticing that one was an old shoe repair receipt. After calculating that Mom had left a whopping seven percent tip, I added another ten to the wad.

Outside Pilar's Table, Mom flapped out her arms to hail a cab. It was eight o'clock, their regular bedtime. "Just wait till this summer, when we'll *really* get a chance to catch up!" Mom told me. She engulfed me in another bonebreaker of a hug and then trundled into the car.

Ariel and Decibel walked me home. They were going to a spoken-word slam at a boxing gym in the Bronx, but first Decibel had to stop by the house and change his shoelaces. I really wished I could join them instead of tapping away at my computer all night. But once inside the apartment, Quinn tackled me with a magnificent arrangement of stargazer lilies and gladiolas, and my mood brightened. "These came for you!" he cried. "You must have been up to some *fine* mischief this weekend!" I took the oversize bouquet and examined the card addressed to "M.S." *Had a nice time chatting with you, kid*, the inside read. *Let me know if you need anything else and good luck on your story. SZ*

"Look!" I bragged, showing Ariel and Decibel the flowers. "This nutty downtown art dealer sent these to me. Aren't they stunning?" Decibel, who'd just tied his thick yellow shoelaces, considered the flowers with a critical expression.

"I only like flowers that is dried," he said, and Ariel clasped his brass knuckles adoringly.

Double Dish

As a child, I had impressive powers of concentration. I could spend afternoons curled up inside the coat closet with a blanket, an Itty Bitty book light, and my black and white marble composition book, concocting tales about disco dancing dragons, or my cat Simon's secret life as a detective.

These days, I have to focus on staying focused, and I'm grateful to accomplish one task a week, let alone sit still for an hour. I don't have ADD, I just have trouble limiting myself to any single activity. While figuring out how much time to set aside for an assignment, I must make allowances for snacking, rearranging my room, pacing, flipping through old magazines, e-mailing, and lip-synching to Dolly. Writing the Serge Ziff profile in one night would be a seriously time-consuming uphill climb. I positioned the lilies and gladiolas on my windowsill, changed into old sweats, placed a one-liter bottle of Coke on my desk, and prayed that inspiration would strike and the story would come spilling out. In retrospect, I'm not sure I would use the words "spilling out" to describe the process that followed. "Giving birth"—a long and painful birth—seems nearer the mark. Still, I was amazed at how quickly I pulled it off. Fourteen CD changes, three phone calls, two trips to the kitchen, and twenty-three deleted paragraphs after sitting down, I'd composed one fairly decent donor profile. Serge Ziff and I could sign the divorce papers, hip-hip, hooray. I was done, and incredibly psyched. I took the article off the printer tray and held it in my hands. Have I mentioned how psyched I was? Though it was twenty past midnight, I was too hyper to sleep and logged on to IM my girls for a round of self-congratulations. My Buddy List, unfortunately, was sparsely populated at this hour, so I composed a group e-mail:

> *Gang,*
> *Guess who just finished her wild goose chase? Lily, you'll have your story tomorrow (or should I say today?). As for the rest of you, I'm dying to catch up. In exchange for your scandalous updates, I can offer a juicy story for the Nikola Ziff Seduces Hollywood folder. Lunch tomorrow at Torre's at 12:30?*
> *Xoxo, Mimi*

After sending the message, I went upstairs for a snack. I'd just opened the fridge when Ariel and Decibel got back from the spoken-word slam. "You should never eat between midnight and dawn," my sister poked her head into the kitchen to advise me. "The food just lodges in your gut, like old gum. I swear."

The next morning I woke up early and remembered my promise to show Harriet the story before handing it in. Before I'd flown down to Bravura, she'd offered to read it over and point out any glaring errors. It wasn't yet seven, which left me plenty of time to jog down to SoHo and drop the article in her mailbox. I took out the square card she'd given me and Mapquested the address printed on it. By the time I got back to Barrow Street, I was sapped and I thought I'd just lay my head on the pillow for two minutes. A short time afterward, the phone detonated inside my eardrum. I looked at my Dolly alarm clock and realized I'd overslept. World Civ was almost over. Crap, crap, and crap with ice cream on top—could I do nothing right?

"Good morning to *you*," Harriet said, and told me she'd read my article over her morning latte. "And what's more, I like it!"

"Mmpph, thank you. It's really OK?"

"It's fine. Well written, funny, informative. It's just . . ." Harriet drew in a breath. "Not right."

I sat up. "What? What's the matter with it?"

"Nothing's the *matter* with it, per se, except that you got Serge Ziff dead wrong. If you come over at two o'clock today," Harriet said, "I'll tell you why."

"Could you possibly tell me now?" I asked. "An afternoon date sounds like fun, but you know I'm enrolled in school, don't you? And Tuesday afternoons I have French Conversation, Creative Writing, *and* Yoga. You want me to cut them all?"

"That makes it sound so tawdry," she said. "You're not *cutting*. You're *prioritizing*."

"Do we really have to do it today?"

"Yup. It's imperative."

I regretted skipping a whole day of school, but as Mom always said, you can't dance at two weddings at the same time. Plus I had a hunch Harriet's request would be worth my while.

And so I sent Lily the dreaded e-mail, asking for yet another article extension, before falling back asleep. Dad must have been on an assignment, because I didn't wake again until eleven, just in time to make my lunch date with the girls. At Torre's, one of our regular haunts, the lighting was comically dim, to the point where you found yourself wondering if everyone in the joint was conducting an illicit affair. I was halfway across the room before I saw that Viv's arm was in a black sling. "Oh my God," I said. "What happened?"

"Motorcycle accident," Viv explained listlessly.

"A WHAT?" I cried.

Pia smirked. "Viv wasn't *on* the motorcycle," she said. "Some incompetent Hell's Angel rammed into her on St. Marks Place and sent her flying."

"That still counts as a motorcycle accident," Viv said.

"Don't worry," Pia teased, "*we* still think you're punk rock. Now, Mimi, what's with sending us a formal lunch invite? Aren't we all family here?"

"I've just been missing you guys," I said, squeezing into the booth next to Jess. It felt nice to be sitting close enough to smell her shampoo. "And I figured this was the most surefire way to see you. And Viv, I'm so sorry about your arm."

"Whatever," Viv said. "Enough about me—let's hear about Bravura."

"Oh, that," I said. Although I'd only arrived home the previous afternoon, Bravura already seemed a hazy memory. All I wanted to do was luxuriate in my long-lost friends' company, not babble on about myself. But feeling as though I owed the girls a little entertainment, I hammed up my account of Bravura, giving extra attention to the Nikola-Orzo hookup.

"Now your turn," I said when I'd finished my recap, and planted my elbows on the table. They all looked around the table and nobody said a word. All this away time had made an insecure wreck out of me, and for a moment I was sure nobody thought I deserved to be caught up on the moments I'd failed to see first-hand. Finally, Jess gave me some love. In the process of applying for summer internships at investment banking houses, she'd met a "beautiful money management intern" at her J. P. Morgan interview. "Before you get freaked out, he's still in college, at NYU," Jess said. "He's from Lexington, Kentucky, and his dad actually *owns* horses—isn't that cute? He sent me a follow-up e-mail. Saying his boss wants to meet me for a second round of interviews. Do you think that's just an excuse to contact me?"

"I think that's just an excuse to do his job," Lily said.

"But what about your writing?" I asked Jess. "Don't you want to work at a magazine or something?"

Jess screwed up her face. "Hmm, let's see. My mom's deep in debt and can barely afford to buy me new sneakers. I could apply for an unpaid job sharpening pencils, or I could make a pile of money and be surrounded by ridiculously hot men in seersucker suits."

"So what else have I missed?" I moved aside so our waiter could put the stone bowl of guacamole on the table. "How'd the rest of you ring in the long weekend?"

"Well," Viv said, "if you must know, you missed a *very* fun dinner party at my place. My parents were in Hong Kong, so it was more party than dinner, but we did spend the day at the farmers' market. My first time there."

"That wasn't her *only* overdue experience!" With a forward lunge, Pia tugged down Viv's turtleneck to reveal a strawberry-shaped hickey.

Finally, the conversation was gaining momentum. Everyone could only pout for so long. "Careful of the arm!" Viv's cheeks turned the color of a Kabbalah string bracelet.

"Pia, you're really one to talk. Why don't you tell Mimi when *Isaac* left, huh?" Lily said, ramming a chip into the guacamole bowl. "The two of them stayed up working on equations till well past the dawn."

Pia glared hard at Lily. "Enough of this libel. Is your brain really *that* incapable of comprehending those two simple words, 'just' and 'friends'? Jesus, what *is* your problem today?"

"Why did nobody warn me we'd have to wear bulletproof vests to lunch?" Jess asked. "Where did my nice happy friends go?"

"Right, pardon me," Lily said. "Not that you can relate, Jess, but sometimes I get sick of talking about guys all the time. And, FYI, Pia, my *problem*, since you asked, is that Ms. Singer was just appointed faculty advisor to the *Bugle* this morning. You may not realize it, but the *Bugle* is my single favorite thing about Baldwin, and with that cow in charge, it's going to become total hell."

"*What?*" I nearly shouted. "The least creative teacher at Baldwin taking over the paper? But *why*?" The *Bugle*'s previous advisor, Sylvester from the math department, encouraged student journalists to "find sources inside your heart" and dropped by the *Bugle* offices a maximum of two times a semester.

"It's serious," Lily said. "I stopped by the office before class this morning, just to check my mailbox, and there she was, rearranging everything, muttering about our 'organizational problems'—can you believe that? I swear, the woman still hasn't figured out that Baldwin and West Point are *not* the same schools!"

"Speaking of Ms. Singer, Mimi, your absence was fondly noted in class this morning," Viv said. "You're becoming a real favorite of hers. I'd *definitely* ask her to write your college recommendation."

"Thanks for the tip," I said, and glanced at Pia's watch. Our entrees hadn't arrived yet, but it was one o'clock. "Not already. I have to go. I'm supposed to be at Harriet's by two."

"But aren't *you* the one who arranged this whole outing?" Jess protested.

"I know, I know . . . " I promised to explain later and guiltily threw a twenty onto the table. I could at least cover more than my portion of uneaten lunch, but Pia pressed the bill back into my hand. A few minutes later, as I waited on the subway platform, my stomach rumbled, so I bought the stale cheese popcorn from the newspaper vendor there. After getting off at Spring Street, I was still hungry, and dropped by Sullivan Street Bakery, home of Manhattan's finest thin-crust pizza. I was polishing off my second and last mushroom slice when I rang Harriet's doorbell a few minutes later.

"Get your Metro Card ready," Harriet said when she answered the door and kissed me hello. "We have quite a journey ahead of us."

At Canal Street, we boarded a downtown train, and Harriet told me only that we were visiting an old friend for tea, nothing more. Several subway transfers later, we disembarked in the wilds of East New York, in deepest Brooklyn. The landscape, a mess of boarded-up storefronts and broken beer bottles, was the bleakest I'd ever seen. Harriet and I walked a few blocks, each more sinister than the last, before stopping outside a graffiti-covered brick warehouse. A heap of old pizza boxes that appeared to have survived years of rainstorms lay in a crumpled stack by the door. Harriet yanked a red wire protruding from the wall and waited until static blared out. She pushed open the heavy steel door and I followed close behind, certain I was about to be mugged. In the flickering light of the freight elevator, I saw Harriet smile. "Get that chicken-shit look off your face! You're in fine hands, I promise."

"Who are we seeing?" I timidly inquired.

"Ezekiel Allen. He's a painter. He used to live in my building, but he had to move a few years ago."

"Why'd he move from SoHo to *this*?"

"Certainly not for the scenery, if that's what you're implying. Common sense, girl." Harriet tapped her forehead. "Some fortunes run dry." As the elevator halted on the fifth floor, she offered one last assurance: "You'll like him. Trust me." The elevator opened directly onto Ezekiel's apartment, a large room with plenty of windows but not very much sunlight. Considering its size, it was a cramped room, with plants and bicycles and copper pots hanging from hooks on the ceiling. Some dangled so low, I had to duck as I followed Harriet across the floor, where Ezekiel waited in the shadows. He was white-haired and slim, wearing a blue denim shirt and circular black glasses that gave him an owlish look. He moved tentatively, as if trying not to disturb a sleeping child. After hugging her friend, Harriet introduced us.

"Welcome to my palace," he said. "I have a different name for every corner of my room. Here's my living room." He motioned toward the largest window. "There's the bedroom." He indicated the couch. "The kitchen . . . "—Ezekiel pointed to the sink and minifridge—"and last but not least, the collapsible laundry room!" He hurriedly folded up a wooden clothes rack and shoved it under the couch. "Have a seat here, in the den," Ezekiel said, leading us to a bunch of floor cushions and a little wooden table with a plate of chocolate-chip cookies on top of it. I occupied myself with these cookies—tasty, by the way—while Harriet and Ezekiel gossiped about people I'd never heard of.

After a few minutes, a whistle sounded and our host padded over to the "kitchen" and assembled a tea tray. While serving the tea, Ezekiel asked me questions about school. He wanted to know about the classes I was taking and what, if anything, I was learning in them. He guffawed when I told him about Russian Dissident Indigenous Crafts. "Sounds very cutting edge," he said. "You mind if I use the phrase for my own work? Could be the recipe for a comeback."

"Be my guest," I said. "Just don't steal my idea of comparing the pottery of the Pukara people to the dishware in the Baldwin cafeteria. Our teacher gobbled up my essay. He loves what he calls 'on-site archaeology.'"

"Whatever *that* means."

"Exactly," I said, then described my work on the *Bugle*. "Last semester it was more of a hobby, but it's starting to get more serious."

"Which brings us to the reason for this lovely impromptu gathering," Harriet said, and told him about my Serge Ziff profile. Ezekial nodded and said in a dark voice, "*That* man."

"So you know him?" I asked, rocking forward on my knees.

"Do I *know* him?" Ezekiel took off his glasses and proceeded to wipe them clean with a paper napkin. "Oh, sure, I know him. In fact, I can't remember *not* knowing him."

Right away, I starting tossing out all the questions Serge had ignored—What had he been like as a young man? How'd he get started as an art dealer? Ezekiel took his time answering. "When we first met," he said, "Sandy Zimmer was this spoiled rich kid from the New Jersey suburbs who, mostly on a whim, decided to sink Daddy's fortune into a little art gallery. The *Times* had just run a big article on me, and Sandy found my studio, dropped by, and seduced me."

I looked up from my note-taking. "He *seduced* you?" First Quinn, now Serge—or, sorry, Sandy Zimmer? Would I *never* hone my gaydar?

"No, not literally, Sherlock," Harriet said with a chuckle. "Ezekiel just means Serge sweet-talked him into dropping his dealer and switching over to his gallery. He vowed he'd make Ezekiel an international star."

"Of 'galactic proportions,'" Ezekiel added, making quotation marks in the air.

"Go on," I said.

"Anyway," Ezekiel said, "around the same time Sandy took me on, he reinvented his personality—changed his name to Serge Ziff and even adopted a lispy European accent." At first, Ezekiel said, he and Sandy/Serge were fast friends. They took the Zimmer's town car to coffee shops and nightclubs and Emilio's, a Cuban restaurant in the West Forties that was famous for its drag queen waitresses. Critics raved about Ezekiel's first show at S. Z. Enterprises, which later became Ziff Projects, and his paintings sold out the first weekend. "Man, those were the days," Ezekiel said. "Running around town, rubbing elbows with movie stars—who all bought my paintings by the truckload, by the way. Sandy and I'd go to this wacky psychic down on Carmine Street to get our fortunes told and then party at Studio 54 till dawn. And no one could get enough of my work—I couldn't paint fast enough to keep up with the demand. For a while, I really believed that signing on with Serge, whom I still think of as 'Sandy,' was the best thing that ever happened to me.

"I know," Ezekiel said when he caught me looking around his grim apartment. "I've often asked myself the same question. Where'd it all go wrong?" About ten years ago, he explained, a leading Hollywood agent named Stewart Indigo came to town and invited Ezekiel to dinner at a swish downtown restaurant. They went out and had a great time, and everything was hunky-dory until the next day, when Serge found out about it. He lost it, Ezekiel said, accusing his "protégé" of being an "ungrateful schmuck" and trying to cheat Serge out of his commission by selling paintings behind his back. Though Ezekiel insisted it had been just a social dinner, Serge couldn't be placated, and he even threatened to drop Ezekiel for his disloyalty.

"So he's not your dealer anymore?" I asked.

"I wish things were that simple," Ezekiel said. "And when I look back on it now, I wish he *had* just dropped me. But no, instead he held me hostage. When I signed on with Serge, you see, I didn't read the contract he gave me, so I didn't know that I was agreeing to give Ziff Projects forty percent of all future sales—for*ever*, for the remainder of my career."

"Are you serious?" I asked. "Surely that's not legal."

"That's what I thought, too. I talked to a few lawyers, though, and they all told me I could try suing him, but it'd be tricky, given the explicit provisions of the contract I'd signed. Plus, in the art world, reputation is everything, and then as now, Serge was an extremely powerful man. He told me if I tried to jump ship, I'd never get another commission again." Ezekiel shook his head. "And I bought it—back then, I couldn't afford not to. Serge still sells enough—barely, but enough—to keep me fed and sheltered, but at the time of the Stewart Indigo fiasco, well . . ." He broke off and took a long sip of tea. "My wife was in the hospital at the time, and I couldn't risk going broke, not even for a week."

"It was horrible," Harriet chimed in. "None of us thought Zeke would pull through."

"I'm so sorry," I said. "Is she—" I stopped as my eyes landed on a photograph of an ethereal young woman that was hanging on the wall. "Oh. I'm *really* sorry."

"Thank you," said Ezekiel, gentlemanly in the extreme. "Our friend Serge wasn't quite so compassionate. I was in no position to move to another dealer and keep only ten or twenty percent of my earnings. So what choice did I have? I stayed with the creep, and with our original arrangement of a forty-sixty split on the very occasional sale."

"Is this a normal scenario?" I asked.

"No, not at all. What can I say? When I signed on, I was young and stupid, and I trusted that crafty jerk. I could've paid him off, but he wanted more cash than I could cough up, and these days, I'm old and stupid, and I don't really care anymore. Serge won—I've dropped out of the game."

There was a silence, during which my pen stopped moving and we all just listened to each other breathing. And then I looked up and saw Ezekiel's tired eyes on my face.

"So now your story might take on a different tone, yes?" he asked.

"If this gets out, won't there be hell to pay?" I sputtered. "What if he stops selling your work altogether? I'd feel terrible if my article somehow made things worse."

Ezekiel got up and emptied the teacups down the drain. "By this point, I'd feel terrible if it didn't get out," he said. "It's time that man had a reality check—past time."

On the train back, I thanked Harriet for setting up that truly illuminating meeting. Any real texture my article would take was to her credit. "I didn't do anything," she said. "You asked the questions. I was impressed—you were a real pro."

When I got home late that afternoon, I ran downstairs to my computer and looked up Ezekiel on the Internet. I came upon images of *several* paintings—violent, swirling images of buildings and landscapes and lopsided women. Ezekiel had been pretty famous once; he'd even been invited to a presidential inauguration, but his production had tailed off dramatically a decade ago. One blogger listed Ezekiel on a "Where Are They Now?" page, speculating that the artist was hiding out in Thailand. Serge hadn't just stalled Ezekiel's career—he'd killed it. Harriet was justified in calling my article "not right" this morning. Serge was a bad man, and I had a responsibility—to Ezekiel, but mostly to myself—to expose him. The question was: Did I have it in me? Baldwin would applaud my courage, that I knew, but what about Serge? How would Nikola react, or She-Michael? I tried to convince myself that they didn't read *The Bugle*, but it didn't do the trick. For a long time, I sat at my desk, terrified by the possibilities.

Down by Law

By MIDWEEK, the halls of Baldwin buzzed with excitement about Friday's winter dance. The theme of the dance, "Against the Law," had inspired contributions from every segment of the Baldwin community. Virginia Lyman spent French class sewing a prisoner number decal onto a vintage bustier, while Leonora Newfield sat in the back sketching a black-and-white striped one-piece suit. Dabney Johnson, head of the theater department, had her tech students hang black strips of construction paper off the lobby ceiling and handcuffs from the classroom doorknobs. They also plastered the bathrooms with mysterious signs like CONJUGAL VISITING PRIVILEGES SUSPENDED and THE RIGHT TO REMAIN VIOLENT. Elvis installed bright red flashing sirens and tested them right in the middle of Zora's morning assembly, and to enhance the maximum-security feel, Yuri Knutz donated a cracked toilet bowl that he'd chanced upon outside a housing project on Wyckoff Street.

The biggest contribution of all, however, would be coming from Max Roth. Zora had great faith in Max's "imaginative vision," and had authorized him to hole up in the art building for the entire week, even if it meant missing classes. I couldn't wait to see what Max would unveil.

But not before I cranked out my own masterpiece. Our garbage-art perestroika mobiles for Yuri's class were due the morning of the dance, so that Thursday after school, I took the 4 train to Viv's house. Viv lived on the Upper East Side, in a sprawling apartment clogged up with aggressive interior decorations. Viv's room was still my favorite part, with framed photographs of rock stars and foreign cities hanging on her walls, which were Indian pink. She and Sam greeted me at the door with an unwieldy contraption of toilet paper rolls and wire hangers. "We're calling it 'Iron Chandelier Understanding,'" Viv said.

"We don't know what it means, either," Sam said, "but Yuri's sure to eat it up. He loves *anything* toiletlike."

I showed them what I'd brought—a box of fishing worms and a brand-new basketball, both items rescued from the Judys' trash.

"Christmas gifts from my father," Judy #1 had said when approached about these treasures. "As if lesbians just lie around fantasizing about sporting goods and fly fishing all day! I tell him we have nothing against normal gifts, like napkin rings and Ann Taylor shirts, but the man doesn't listen."

"I have an idea," Sam said, taking the basketball. He ran into the kitchen and came back with scissors. "Now stab it," he instructed me. I leveled the scissors at the ball, and the three of us watched the air hiss out. Flattened, the bright orange basketball supplied a perfect stand for the perestroika chandelier. Once we'd suspended our artwork from a shower rod in one of the Steinmanns' guest bathrooms, I got ready to go. I wanted to finish my World Civ homework that night, so I could devote the weekend to rewriting my Serge Ziff article.

At the door, I waited for Sam, assuming he'd be accompanying me on the crosstown bus to the West Side. Instead, he lingered at Viv's side and scrunched up his face. "Hey, Mimi?" he said. "About tomorrow night?"

"What about it? Aren't we all meeting up first at Pia's first? Or what—you two not going anymore?"

"That's just the thing," Viv said quickly. "We're still going, but, like, we were thinking about going, you know—*together*."

"Yeah, I know, Pia told me already. Are we still meeting at her place first or what?"

Why were Viv and Sam looking at me like that?

"No, Mimi," Viv said. "That's not what I meant. I meant *together,* as in, the two of us." She reached up and took Sam's hand. "You know, kind of like a date?"

"Oh, of course, I get it." But actually, I didn't. Viv and Sam were dating—when had that happened? Weekend hickeys were one thing, but *dating*? In my limited Baldwin experience, dating was a big deal, a radical statement that almost no one made. "That's fine, then," I said, and stumbled backward into the hall. "I'll just go with Lily and Pia and Jess—I'm sure we'll see you there."

"That's another thing," Viv said. "We've all kind of talked about group dating, you know? We'd thought it'd be fun. Which is why . . . well, Pia's agreed to show Isaac in public for the first time, and Jess is bringing the banker guy who interviewed her for a summer job."

Sam took a little red rubber ball out of his pocket and started bouncing it around. He refused to look at me. How was he suddenly tighter with all my friends than I?

"Oh, really? Then I'll just go with Lily." Despite Lily's recent orneriness, she'd appreciate that at least one of her friends was a boyfriendless loser like herself.

"Mimi, there's no need to get all touchy," Viv said. "It's not like we were *trying* to exclude you. You just weren't around when we talked about it, and whose fault is that?"

"You're right," I said. I had been so busy lately. But did I really deserve to be punished for it? It wasn't as if I'd gone out and found a new group of friends.

"And while we're on the subject, by the way," Viv said, "you should know that Lily has a date, too—or sort of. Her mother set up her with this Trinity guy whose investment portfolio was just written about in *New York* magazine."

"She didn't want to be obsessing over Harry Feder all night, you know?" Sam added.

Well, wasn't this just the final blow. Not only did Lily have a date, but Sam was discussing her B. J. Harry hookup—which she'd still never mentioned to me. "Oh," I said.

"But listen," Viv said, "why don't you bring someone, too?"

"Maybe I could've if I'd known more than a day before the dance. *Now* who I am supposed to invite, my dad?" Nobody said anything for a little while.

"Boris was thinking of going," Sam said, finally. "I can call him if you want. We're all going to Pia's first, for a little preparty, and I'm sure he'd be down." It was amazing how little it had taken to become everybody's number one pity case.

"Thanks, but no thanks," I snapped. "I'll be perfectly fine on my own." With that, I tore down the hall, fuming with every step. Sam had some nerve, trying to fob me off on his friend like that, a near stranger! Who said I couldn't get my own date? An hour later, after rejecting various possibilities (Quinn? Ricky Marino, my favorite Bravura Islander?—nah, both too grown up and cool, not to mention too obviously gay), I became upset. To avoid brooding on my datelessness, I began work on my article.

I skimmed it and realized it still seemed flimsier than I would have liked. Deciding I needed a quote from a specialist to make the story sound more credible, I tracked down the home phone number of Ira Finkelman, a professor at Columbia University who'd published an online article called "Do-Gooding/Do Badding: The Dark Side of Philanthropy."

When Dad popped down and invited me to join him, Ariel, and Decibel for dinner at John's Pizzeria, I accepted without hesitation as much for my sake as his. Over buffalo mozzarella bruschetta, I told everyone about the big event at Baldwin, and Decibel beat-boxed his approval of the dance's illicit theme.

"You *make* da law, I *break* the law," he rapped, pulling at a strand of mozzarella.

I turned to Ariel. "I know you'd be older than everyone there," I said, praying she wouldn't read the desperation on my face, "but you wouldn't possibly want to come along, would you?" I should never have doubted Ariel, whose collegiate fixation on Kappa mixers was the logical extension of her high school fixation on debutante balls. She could imagine no better way to spend her last night in New York. "We'd *love* to go—it sounds totally fun! It's seriously *in* Brooklyn?"

Though temporarily cheered, by the next morning I almost wanted to cancel on my sister. The potential to feel lonely at a dance where I was the only person without a date was too daunting. Over breakfast I tried telling Ariel that I should probably stay in and work on the huge essay Ms. Singer had assigned, but Ariel saw right through my pathetic excuse and told me she wasn't going to let me wiggle my way out. "We're going to have fun," she said. "More fun than if I let you spend the night on the couch with a pint of mint chip."

That evening, while getting ready for the dance, I started to mope about being the only unattached girl in the room. "I just feel so lame," I said to Ariel. "Every single one of my friends will have a date except me."

"God, Mimi, is *that* all you're worried about? Listen, dating is like acid-washed jeans—totally over. Not even Kappas go on dates anymore."

"But aren't you and Dec dating?" I asked.

"We're chilling. Totally different. And besides," she said fondly, "you do *too* have a date. In fact, you have two dates—me and Dec!"

Because Decibel thought it was "ghetto" to be seen in taxis, that night we climbed out of the car around the corner from

Baldwin. Half a block from the school, we could hear "Smooth Criminal" by Michael Jackson blasting out the open windows. Ariel and Dec exchanged approving looks.

In the Undercroft, Arthur Gray was manning the coat check, accompanied by a pudgy man in a police uniform, who had a bright yellow handlebar mustache that stuck out several inches from his face. "Hey, you, tall girl, you underage?" the cop asked me.

"Is that a real cop?" I whispered to Arthur.

"Not exactly," Arthur said. "But Officer Padin's a genuine museum guard, and in my book, that's pretty close. I met him on his lunch break at Starbucks yesterday. We got into a heavy talk about geopolitics, and pretty soon I'd convinced him to show up at the dance to balance out the lawlessness. Told him he might meet some hot teachers. Isn't he awesome?"

Officer Padin had just sprung in front of my sister and was now shouting, "Hands up, lady! Give me your coat or I'm taking you to central booking!"

Decibel jumped in front of his beloved. "She ain't packing, officer, I can vouch it."

"You! Freeze!" Officer Padin yelled, caressing his mustache. "Hands up!"

Arthur hooted and cheered.

"That's what you want?" Officer Padin asked his friend.

Arthur told him he was doing a great job, then trooped upstairs to the dance. Ariel couldn't believe how tall and skinny my school was, and I told her it looked much more normal during the day. But when we walked into the high-ceilinged cafeteria, even I was impressed—it really had been transformed into looking like a federal prison. And I thought Texans took their party decorations seriously. The room, usually flooded with sunlight, was dim and shadowy. A squad of seniors in orange jumpsuits were doing jumping jacks by the servery, and in the center of the room the drama kids, decked out as prison wardens, were patrolling a large metal cage that contained a bunk bed, a toilet, and a large, muscular man. When she spotted this convict, Ariel let out a resounding squeal. "Dec, look! Priz *totally* pulled through!"

Huh? Ariel had been in New York for less than a week and already she knew someone at my school dance? I must say—it was pretty irritating. I had no choice but to trot behind my sister to the cage, where Decibel welcomed the prisoner with a familiar, "Hey, man."

"You look *so* tough behind bars," Ariel told the thug. "You're the hottest ex-con ever! Oh, hey, meet my little sister, Mimi," she said, pushing me against the cage. "Mimi, Priz; Priz, Mimi."

"The pleasure is all mine," the inmate said, then leaned forward to ask Dec: "Yo, you really think there gonna be record execs here?"

I missed Decibel's reply because my attention was suddenly arrested by the glowing white tent in the back corner of the cafeteria. Max's exhibition, I thought, and smiled inwardly. Though tempted, I restrained myself from checking it out right away. Better to wait a bit, play it cool. While biding my time, I meandered around the room confirming that my friends still hadn't shown up; they were probably having too much fun at Pia's couples-only preparty. On my way back to Big Priz's cage, I resolved to have fun myself, or at least *pretend* I was having fun. So I started dancing by myself, shuffling back and forth, determined not to feel sad or lonely or pathetic or ditched or deformed for not having a boyfriend, and after a while I was actually enjoying myself a little. After a few songs, Amanda France cantered up to me. "Hey, Mimi!" she cried. "Mind if I join you? Dancing's a *great* cardiovascular workout, but everyone at this stupid school is too ironic to just go for it."

It was true, I thought. The cafeteria was packed with students—many drunk, but almost none dancing. "Totally," I said, and Amanda took her place next to the cage, and for a good half-hour the two of us danced side by side, bobbing and bouncing and swishing our hair, while Big Priz egged us on. I was red-faced and sweaty by the time Amanda left me to find her best friend, Courtney Sisler: "She gets *so* freaked out on her own at social events."

When, a few minutes later, I saw my friends roll in, I stubbornly kept dancing—let them find *me*. Viv was the first to rush toward me, crying, "*There* you are!" Her breath smelled like licorice and alcohol. "You are a total freak for skipping our pre-dance festivities. So, how were Max's paintings? Is he really and truly the next Leonardo?"

I shrugged, feigning indifference. "I dunno." Viv had seen my reaction to the double-date setup in her building the previous day, and now her fake exuberance put me off.

"Yeah, right," Viv said. "C'mon, let's go check it out." As we walked outside the tent, I asked Viv where Sam was. "Oh, he's around," she said, shrugging. "Hey, I actually wanted to ask you . . . well, Mimi, are you *sure* you don't mind? About me and Sam, I mean?"

"Why on *earth* would I mind about you and Sam?"

"I don't know," she said. "You just seemed so weirded out about it last night."

"Viv, that's *not* why I was—"

As I spoke, the crowd thronged forward, propelling us into the tent. There, for once, my height came in handy. I stood on tiptoe and studied the paintings over everyone else's heads.

The first picture showed a pouting girl with long reddish hair, her face framed by black vertical stripes meant to resemble prison bars. The girl seemed oddly familiar, and I angled forward to inspect the canvas. Something about that blank, conceited expression—"Tinsel Mulchgarten!" I practically bellowed.

"I know that girl," I told Viv, who was too short to see the painting. And what's more, I thought, I know that picture of that girl. As I moved to the next painting, my mind reached back to the afternoon when Fenella had dissed Tinsel's photo spread in *Teen Vogue*. Here, in Max's second picture, Tinsel was sitting on a park bench, wearing handcuffs and holding a candy-cane umbrella. Yep, I was right. The great visionary Max Roth had copied his great masterpieces from *Teen Vogue*. Talk about a royal disappointment.

He'd scruffed up Tinsel's outfits, swapped summery gowns

for ripped jeans and moth-eaten T-shirts, and added some decorative prison-themed details, but otherwise, the portraits were identical.

Max certainly had a strong technique, a talent for accuracy or verisimilitude or whatever you call it. His portraits of the unbearable Tinsel Mulchgarten were unmistakably the unbearable Tinsel Mulchgarten. But (and I acknowledged this with a sharp stab of disappointment) that was all they were. As I pushed from painting to painting—Tinsel incarcerated on a gold four-poster bed, Tinsel ballroom dancing in prison stripes—I could no longer deny the truth about Max. He had skill, but no soul.

At the far end of the tent, Max stood accepting compliments from the Baldwin student body. He looked adorable in a rumpled light gray sports coat, but I'm not sure that fully explained my sudden squeamishness at his proximity. I stalled at the second-to-last painting and waited for little Viv to locate me.

Max had already spotted me at the front of the receiving line, and when he waved, I knew I was trapped. "Thanks so much for coming," he said to me.

"Well, I was already at the dance," I said, trying to keep it light.

"So how'd you like the paintings?" he asked. He smiled, and his left dimple deepened.

"Well, they're very . . ." I hemmed, searching for a charitable response. "Evocative," I came up with, finally.

"Thanks," Max said, but his eyes had already roved past me. I started to gratefully edge away when I heard a familiar angry voice behind me. I turned in surprise—I hadn't seen Nikola Ziff on Baldwin property since the first day of the semester, when she'd rammed me into the stairway wall. "Hey, Nikola," Max said warmly. "How's things?"

Wait a minute—how did those two know each other?

"It was going fine until now," Nikola spat. "But I have just one question for you, Max Roth. What was your inspiration for this project? Was it your *hormones?*"

"It's a commentary, " Max answered, unfazed.

"On *what?*" Nikola threw back her platinum mane. "The shallowness of contemporary culture?"

"Actually, yeah, sort of," Max said. "I wanted to convey the ritual plasticization of individuals, an all too common problem these days."

Maybe my timing was off, but I chose that instant to tap Nikola on the shoulder and say, "Hey, what's up? Have you seen Orzo since we got back?"

Nikola stared at me as if I were a pervert whose face was pressed against her shower curtain. "What are you *talking* about?" she spat. "Who *are* you?"

I careened backward out of the tent. To think I'd mistaken Nikola for a decent human being! I felt pathetic, ridiculous, and all the more so because Max Roth had witnessed the insult.

Viv found me outside the tent a few minutes later. "Hello, can you spell 'lame' in all caps and billboard-high letters?" was her only reaction to Max's exhibition. Her conclusion cheered me, for Viv had a real handle on contemporary art, if only through osmosis from her older sister.

Viv and I crossed the cafeteria to the cage, where the rest of my friends were milling around Big Priz. To my relief, the group didn't look excessively coupled off. Ariel, Lily, and Pia were deep in conversation, as were Decibel and Priz, while Jess was busy entertaining three guys I'd never seen before—one skinny with round glasses; the second overdressed, preppy, and slightly older; the last on the heavy side with greased-back hair. Ah-ha— the mystery dates, maybe?

"Your sister is *so* over the top," Pia said when I joined their conversation. "She's been telling us about her sorority."

I smiled noncommittally. Ariel was indeed over the top, but with Pia, I could never distinguish between flattery and sarcasm. Was she mocking Ariel?

"Yeah," Sam said, "can you *believe* she got Big Priz to come to a high school dance?"

"What's the big deal about that?" I asked. "What else would he be doing?"

"What do you mean, what else would he be doing?" The question flabbergasted Sam. "He's *Big Priz*. What *couldn't* he be doing?"

I was totally lost. "Sorry, but who's Big Priz?"

"What do you mean, *who's* Big Priz?" Jess repeated in astonishment. "You're joking, right?"

Pia murmured something into the ear of her escort, and even pop-culturally out-of-it Lily gawked at me. It finally fell upon Viv to explain. "Mimi, Big Priz is the guy who did 'Jail Bait,' only the best hip-hop single of all time!"

"Yeah," Sam helped out, "surely you've heard it—with the

Isaac Hayes sample? It was playing everywhere last summer, I'm *sure* it made its way to Houston."

"Oh, yeah," I lied. No wonder kids had been circling Big Priz's cage all night, pointing and whispering. "Of course. What were his other songs again?"

"That's the tragedy," Viv said. "He doesn't *have* any other songs. Right after he hit it big, he was busted for his involvement in a pizzeria shooting in Queens. He was *totally* innocent, but he refused to rat on his friends, so they hauled him off to Rikers on a manslaughter two conviction."

"He got out in ten months," Sam said, "but that's an eternity in the music world, so he'd pretty much fallen off the map. That is, until your sister and Decibel ran into him on the J train, which he was riding home from a visit with his parole officer."

"I would *love* for our sisters to meet, by the way," Viv broke in enthusiastically. "I think they'd really hit it off—they have *so* much in common."

At this high praise from Viv, I glanced over at my sister, who was gyrating with the music. "You befriended a famous rapper on the subway?" I asked her. "Seriously?"

"Sure," Ariel replied, without losing the beat. "We're trying to talk him into coming back to Austin with us so we can work on cutting his comeback album there. Dec's dad might even let Priz stay in the guest room. Though generally Professor Rosen prefers Danish exchange students."

"Wow." I was genuinely awed. "Whenever Dec and I go anywhere together," Ariel added, "we always meet the coolest people. It's almost, like, cosmic."

"Cosmic," I echoed, as Boris Potasnik shimmied up to the cage. "Sorry I'm late," he said. "I had a near run-in with Nikola Ziff by the coatcheck and had to hide out in the phone booth downstairs. The engineers of those things should take into account that some people might be taller than five-foot-seven." Boris patted down his hair and looked at me for sympathy. Yuck. I still had trouble imagining Boris Potasnik with Nikola Ziff. Not that he was out of her league—not at all. Boris was cute, hilarious, and loaded. The mystery to me was what he saw in her. Nikola was hot, true, but she was also shallow, self-obsessed, and—as I'd just discovered—pretty cruel, too.

"Lucky you caught us—we were all actually on our way out," Pia said, which was news to me. "There's an after-party." As she spoke, the deafening rap music faded out, only to be replaced by the live version of Johnny Cash's "Folsom Prison Blues." When Johnny sang, "I shot a man in Reno—just to watch him die," Priz pounded his chest and solemnly declared, "Johnny's the man!" I clapped in agreement, but everyone else interpreted this change of tempo as an exit cue.

"A slow jam at this hour is Elvis's special way of saying good night," Lily told me. I joined the crowd of students filing from the cafeteria, pausing at the door to watch a hapless freshman retch into a trash can. Behind me, the theater kids were dismantling Big Priz's cage, and Max was wrapping his canvases in protective pillowcases.

"Lovely view, don't you think?" Boris asked, stealing up behind me with my burgundy coat.

"Hey, where'd you get that?"

Boris appeared to be too mesmerized by the vomiting under-classman to reply. "What do you think he had for dinner?" he asked. "My money's on baked ziti and Brussels sprouts." And then, unexpectedly, he reached out his arms and crisscrossed them around my waist.

"How about the last dance, Schulman? You can't be from Texas and ignore Johnny Cash."

I looked around the room.

"He's actually from Arkansas," I said, but I'd already placed my palms on his shoulders. We'd just started swaying when the cafeteria lights came on and Pia appeared.

"Hurry up," she called. "Everyone's waiting in the limo."

I dropped my arms, and Boris and I immediately made our way over to her.

"Where are we off to, anyway?" he asked.

"Only the most paparazzi-infested nightclub to grace the Meat Packing District in at least a week," Pia said. "Dis/Play—do you know it?"

"It sounds fun," I said, and it did. But Ariel was leaving New York in the morning, and I felt a sense of obligation to her for playing my "date" at the dance—if not for her, I probably would've had a tub of mint chip hardening in my stomach. On the curb next to the Pazzolini limo, I told Pia, "I really should hang with my sister tonight." Then another legitimate excuse came to me. "Also, I really need to be clear-headed to write my article tomorrow."

Pia's lip curled upward. "News flash, Mimi? Your sister's coming with us. She already called your dad from the limo, and he's agreed to suspend your curfew in the name of family bonding. Oh, and P.S., the subject of your article just so happens to own Dis/Play."

"What?" I was very confused. "Serge Ziff owns the place where you're going?"

"Yes, dumb-ass, the place where *we're* going—get in already!"

"MIMI, THIS IS TOTALLY AWESOME," Ariel said when I squeezed onto the seat, and with some satisfaction I saw she was right. If someone had told me a year ago that I'd be cruising over the Brooklyn Bridge in a stretch limousine with diplomatic license plates, I would've laughed out loud. Over the last few months, though, I'd grown accustomed to the insane glamour of my new lifestyle. Ariel was right: this *was* awesome.

There I sat, squashed between rap-superstar ex-convict Big Priz and Boris Potasnik, the high-living son of a notorious Russian slumlord. Sharing the black leather seat with us was my sister Ariel, who never gave me the time of day in Texas, and her white rap-impresario boyfriend, a professor's kid who'd legally changed his name to Decibel. Jess Gillespie and her new admirer, Trevor, the investment-banking intern from Louisville, were sitting Indian-style on the limo floor, speaking quietly and neglecting the rest of us. In the opposite row, Vivian Steinmann, daughter of one of the most feared defense attorneys in the country, sat folded into the lap of my freckle-faced childhood friend, Sam Geckman. Next to him Lily Morton was trying to avoid physical contact with her tedious blind date Andrew

Gertz, a tenth-grader at Trinity who thought mutual funds made for fascinating cocktail party conversation. On Andrew's left, Pia Pazzolini, the one in charge of the limo, was leaning into Isaac Levinson, the bespectacled and extremely uninternational guy she'd picked up in her advanced placement calculus class at Columbia.

On the other side of the divider was Isaac's predecessor Guillermo, Signor Pazzolini's hulking chauffeur. Despite the driver's bee-stung lips and thick Italian accent, pale, shrimpy, adolescent Isaac seemed a definite improvement. Not only was Isaac closer to Pia's age, but he, too, was a card-carrying member of the Nerd Club.

I only regretted that, unlike the other girls, I hadn't already met Isaac before. Ever since their visit to Nona in Massachusetts, my friends' lives had sprouted in all sorts of different directions, and I hadn't been around to watch. I was like one of those Wall Street dads who never sees his kids from one birthday to the next, except with a lousier pay stub.

Unable to follow the schizoid exchanges whizzing back and forth inside the limo, I asked Big Priz about his comeback album plans. When we got to Dis/Play, and made our way past the bouncers, I experienced a twinge of disappointment. Maybe Bravura Island had raised my expectations unreasonably high, but Dis/Play was seriously pointless. It was empty except for a sprinkling of Baldwinites near the bar—all of them admitted into the club, like us, for the dance's unofficial after-party. It was already past midnight and nary a denizen of New York's after-hours club scene was in sight. I recognized some people in my

World Civ class, a few faces from the *Poetry Review* circle, and Porter Yurnell from Russian Dissident Indigenous Crafts. At the bar, Arthur Gray's pet security guard, Officer Padin, still in his blue uniform, was stroking his golden mustache while good old Arthur twirled on a barstool, signaling in vain for the bartender.

"It might help if he'd left his backpack at Baldwin," Pia said. She slumped onto a barstool and the rest of us grouped around her. We weren't really talking, with the exception of Andrew Gertz, who was babbling about futures and bonds.

"Where is everybody?" Lily asked. "We might as well be in the *Bugle* office."

At that moment, a figure on a barstool swiveled to face us. It was buck-toothed Vikram Mohini, the *Bugle*'s layout king. Obviously thrilled to be inside a nightclub, he smiled broadly at Lily.

"Oh, for God's sake," Lily muttered. "Next thing you know, Ms. Singer is going to walk out of the bathroom."

"Should we proceed to the Potasnik pad, then?" Boris suggested. "My family's out in Vegas and the fridge and bar are stocked."

"No, listen," Viv said, "my sister said the VIP area is actually cool."

"Well, then, shall we?" Pia said. Mia Steinmann didn't dole out endorsements lightly.

"The only problem," Viv said, "is you've got to get on the list. Maybe Mia's in the neighborhood. She could definitely hook us up."

On her way outside to call Mia, Viv brushed past Blowjob

Harry, who had just arrived. Next to me, Lily groaned, "Oh, *no*," as Harry drew near us with a petite, curly-haired blonde on his arm. Mistaking Lily's cry of despair for disagreement, Andrew Gertz's financial convictions became more animated.

"As long as you're shooting for a balanced portfolio," he insisted, "there really are no taboos."

"Don't worry," I whispered into Lily's ear. "We can always leave if you want."

"No, it's fine," Lily said gruffly. "I'm just tired—I just need to sit down or something."

And so we found two barstools and waited for Viv, who eventually returned with her sister in tow. "See? I knew she'd be nearby," she said. "She was still in the middle of her Urban Beauty performance piece when I found her, so it took a while."

That night, Baldwin legend Mia Steinmann had on a violet tunic, gold platform wedges, and a garland of twigs around her forehead. "Urban Beauty is a reminder to all those urban rats who just race down the streets without any real presence of mind," she told us. "We need to look closer at the world around us, take time to be of the moment."

I nodded, awed as ever by Mia's bizarre brilliance. Viv's older sister was across-the-board exceptional, and not just for her ability to look stunning in bed linens and bark. It was Mia's impenetrable self-confidence that floored me. She knew everyone worth knowing in New York and yet she was always alone, publicly, proudly on her own. In a million years I could never imagine cruising the Meat Packing District all by myself, draped in a sheet.

Mia directed us to Dis/Play's chrome spiral staircase, and Vikram watched us walk away with a pained expression.

"My mom's picking me up in five minutes. Can you hold off until then?" he pleaded. Harry broke away from his poodle date and called out to Lily, "Hey, wait—where're you guys heading?"

Pretending she hadn't heard, Lily straightened her posture and kept moving. Such were the privileges of tearing through nightclubs with Mia Steinmann.

Upstairs was a large steel door similar to the forbidding dungeonlike entrance to Serge's art gallery. Mia pounded on the door and a rectangular panel slid open, revealing a pair of squinting eyes. "They're cool," Mia said, and abracadabra, the door opened, leaving Viv's sister free to slink back downstairs and find another street corner to perform on.

The VIP lounge was dark and musty, like a sleazy bar in Texas, and about as unhappening as Dis/Play's ground floor. With our choice of seats, our group settled on low-slung sofas underneath an oil painting of Michael Jackson making out with a mermaid. Boris studied the canvas with an amused expression. "I've often wondered what that would look like," he said over the generically thumping music. "Now I know."

At least the artist has *some* imagination, I thought, remembering Max Roth's insipid Tinsel Mulchgarten tribute.

Across the table, Jess was batting her eyelashes at Trevor, Pia was wriggling into Isaac's lap (they were both so little!), and Sam was scowling at whatever Viv had just said. Lily looked miserable as Andrew blabbered about his personal finance "Internet tabulation service." Next to them, Dec, Ariel, and Priz were tossing around song ideas. Meanwhile, Boris called the waitress over and shocked everyone by ordering a two-hundred-dollar bottle of vodka. I stand corrected: shocked everyone except the waitress, who didn't even demand to see his ID. I guess once you made it into the VIP lounge, you received VIP treatment.

"Wow," I said, contemplating what two-hundred bucks could buy me: a week's worth of fabulous thrift store outfits, with cash left over to take my whole family out for Mexican food. "I can't believe you bought that."

Boris threw up his arms. "Why not? It's a great deal. Check it out"—he pointed at the menu—"it comes with all these juices, free of charge, see? Peach nectar, mango concentrate, even pear!"

After our waitress unloaded a fancy silver tray on our table and gave Boris a conspiratorial look, I went for the cranberry juice, without vodka. It was late, and I was tired—plus, I needed to stay in top form and knock off my stupid article in the morning. As my friends took turns with the vodka and the room started to fill up, I sipped at my juice and absently stared at a black door across the room. Every now and then it would open to admit a man of Neanderthal dimensions and a thick head of black hair. I watched as he clomped through the V.I.P. area, occasionally stopping to accost a club-goer. Some of these exchanges lasted only a few seconds. Other times, the Neanderthal would chew the fat for several minutes before leading the club-goer past the swinging door. In our first half-hour in the VIP lounge, three people followed the Neanderthal down this passage. Could this be some weird sort of sex thing? I wondered. "Explain something to me," I said to Boris. "We've gone through two checkpoints to get here. The music is generic and way too loud, the vodka costs five hundred times what it would at a liquor store, and all we're doing is sitting on a sofa, talking to the people we came with. So this is better than kicking back at home how?"

"What, are you out to meet someone?" Boris asked. "What about that guy talking to your sister? He seems pretty nice."

"Big Priz *is* nice," I said. "Extremely." Boris had missed my point. I simply didn't understand why people spent their evenings in overpriced lounges like this; I would've preferred hanging out at Boris's house. "I'm going to circulate," I told him. I got up and was backing away from the table when I bumped into the Neanderthal. Up close I could see there was no obvious line where his head hair stopped and his facial hair started.

"How's it going?" he asked me, smiling and angling his extremely large body toward me. "Having a good time tonight?"

"So-so," I answered honestly. "I'm actually getting a little bored."

"*Ah.*" Neanderthal leaned in a little closer. I tilted a little further back. Because I'm nearly six feet tall, I wasn't used to feeling this feminine next to a man. "So," he said, "you're a girl who likes things to move a little faster, is that right?"

"Uh, I guess you could say that," I said. I looked over my shoulder and tried to catch Boris's eye, but he was studying the selection of vodka mixers.

"Looking for any kind of fun in particular?" Neanderthal inquired.

"You know, I'm pretty open to fun, so long as it's, um, fun,"

I said, immediately regretting the accidental innuendo.

At this, Neanderthal leaned even closer. "Well, how's *this* for fun? I've got uppers, downers, sideballs, sidecars, shack, and tungsten babies—any of that appeal?"

I jumped three feet in the air. "Are you trying to sell me *drugs?*" I blurted out.

Maybe that wasn't the best move. Talk about faux pas. The Neanderthal's jaw fell open and he balled his hairy hands into fists.

"I—I—I—" I tried to explain.

Suddenly, Boris's voice sounded in my ear. "Sorry, man," he said. "Is my cousin giving you a hard time? She's just in from Texas and hasn't spent much time in the big scary metropolis. Don't mind her. Please." Boris squared his shoulders and faced the Neanderthal. And oh, the joys of tall men! Though Neanderthal weighed twice as much as Boris, they were almost the same height and the bluff succeeded.

"Well, get her out of here, then," Neanderthal grunted before pounding back behind the swinging door.

"Smooth, Schulman," Sam said when I convulsed back to the table.

"Thanks for helping," I said. I could hear the terror in my own voice. "Jess, could you pass me my purse? I'm totally out of here."

"I'm coming with you," Boris said. "Like I said, it's a big, scary metropolis out there, and my little cowgirl cuz' requires constant supervision. No telling what trouble she'll get into."

"Don't worry," I told him. "You've already done enough tonight, seriously. You barely touched your drink. I just need to go—"

I never finished the sentence because at that moment a seismic change occurred in the room. Several waitresses yanked walkie-talkies from their aprons and began frantically punching buttons. Neanderthal ducked behind the swinging door, and Arthur Gray and Officer Padin came sauntering up to our table.

Boris put it together before I did. "Holy shit," he said. "They saw the *cop* and flipped."

"Officer Padin?" I waved at Arthur Gray's harmless handle-bar-mustached companion. "What about him?"

"The people working here think some kind of drug bust is going down," Boris whispered.

"Really?"

I was more convinced when Officer Padin, after one disappointing sweep of the room, turned around and left the VIP area. The second he departed, the swinging door creaked open again, only this time it wasn't the Neanderthal standing behind it. No, it was my old friend Serge Ziff, who evidently was in cahoots with the drug pusher. As Serge surveyed the room and saw no trace of a policeman, his facial muscles started to slacken. But then his gaze landed directly on me, our eyes locked, and Serge lost it.

"What's *she* doing here?" he screamed at the Neanderthal. His hysterics continued, and I could read his lips as he commanded: "Get her *OUT!*" Talk about making your guest feel unwanted. Lightning-fast, the Neanderthal pounced on me and hoisted me into the air. He carried me down a service staircase and out the back door, muttering some very ungentlemanly things along the way. When he pushed through a set of doors leading onto the street, icicles immediately formed in my nostrils. The coarse hairs on his arms shot up, thick and black as spider legs. "Sayonara, sister," he said. And then, as nimbly as he'd plucked me up, Serge's henchman bent down and deposited me into a pile of garbage bags. Talk about rude! The scent of curry and melted butter came wafting from the Pakastani samosa shop next door. It smelled delicious, but for once I wasn't hungry.

You Cold, Cold Fish

BORIS FOUND ME OUTSIDE THE SAMOSA SHOP, sobbing hysterically and flagellating in vain for a cab. Several drivers had already pulled up, only to speed off when they saw—or smelled—me up close.

"Take a shower, kid!" the third taxi driver yelled before revving up and away.

"I'm reporting you to the Taxi and Limousine Commission!" I yelled back.

"I don't know if I'd take you, either," Boris said. "Hey, close your eyes for a second." I complied and he wiped a foreign object off my lid.

"What was it?" I asked.

"Let's just say it wasn't an *it*." Boris told me. "It was either a *him* or a *her*." Boris's sense of humor, however endearing, served no purpose at this stage. He stepped into the street and after several attempts flagged down a beat-up Cadillac. The driver rolled down his window and gauged me doubtfully, whereupon Boris exchanged a few words with him and pulled a bill from his wallet. When the driver grinned his assent, I saw he was missing a tooth in the back of his mouth.

"What are you doing?" I hissed as Boris tried to escort me into the car. "This isn't a taxi! Haven't I had enough danger tonight?"

"Chill, Mimi." Boris gently placed his hand on the back of my neck. "There's a 'T' on the license plate, which means it's a car service. It's fine. And don't worry, I'm coming along for the ride."

Concluding that I had no choice, I climbed in after him. I was desperate to be home, but though it was well past midnight, traffic was intense, and we stalled at several lights. As the car turned off Tenth Avenue, Boris startled me by clamping his hands around my filthy wrists. I cut my eyes over to him, expecting some sarcastic disclaimer, but my usually convivial friend simply gazed out the window, his hands gripping mine all the while. After what felt like an hour, the car turned onto Barrow Street and pulled up outside my house. The Upstairs Judys' lights were still on, and I jealously imagined their mellow evening at home, maybe with some takeout Moroccan food and documentaries on DVD.

"Hey," I said softly to Boris, trying to extricate myself. "This is my stop."

Boris showed no sign of having heard, even after the driver groused, "Move it or lose it—I don't got all night."

I shook my hands free and told Boris I was going in, then offered him cash for the carfare, which he wouldn't accept. He just stared abstractedly out the window. As the car pulled away, he barely even glanced at me.

Although I hadn't touched any alcohol at Dis/Play, I woke up early the next morning with a pounding headache, intensified by the knowledge of the work that lay ahead of me. I needed to stock up on provisions and decided to get them at the bagel shop on West Fourth Street—a greasy egg and cheese sandwich, some black-and-white cookies (Decibel's favorite New York dessert), and a two-liter bottle of Coke sounded perfect.

I tiptoed upstairs and tried hard not to disturb Ariel and Decibel, who were sleeping on the living room floor. Outside, the streets were quiet and peaceful, abandoned except for a few dedicated dog owners. I enjoyed the sensation of inhabiting my own private city and took my time walking down the street. When I got back home, everyone was still asleep, so I silently tiptoed downstairs, propped myself up against my pillows, and began plotting my article in the Goat Show notebook. But I was still tired, and I'd only written a few words before drifting back to sleep. The next thing I knew, Decibel was standing above my bed in a silver Mylar jacket and rapping into the cordless receiver. "Hottie's got a hotline, it be ringin' for ages, she be popular as a call girl listed in the"—Decibel stopped to search for the perfect rhyme—"White Pages!"

"Thanks, Dec," I said, and took the phone. The house really would be lonely after he and Ariel returned to Austin that afternoon. Decibel was an acquired taste, that I'll admit, but he was also fun to have around.

"Well, thank God *some*one's home," Harriet Yates sighed into the receiver. "Now, listen, I hate to bother you, but I have an extremely asinine favor to beg. I'm supposed to be at home all day waiting for a shoe delivery from my cobbler in Buenos Aires. They're a gift for Yolanda, my former editor at the *Voice,* and it's urgent that I give her at least one birthday present before she croaks. She's having a garden party tomorrow afternoon, and I just—"

"Slow down, Harriet," I said, rubbing my eyes. "I don't exactly see what the problem is."

"The *problem*," Harriet panted, "is that I'm supposed to be in Connecticut in an hour, and I don't know what to do. His courier system's pretty primitive, and I already snoozed through the first delivery attempt. If I miss this one, they'll send the shoes back to Argentina, and I'll have screwed up again and Yolanda will pretend she doesn't care, but will she ever. And can that woman *ever* hold a grudge, Mimi, you have no idea!" Harriet paused to catch her breath. "What I'm trying to say is—well, what I need is for someone to wait at my apartment and answer the door when it rings. You up for it, champ?"

I considered the request. Holing up at Harriet's would mean missing Ariel and Decibel's farewell brunch at the Miracle Grill, which served the best chicken fajitas in town. I'd been looking forward to the outing, particularly the charcoal-grilled fajitas, and I knew Dad would be hurt if I ditched. On the other hand— and most importantly—I'd already eaten breakfast, and I might really benefit from some peace and quiet. Not only that, but Harriet had introduced me to Ezekiel Allen, no small favor. "I have to spend all day on my article," I said finally, "so if you can guarantee a peaceful environment, I'll be right over."

"You're a *life*saver!" Harriet cried. "Peaceful's my middle name!"

"By the way, why Connecticut?" I asked, already up and piling on the winter wear. "I can't picture you going anywhere not accessible by subway."

"In my dreams," she said. "One of my oldest friends, Liesl, is having an engagement shower for her daughter, and however much I hate suburbia, Bettina's my goddaughter and I've been unbelievably lousy at this whole role model business." Harriet chuckled. "I once ran into Bettina at a restaurant and introduced her as 'Bethany.'"

"It's her fault for having such a silly name," I said. "Oh, and Harriet, you'll never guess. I ran into Serge last night and he—"

"Hold that thought," Harriet told me. "I need you over here ASAP. Put it in the story and I'll read it when I get home."

After I'd finished getting dressed, I knocked on Dad's door. When he said "Open, sesame," I walked in and found him propped up in bed watching TV. A divinely trashy woman on the screen was pleading with a man: "Don't go. My heart will melt." Uh-oh, I thought, but I tried to sound sunny when I asked, "What's this, *Masterpiece Theatre*?"

"It's about a woman who falls in love with a Canadian hockey player," Dad said somberly. Yep, the pre–Ariel departure blues had already taken hold. Even years ago, Dad's eyes would mist over when dropping off me or Ariel at a sleepover party. He always went on about needing his daughters near him at all times and became downcast whenever one of us left. Now it was worse than ever, since he so seldom saw Ariel.

"Cheer up, Daddy. Ariel goes to college, remember?" I reminded him. "So even if we were in Houston you wouldn't see much of her."

"Since when did you become Miss ESP?" Dad asked me.

"Since always." I sat down on the edge of his bed. "Now, listen: You remember that cool woman I told you about, Harriet

Yates?" When Dad nodded uncertainly, I added, "*You* know—she's an old friend of Fenella's. Well, anyway, she needs me to go over to her house today and wait for a delivery. Do you mind? I'm not abandoning you, I swear—I just have a lot of work to do, and she needs a housesitter." Dad didn't answer, just shrugged dejectedly. I gave him Harriet's number, which he mindlessly placed on the bedside table, and kissed his forehead. "Daddy, listen, I *really* wish I could come to lunch with you, but I can't bag on Harriet, not after she helped me on the article. Besides, I'll be there in spirit, especially if you bring me a doggie bag of fajitas."Someone chuckled, but it wasn't Dad. It was Ariel, standing in the doorway.

"You refused to eat when you were a baby," she said. "When did you become Miss Piggy?"

"I dunno," I said just as the lady on TV screamed at her lover: "Damn you! I always knew you were a cold, cold fish!" at which Dad, Ariel, and I started laughing uncontrollably. A few minutes later, when I told Ariel goodbye, she threw her arms around my neck and melodramatically bawled, "You cold, cold fish!"

Our love-in on Dad's bed left me with a feeling of contentedness that was rare these days. Sometimes I forget, I guess, how nice it is to have a family. I set off cheerfully for Harriet's; even with my laptop in tow, I was bouncing, almost skipping, down the icy streets, which had grown more congested since my first trip outdoors. But then something happened. A few blocks from Harriet's, I caught sight of a familiar strawberry-blond head of hair in an Italian restaurant on Spring Street. I stopped to peer through the window, but the tiara had already given her away. It was Tinsel Mulchgarten, comically overdressed as always, sitting alone with a Pomeranian in her lap. I was about to back away when—and I can't believe I didn't see it coming—Max Roth sidled up to her table and took the empty chair across from her. It was like watching a train wreck, I swear. I stood there transfixed as he reached across the bread basket to scratch the Pomeranian behind the ears, then tenderly stroked Tinsel's porcelain cheek. So that's it, then, I thought. Max and Tinsel sitting in a tree. As I walked away, I can't say I felt sad exactly, just deflated. In itself, Max Roth's affection for Tinsel didn't bother me. If he wanted to cozy up to that vapid socialite, who was I to stop him? What bothered me was that the boy I liked—the sweet, brooding artist who devoted Sundays to his Bubbie and sometimes smiled in my direction in World Civ—no longer existed.

When I got to Harriet's, she was already in her zebra-striped coat. With dizzying speed, she pointed me to the stocked refrigerator, promised to be back by dinnertime, and barreled out the door. After she left, I explored her apartment, with its oversize furniture in childish colors, its walls surprisingly uncluttered with art. In the kitchen, tools were displayed in an old-fashioned hanging shoe organizer. Harriet had labeled every pocket with a description of its contents: "cheesecloth," "eyedroppers," and even "chicken scissors." I loved it, Harriet's home; it really was peaceful, an appreciated sanctuary after the Max fiasco. And sure enough, when I finally sat down at my laptop, I immediately plunged into a weird work trance. Afterward, I remembered nothing of hammering away at my article or scarfing down a bag of oatmeal raisin cookies or answering the doorbell downstairs. I hardly even remember my hundreds of attempts at getting the first paragraph just right. All I know is that when Harriet came home just after seven o'clock, I was sitting at her dining room table, surrounded by oatmeal crumbs, a cardboard box with an Argentine postmark, and a finished piece on Serge Ziff. Harriet's eyebrows twitched as she read over my story once, and then twice. I watched her anxiously, hoping she didn't hate it.

When Harriet put the paper down, she looked at me intently for a few seconds and shook her head before exclaiming, "You did it, champ! This is going to be big. I can feel it. I wish I weren't off to Delray Beach tomorrow, but my little sister's been clamoring for me to visit for months now. But be sure to call my voice mail with updates, will you? I can't *wait* to hear how this goes down."

After a celebratory bottle of grapefruit-infused sparkling water (Harriet's choice), we walked to Chinatown, where we feasted on crab dumplings and ginger ice cream (my choice). Then, as a shoe-patrol thank-you, Harriet treated me to a seaweed-wrap massage at a Chinese salon eight stories above Canal Street.

As I settled onto a sheet of wax paper, I wondered how I'd started hanging out with a woman nearly four times my age. My mother no doubt would have some Oedipal-Freudian-whatever explanation: Stanley would just congratulate me. In World Civ last semester, he'd always yammered on about how Asian civilizations, unlike ours, respect and cherish their elders. "Remind me to make a habit of finishing stories at your apartment," I told Harriet as two men performed a "four-handed tiger knead" on my calves.

Next to me, Harriet managed a "sure," and smiled dimly as her masseur ran a huge yellow feather over her forehead.

Dead in the Water

THE NEXT AFTERNOON, I woke from a dream in which Serge Ziff and I were racing each other on a dusty NASCAR track, while Boris Potasnik sat on the bleachers, waving colored flags and mouthing something to me. I couldn't understand him, so I just kept grinding my foot into the accelerator. Then Serge's car zoomed ahead of mine, and clumps of dirt flew off his wheels and into my eyes, and I was swerving into a ditch when—

I shot up in bed, short of breath.

My mother believes that dreams represent our unconscious world, but there was nothing subtle or encoded about this one. I'd finished my article, and I even liked it—I just didn't know if I'd be brave enough to send it.

At least it was Sunday, which meant that Ulla probably wouldn't see the article until the following morning, and I could still enjoy an evening with Dad before dealing with Ulla's awful "tweaks." It was also time—past time—to move on with my life. With freedom in mind, I hauled myself out of bed, flipped on my computer, attached the article, and hit Send. When I went upstairs, lightheaded with relief, I found Dad sitting at the breakfast table, thumbing an old Science section of the *Times*.

"Do you have any idea what time it is?" he asked me. "I was beginning to feel like a nursemaid in a World War Two movie—will the proud soldier never stir?"

I bent down and hugged my father, who had newsprint smudges on his forehead. I took a seat across from him, and as I admired his newest salt and pepper shaker set, figurines of Ronald and Nancy Reagan in their prime, I thought about how little quality time the two of us had spent together in recent weeks. Once again, he'd got lost in the shuffle of my ridiculous life. "How's it going?" I asked guiltily. "Seems like you've been working pretty hard lately."

When he first moved back to New York, Dad had focused on rekindling old professional connections, efforts that quickly paid off in the succession of freelance gigs he'd scored. "Sure have," he said now. "I just landed a commission from *Urban Nature* to shoot pictures of city squirrels. Pretty exciting stuff," he said unconvincingly, "and the pay's nothing to scoff at."

"Cool," I said. "So that's it, then?"

"That's it what?"

I looked at him hard and didn't say a word.

"That's pretty much it," Dad said, looking down at the breakfast table. "That and, well . . . you should know that . . ."

"Yes?" I coaxed.

"Fenella and I . . . how should I—well, let me put it this way. She and I saw each other last night, after your sister left, and we, well . . . we decided to take a step backward."

"But why?" I asked Dad, genuinely sorry for him.

In fumbling fragments, Dad told me that Fenella had invited

him to accompany her to the Basel Art Fair in Switzerland that May. At first, Dad said, he'd accepted enthusiastically, and they were already comparing hotels and rental cars when Fenella stumbled across the suitcase that years ago Mom had plastered with duct tape so that Dad would be able to pick it out on the baggage carousel. Appalled, Fenella had whisked him off to the luggage department at Barneys and together they'd chosen a classy tweed carryall. But as they stood in line to pay for it, Dad had a sudden change of heart. He wasn't sure he wanted it anymore, he said—not just the suitcase, or the trip, but the whole shebang.

"I told her that I *liked* my disgusting suitcase, and I didn't need any tweed in my life, now or ever. It was awful, Mimi, really awful," Dad said. "I was already a little blue about seeing Ariel go, and by the time I'd gotten everything off my chest, the Italian tourists behind us were staring at us and pointing. Poor Fenella—I'm afraid I really embarrassed her."

"So you really think it's over?" I asked. "It wasn't just a blowup?"

"I'm not sure," he said and sighed. "I think it might be. I really do want to stay friends with her—she's great, whether you see it or not." I felt another stab of guilt and wished I'd treated Fenella better early on. "She's one of the most interesting people I know in New York, after you and Quinn, of course. But, well, seeing your mother the other day . . . " Dad broke off. "Well, what can I say, Mims? It's been hard for me, this."

His eyes brimmed with tears and so did mine. The poor sweet

man. He, too, was having a bumpy ride back; only unlike me, he'd valiantly concealed his problems. As for Fenella's disappearance, well—I wasn't as psyched as I'd expected. Scarecrow frame and jangly charm bracelets aside, she actually wasn't that bad. I knew only one thing for certain: my dad needed me, and for once I'd be there for him.

And so, I invited my dad on a date. "Takeout schmakeout," I said. "I want to get dressed up and go out and paint the town beige." (That, believe me, was one of Dad's favorite expressions, not mine.)

We got dolled up and went to Wallse, an overpriced Austrian restaurant on West Eleventh Street, and feasted on Wiener schnitzel and tafelspitz and rostbraten and other delicacies with nasty names. I wore a long pink dress from the Goodwill in Houston, and Dad wore a houndstooth blazer with suede elbow patches. The outfit combo prompted Dad to observe that we looked like Scarlett O'Hara and Sherlock Holmes. "Could be worse," I replied.

Dad's failed romance never came up at dinner; we were too busy reminiscing about Ariel's attempt to toilet-train Simon and gossiping about Serge Ziff. Dad hadn't read my article yet, but he'd actually dug up some of his own dirt on Serge, who represented a woman in Fenella's book club. "I can't believe you didn't tell me before!" I said after learning that, a few years ago, Serge had sent his lesser-known artists gifts of can openers from the Home Shopping Network for Christmas. "It's elemental, Watson," Dad said in his best Sherlock Holmes voice. "Some dads can be discreet." We ordered blackberry crepes for dessert and Dad ordered a glass of port. Without Fenella around, there'd be less espresso in our lives. It was the most fun I'd had out in several months, and before going to bed Dad and I vowed to step out again soon.

My next three days at school were dull in a good way. Lily said my article had blown away her expectations, and Ulla never contacted me about "tweaks," which led me to assume that she liked my article and would be running it as is.

But Wednesday, following an afterschool visit to the charity stores on West Twenty-third Street, my dad met me at the door of our brownstone with a grim expression.

"What?" I asked him. "What's going on?"

"I'm not sure," he said. "Zora Blanchard has been calling here all evening. She wants you to come to her office tomorrow morning at seven-thirty for a meeting."

"At seven-thirty in the *morning?*" The hour seemed obscene, but then, Zora's coffee intake gave her a real advantage over the rest of us. "What else did she say?"

"Very little. When I tried to press for details, she referred me to the Baldwin Bill of Rights. But as your father, I'd appreciate it if you'd fill me—"

The phone jangled again, and Dad picked it up quickly. "Oh, hi, Lily," he said, and passed me the receiver.

"I thought you'd be Zora Blanchard," I told my editor. "Apparently she's been calling me all afternoon. How warped is that?"

"More warped than you know," Lily said. "That's actually why I'm calling. I'm not sure how, Mimi, but Zora seems to have gotten her hands on your article, and let me tell you—she is *not* happy. She says if Serge sees it, he'll withdraw his pledge, and Baldwin can kiss the new gym goodbye."

"But Lily, it's dirty money—why would Baldwin even want it?" I caught Dad's eye, and he nodded. He was troubled, I saw, but not angry, or not at me.

"That's not for you to worry about," Lily told me. "Right now just concentrate on escaping Zora with all major organs intact. From what I hear, we should seriously consider showing up to tomorrow's meeting in bulletproof jackets and Humvees."

"We?" I repeated. "You're coming with me?"

"Yeah, obviously," she replied. "I'm your editor, aren't I? I assigned the article, and I'll stick by it no matter what."

"You are the best friend, ever, in the whole wide universe," I said, and meant it. The panic set in only later, over dinner. I couldn't eat Dad's special caramel pancakes, and neither could I focus on his deliberately upbeat banter. I felt jittery, nauseated, tense.

The next morning, I woke up still feeling all of those things, but also tired and ill. I selected my clothes to reflect my serious side: gray wool pants, a white button-down shirt, and a boys' argyle vest I'd recently bought at the Salvation Army. When I arrived at Baldwin, I saw that Lily had the same idea; she'd forsaken her sweatshirts and donned a V-neck sweater for the occasion.

"You made it," Baldwin's high-strung headmaster stated flatly when we showed up at the appointed time. With her mug-bearing arm, she ushered Lily and me into her office, a room whose every surface was speckled with coffee stains. The smell, too, was overwhelming. Even the squeaky leather chairs where Zora motioned for us to sit reeked of her favorite stimulant. I had hardly eaten since lunch yesterday, so the all-pervading odor only sharpened my queasiness.

Zora got straight to business, snatching a mockup of this week's *Bugle* and ripping it open. I wondered how Zora had seen the paper so far before its Friday publication—wasn't the *Bugle* supposed to be the Baldwin student body's "independent voice"? As Zora flipped through the paper Hebrew school–style, last page first, she mumbled a running commentary to herself: "Now, let's see here, quite an interesting issue this week . . . Here on the features page, 'Ten Ways to Update Your Look Without Spending a Dime'—very cute, I like that. . . . And oh, look, in the Q & A section—'Baldwin Teachers' Favorite Excuses for Cutting Class.' Adorable."

Zora pushed back her reading glasses when she came to the editorial page. "And what have we here? 'Stop the Snapples,' an opinion piece about the new vending machine that accuses Snapple of anti-union tactics." She shuddered like a good liberal.

Zora folded the paper closed and let her eyes rest on the front page. And then I saw it—my article. The editors had put it on the front page, right up at the top, for all of Baldwin to behold. Too sickened to be pleased, I concentrated on breathing and not dry-heaving. "Oh, and look here," Zora said. "A little article claiming that the savior of Baldwin's bank account is a liar, crook, and drug trafficker." She dropped the paper, whipped off her reading glasses, and stared at me. "Now, this, Mimi, well—I'm not sure I find this very cute." Zora looked at me expectantly. "So, let's think logically here, Mimi, shall we?" she went on. "If *you* had just pledged seven figures to an institution, would *you* be impressed with this article?"

"Um, no?" I croaked with great effort.

"'Um, no,' she says," Zora told her coffee mug. "Well, Mimi Schulman, that is absolutely right. You wouldn't be impressed at all—in fact, you might even be a little angry."

"But Zora," Lily bravely interjected, "we checked out the sources, and it's all true. This is the biggest thing to hit Baldwin since grades were abolished."

Zora, however, was still conversing with her coffee mug. "What a slam dunk, really! Who'd guess that Baldwin's patron saint could be such a lowlife? And to think he's been getting off scot-free for decades!" The roller-coaster intonations of Zora's voice recalled Mikey the Magician, Houston's premier birthday party entertainer who'd recently pleaded guilty to two counts of assault against a counter-girl at Taco Cabana. There was a knock on Zora's door, and Ms. Singer strode into the room. Without acknowledging me or Lily, the *Bugle*'s new faculty advisor took a seat on the couch. And suddenly, I understood. This hardhearted shrew in the charcoal gray suit—of *course* she had betrayed me.

"The paper hasn't been sent to the printer yet, so we can recall the story without losing a dime," Ms. Singer said, addressing Zora as if Lily and I weren't there.

"You're not seriously recalling the story—are you?" I burst out. I'd worked my ass off on that article and they were just going to flush it down the toilet, like it never existed? "You can't just can—" I was stopped by another knock on the door. This time it was Ulla Lippmann who walked into the office, Ulla who hadn't said a word about my article to me but had nevertheless given it front-page treatment. "I am *so* sorry for being late!" she groveled to Zora. Like Ms. Singer, Ulla completely ignored me and Lily on the couch.

"We're just wrapping up," Zora said. "I guess there's nothing else we can do at this point except make absolutely certain that Friday's paper contains no slander about Baldwin's benefactor." Then, flinging the *Bugle* mockup onto the coffee-stained files on her desk, Zora peered down her nose at me. "And in the future," she added, "some of us might want to consider thinking before acting." When the conference was over, Lily and I wandered, dazed, into the lobby, with Ulla a few feet behind us.

"What happened?" I turned around to ask her, still without suspecting our controversy-hungry editor-in-chief had played a part in the fiasco.

Ulla stopped to gurgle some spring water from the dispenser. After wiping her sleeve over her mouth, she told me she wanted to talk. "In *private*," she added.

"Well, ex*cuse* me," Lily said. "I think I have a right to know what's going on, too, but have it your way. I left my iPod in the Undercroft, anyway, so I'll take my exit."

After Lily left, Ulla surprised me by blubbering out a long, incoherent apology. I stopped her at the twenty-fifth utterance of the word "sorry" and asked her to start over. Nodding, Ulla flicked her fluorescent rubber bands with her tongue. "Monday night," she said, "Vikram Mohini and I were in the *Bugle* office, fine-tuning a few layout issues, when Nikola Ziff stopped by. I know what you're thinking—spooky, right? That's what I thought, too, even after Nikola said that she wanted to write something for the paper and invited me and Vikram out to dinner to swap ideas." As she spoke, Ulla kept her eyes on her feet, watching her weight shift between them. "Vikram," she said, "needed to rest his chronically fatigued eyes, and as for me, well—I just couldn't get over the surrealness of the whole thing. Nikola Ziff hadn't spoken to me since the third grade, and I couldn't believe she even knew my *name*. I was so . . . " *Snap!* went a rubber band across the lobby. "Flattered, I guess." Poor Ulla, I thought, looking at the horsy girl whose mouth was permanently haloed with spittle. I could relate: I had experienced a dizzying ego rush every time Nikola had summoned me to tag along with her, Orzo, and Ricky on Bravura Island. "Dinner was pretty awkward," Ulla was saying. "We went to this shady mobster Italian joint on Court Street—the one where all the waiters trade off the same toupee? And the whole time, Nikola kept making these really stupid article suggestions—they all sounded more like bad movie plots than newspaper stories, but I was still so excited to be seen in public with her, you know? Of course, she left after the minestrone, and after that I lost my appetite. Still, I didn't figure it out until Vikram and I got back to the *Bugle* office and the proofs we'd been working on were gone." Ulla snuffled. "Vanished into thin air. Nikola must've snatched them when I went to the bathroom to brush my teeth and Vikram was putting in his eye drops. Mimi, I'm so sorry, I . . . I don't know what else to say. I guess it's my fault for getting starstruck."

How could I be mad, with Ulla Lippmann groveling at my

feet, begging my forgiveness for getting snookered by nasty Nikola? Considering the insanities I'd committed in the name of popularity, how could *I* judge anyone else's social ambitions? "That's why I didn't call you about edits," Ulla said. "I *knew* something like this would happen; I just wasn't sure when. So I swore Vikram to secrecy and we started over on the layout, as if nothing happened."

"But what about Nikola?" I asked. "Have you talked to her since?"

Ulla snorted. "Are you kidding? Third grade was nine years ago, Mimi. At this rate, I'll be thirty before Nikola speaks to me again."

At Ulla's almost wistful sigh, I felt another stab of compassion. Nikola was a truly first-rate manipulator, cozying up to Ulla to sabotage my article. The question was, why'd she bother? Even if Serge had mentioned our run-in at Dis/Play to his daughter, I couldn't imagine Nikola giving a damn. She didn't seem scandal-shy, nor did she strike me as the protective type. On Bravura, she'd brought up her father only to rail against his "pathetic" decision to invite Tinsel Mulchgarten along. But who was I to presume to understand what went on inside someone else's family, when I barely understood what went on inside my own.

Inside the Inferno

To DESCRIBE MY INDUCTION TO NEW YORK society as an emotional roller coaster would be a gross understatement. The last six months had been an emotional Around-the-World-in-Eighty-Days, and I was in a perpetual state of whiplash.

Of the many traumas I'd endured this year, two moments stood out. The first: that night in early December, when I was sitting in the hospital holding Lily's hand as she wept over her mother's mental breakdown, seconds before Pia, Viv, and Jess charged into the waiting room with the news that Sam had posted my private ramblings on the Internet, and just like that, my house of cards had come crashing down. The second memorable moment occurred exactly twenty-four hours after my tête-à-tête with Zora Blanchard and Ulla's confession. When I arrived at school on Friday, I immediately sensed something was amiss. A thick silence was stalking me down the halls and at my approach, my classmates' voices dropped to low whispers. When I passed Leonora Newfield on the staircase and innocently asked her about our World Civ terms sheet, she just muttered, "Dunno," and kept walking. On the ninth floor, I said hello to a trio of theater kids, who burrowed into their lockers in response. Why is it that when you're having the time of your life, it all flies by in a second, but when you're in abject misery, every single minute drags on endlessly? I was walking slower than normal, sometimes stopping midstride because I was too overwhelmed by the sheer awfulness of Baldwin's wholesale rejection of me to remember how to operate my limbs. What had I done to deserve this? Once, in seventh grade, I had accidentally tucked my uniform skirt into my underwear and walked halfway across the lacrosse field before detecting a cool breeze on my backside. Recalling that humiliation, I checked to make sure I hadn't committed a similar blunder that morning. But nope, my fly was securely at its northernmost point of my low-rider Levis, and my Goat Show notebook was still in my backpack, hidden from human eyes.

Why, then, did I feel so ugly and ostracized? It was only when I entered the student lounge that the pieces began to fall into place. There, thumbtacked to the large cork wall, was the *Baldwin Bugle*. It was unusual for the *Bugle* to get top billing; the lounge's bulletin board was usually reserved for psychedelic film festival announcements or flyers for banjo lessons from local potheads. I hopped over several backpacks to investigate, and that was when I saw it: my tell-all profile of Serge Ziff, front and center on page one of the *Bugle*. The headline read: "BALDWIN DAD GIVES SCHOOL $1 MILLION, BUT WHERE'D HE GET IT?" Underneath, in a slightly smaller font, ran the subhead: "A Journey from Disco Inferno to Infamy."

"You did it!" said a familiar voice behind me.

I spun around to see Lily Morton, clapping. At her side was Ms. Singer, with erect military posture and a menacing frown.

My knees buckled, and I steadied myself against the wall. The printers must have screwed up, and now I was going to pay for it. It took all my strength to declare, "I swear I had *nothing* to do with this!"

"Of course you didn't," Lily said. "Why don't you ask Ms. Singer who did? She's the faculty advisor."

"What do you mean?" I asked. I still couldn't bring myself to look directly at Baldwin's meanest educator. The bell rang, signaling the start of first period, and World Civ. But obsessively on-time Ms. Singer didn't budge. She just stood there, looking at me, until well after the bell stopped. There was a silence and then she said, "Oh, Mimi, you should know me better than *that*."

Mimi! The same martinet who always called me Ms. Schulman had addressed me as Mimi! What could this mean?

"So maybe I fudged it a little in Zora's office," she said, "but I never *seriously* considered pulling the plug. You showed real integrity in that article, and set an estimable example for the rest of the school. Forget about Zora. She's just a coward."

First she calls me by my first name, next she criticizes her boss—would wonders never cease? I'd never heard a teacher publicly criticize Zora before; it just wasn't done.

"But she's going to freak!" I cried. "What if she fires you?"

"Let me tell you something, Mimi," Ms. Singer said. "I've known Zora for a long time. About twenty-five years ago, we sat on a charity committee together, bringing marginalized poets to give readings in high-security prisons. We really hit it off, so when I came to Baldwin I'd looked forward to rekindling our acquaintance. But the way she handled this whole thing, well—

I can't remember when I've ever been this disappointed in someone. All you were doing was exercising your First Amendment rights, and as the *Bugle*'s newspaper advisor, I must commend your bravery." Was this the same tyrant who'd dismissed me as a dumb slacker and mocked my esoteric knowledge of the leisure activities of Mary, Queen of Scots? It was too much information to process at once.

"As for firing me," Ms. Singer went on, "they wouldn't dream of it. When my last employer tried that, I won a nice chunk of change in a sex discrimination lawsuit. The Baldwin higher-ups know all about it—in fact, Campbell Biers's wife was my attorney."

Cambell Biers was the chairman of the Baldwin board of trustees and one of Fenella von Dix's loftiest contacts.

"For the time being, Mimi, you're the one we need to worry about," Ms. Singer said. "There may be certain . . . repercussions for you down the line."

"I saw Zora in the hall just now," Lily said. "She's tearing through the halls like a rabid coyote, splashing coffee and screaming your name. She practically shoved John Loman down a staircase because she—" Lily broke off as Zora tore into the student lounge, frazzled and furious, all but foaming at the mouth. Her salt-and-pepper bun had come undone and her hair hung wildly over her shoulders, like a sorceress's in a medieval fairy tale. Coffee dribbled like blood from the sides of her mouth.

"Mimi Schulman!" she screeched. "Don't even think of going anywhere!" She had nothing to fear: I was already frozen in place. As the sound of Zora's purple clogs across the floor reverberated through my brain—*clomp, clomp, clomp*—the rest of the universe shrank out of focus. Lily, Ms. Singer, the pile of coats on the floor—it all just disappeared, and nothing remained to shelter me from Lady Caffeine Breath. She stopped inches away from me and, wheezing, ripped the newspaper off the wall, exposing a flyer for an Electro-Klezmer retreat in the Catskills. Without her reading glasses, Zora had to hold the paper at arm's length, and as she began to read my article out loud, she squinted at what she thought were the most offensive passages: "*While few dispute Ziff's prominence in the New York art world, some detractors question his business methods* . . . Wonderful opening line, Mimi, very impartial." Zora wheezed again, once, twice, as her eyes scanned the page. "Mmph, I especially like this part down here, when you get to the explanation of 'devil dealing'— it's *very* inventive." She read on: "*This practice, favored by theater agents and publishers in the late nineteenth century, involves indenturing new talent by forcing artists to hand over a disproportionate percentage of future earnings should they ever switch to another dealer, thereby preventing any defections. Whereas most major dealers tend to lose around a third of their clients, Ziff's defection rate hovers around three percent.*"

Zora paused to look at me. "Oh, and this sweet little interview, Mimi, this is very human interest, very touching, hearing what that sad sack dead-ender Ezekiel Allen has to say. "'*I feel paralyzed,*'" Zora read in an obnoxious whimpery voice, "yes, that's a real heartbreaker. But you really clinch it with your trenchant analysis of the Baldwin donation. Here we go, this part: *Ziff's donation to Baldwin is the largest in the history of New*

York independent schools. *'Giving money to a school helps cement a reputation as a warm-hearted, child-loving do-gooder,' observed Ira Finkelman, a professor at Columbia University who specializes in the politics of philanthropy.*

"Sorry, Professor Finkelman," Zora said with a sneer, "but we've got to keep moving to the real coup de grace, the unsubstantiated rumors of—well, Mimi, I'm not sure *what* you're implying here. If you're trying to be opaque, you've succeeded with a real bang. *But where did the money come from? For years, rumors have dogged Ziff on this subject, but the dark horse impresario has maintained a mysterious profile. On a recent visit to Dis/Play, Ziff's Chelsea nightclub, several witnesses observed illegal drug transactions in the VIP lounge, in the presence of Ziff.*"

Without even finishing the article, Zora threw down the paper. She took another step toward me, then another, and soon I could smell nothing but her rancid coffee breath. At least I had an eight-inch height advantage over her, I thought, so I could keep my eyes fixed firmly above her head, on the cherry red "X" of the Exit sign. "Well?" she demanded, shaking my shoulders. "Exactly what do you have to say for yourself?"

I opened my mouth, but no words squeaked out. My throat and vocal cords had stopped functioning. I was still trying to reply when Ms. Singer inserted herself directly between me and Zora. "That's enough for today, Zora," Ms. Singer said in the disgusted tone she employed when Arthur Gray wore fake mustaches to class. "Let go of her this instant." With this, Ms. Singer grabbed my wrist and yanked me out of Zora's grip. "Ms. Schulman has had a very trying morning, so I'm sending her home for the remainder of the school day. Ms. Schulman, you're dismissed," she said, pushing me toward the Exit sign. "Ms. Morton, if you'd care to escort her home, you, too, will be excused from classes today."

"You can't do that! I override her—" Zora sputtered as Lily hustled me out the door. In a daze, I followed Lily out the Clinton Street service entrance. She led me to the diner on Clark Street and ordered two hot chocolates to go. While we waited for the waiter to squirt whipped cream on our drinks, she popped outside to make some calls on her cell. A minute later, when she came back inside, I was too shaken to ask whom she'd spoken to. She guided me by the elbow into a yellow cab and gave the driver my address. When the driver flipped the meter, my eyes welled up; I was going to be a complete, red-nosed wreck before we reached the Brooklyn Bridge.

"Everything's going to be just fine," Lily said, reaching over to hug me. "Your Dad knows what happened and he and Quinn are waiting for you."

Even after the cab deposited us on Barrow Street, I was still too unsteady to handle keys, so Lily had to ring the doorbell. Instantly, my dad rushed into the front hall to let us in, whereupon I flung myself into his arms and immediately began crying again. "Uh-oh, you might not be ready for this," Dad said as he led us toward the apartment. "Ready—?" I braked in the doorway. "Surprise!" a chorus of voices called out, and through my tears I made out the faces of Pia, Jess, Viv, and Quinn. In one coordinated motion, the group lunged forward and engulfed me in a messy hug.

"You *guys*"—I was gushing—"you guys are beyond the best. I can't believe you ditched school for me."

"No offense," Pia said, "but skipping Baldwin isn't exactly a blood sacrifice."

"Yeah," Quinn seconded, "I'm supposed to be making prints of your dad's squirrelscapes, so this is a paid vacation!"

"But wait—how did you all even know?"

"How could we *not* know?" Jess tipped her chin at the coffee table, which was stacked high with fresh copies of the *Bugle*.

"We had to rescue them from Nikola," Viv said. "She was busy feeding them into the paper shredder in the puppetry studio."

A few minutes later, Pia took me downstairs to my room to get me cleaned up. "Wouldn't it be nice if people could tell you to get fixed up for your surprise party without spoiling the surprise?" she asked as she helped me remove my smudged eye makeup and pick out an outfit—white tights, a swirly patterned skirt, and a simple white pullover. Pia said I looked "very Alice in Wonderland" but on our way back upstairs, she noticed a "chromatic imbalance" and marched me back to my bedroom, grabbed a stringy Mexican belt off my floor and tied it around my waist. "Perfect!" she declared. When Sam and Boris arrived a half-hour later, they both complimented me on my outfit. I'm sure any *real* kick-ass journalist would want the attention focused on her talent, but I was secretly pleased that Sam said I looked like Frida Kahlo and Boris pointed out that I had much better eyebrows. As he spoke, Boris realized he was holding a bouquet of purple flowers and handed them to me. I effusively thanked him and Sam, assuming it had been a joint purchase.

Dad, meanwhile, called Village Bagels and ordered orange juice, bagels, and multiple flavors of cream cheese. When the delivery man showed up, Dad patted his pockets for his wallet, while I took the bags into the kitchen and dumped the bagels onto our largest serving platter. I'd balanced the tray in my arms and a serrated knife on the tray, and I was heading back to the living room when Dad intercepted me. "Easy there," he said, lifting the knife off the platter. "This is supposed to be a party, not a bloodbath. And besides," he said, "you obviously don't know rule number one of New York entertaining yet."

"What's that?" I went back into the kitchen with him.

"You *never* ask guests to cut their own bagels," Dad said, and began slicing a cinnamon raisin. I reached over and grabbed a poppy seed bagel, but Dad shooed me away. "Rule number two," he said, "is too many cutters spoil the bagels."

"Oh," I said. "I wasn't trying to cut it—I just wanted a bite."

Dad laughed. "Which brings us to rule number three!"

"What, that I'm a hog?"

"No," Dad said, "that's not a rule, that's a given. Rule number three, Mimi Schulman, is that I'm proud of you. You wrote a terrific article." He put down the knife and smiled at me, and I choked up with tears yet again. In the living room, Quinn was blasting cheesy eighties music but when I came in with the bagel tray, he put down a stack of CDs and presented me with a blond wig and a pair of huge black sunglasses.

"I bought them for you on Bleecker Street after getting Lily's phone call," he said, snapping the wig onto my head. "I love the witness protection look."

After eating (and after Boris and I had sampled every flavor of bagel), the baboon dancing got under way. I jumped onto the couch, which Viv and Jess were using as a trampoline, and Jess whispered to me, "You know, if we took him shopping for a day, Boris would be pretty cute!"

I blushed, but Lily spared me the awkwardness of responding by shimmying up to demonstrate a dance move she'd just invented. It involved dipping her head to her knees and whipping her ponytail back and forth. She looked happier than I'd seen her all semester, and I imitated her movements, thrilled that she was in such a good mood. This *Bugle* controversy had really brought Lily back to life. And then, louder than a firecracker, the phone rang. Dad rushed across the room to take the call, and from the sudden whiteness of his face, we could tell it wasn't a telemarketer on the other end. Jess, Lily, and I froze in place on the couch, Quinn silenced the stereo, and Boris put his plate down. "Mm-hmm, I'm aware of that . . . mm-hmm . . . ummm . . . " Dad mumbled for a minute. He crossed over to me, mouthing "Sorry" as he passed me the receiver.

The intervening hours had done little to mellow Zora Blanchard. She was still thoroughly *pissed*, and pelleted me with threatening phrases that included "unaccountable hubris," "legal team," and "provisional suspension." "This concerns the future of the finest progressive school in the *nation!*" Zora roared. "We were just ranked number two for college admissions by *U.S. News and World Report*. People are *paying attention!*" Pant, wheeze, and then, right before slamming down the phone: "The board has just called an emergency meeting, so expect to hear from us soon!" When it was all over, everyone swarmed me, badgering me for an instant replay. Though I tried to reconstruct our one-sided conversation, the only words I could remember were "provisional suspension." "So it looks like we'll finally get to spend some serious time together, Dad!" I said cheerfully. My father looked at me, droopy and mournful, and I couldn't deal. I leaped off the couch and raced over to the stereo, which I cranked up even louder than before. "Can we just dance now and commit suicide later?" I beseeched everyone. "*Please?*"

Sam was the first to help get the dancing going again. "I'm impressed," he said, bunny-hopping up to the couch. "If you get kicked out of Baldwin, I'll still be your friend." I never wanted that party to end, but by midafternoon, Quinn had to take off to an interview for a gig photographing a bar mitzvah on Long Island.

The girls dispersed next: Pia to tutor; Lily to prepare for another family dinner; Jess to rock-climb at Chelsea Piers with her investment-banker beau. When it was her time to go, Viv lolled in the doorway, waiting for Sam.

"Aren't you going to help me with Islam?" she playfully asked him.

Sam didn't budge. "It's Friday night," he said. "And right now I think Mimi needs me more than you need help with Islam."

"Fine, then," Viv snapped, and flounced out the door.

"She could've stayed, you know," Sam said when he saw my worried expression. Then, to Boris, who was next to him on the couch, he asked, "So, what now, big guy?"

"My question precisely," Dad said from the doorway. Over the course of the afternoon, he'd modified his attitude, and was now putting on a brave face, for my sake. Blessed man, he'd even agreed, after much pleading, to conceal the news of my provisional suspension from Mom, at least until we'd heard more from Baldwin.

And that night, it was Dad who took us out to dinner at the burrito bar around the corner. We all pigged out hardcore, and when we got back home, Dad gripped his stomach, moaned, "Ugh, I need to lie flat for a minute," and excused himself. I'd overeaten, too, but instead of falling into a food coma I flung my nervous energy into a huge housekeeping campaign. Why dwell on Zora when I could unload the dishwasher and Windex the hallway mirror and clear the refrigerator shelves of prehistoric condiments and scrub the counters and alphabetize the spice rack? Boris and Sam sat at the kitchen table and watched me execute these tasks. Once every surface sparkled, I led my useless companions downstairs, and continued the cleaning frenzy in my personal domain. Sam sprawled across the floor to practice the "corpse pose" he'd learned in yoga class at Baldwin, while Boris lowered himself into the armchair.

"I call this the 'lazy-ass' pose," he said. As I hurled socks into the hamper, I suddenly realized that neither Boris nor Sam had offered to pitch in. "Explain something to me," I said. "Why are guys of our enlightened generation unwilling to help out with domestic duties?"

Sam didn't answer, just breathed deeply in "corpse."

"Hmm, let's see—because they're boring?" Grinning, Boris reached down into the hamper, grabbed an armful of socks, and wound back his arm as if to pitch them across the room.

"Don't you dare!"

"Why don't you sit down?" Boris said, depositing the socks back into the hamper. "You're driving yourself crazy. Here." He got up and scooted onto the armrest so I could take over the chair. And then he asked how I was feeling.

"What do you mean, feeling?"

"You know. You've had a kind of crazy day. Or do you normally get suspended, provisionally or otherwise?"

"Oh, that." I threw up my arms. "I'm not feeling much at all right now, actually."

"Lucky you," Boris said. "If I were expelled, I'd be freaking out."

"Yeah, I *am* lucky. Lucky I don't have your crazy-ass dad to inspire terror," I retorted. "And for your information, I was *not* expelled. I was provisionally suspended." I looked to Sam for support, but he was really committed to the dead pose.

"Of course," Boris said. "Sorry."

I pushed myself off the chair. If I stayed still, the doubts would take over, so I dropped down and stuck my head underneath the armchair, where I unearthed the missing halves of three pairs of shoes and about six months of dust. When I emerged, Boris was back in the armchair, his index finger at his lips. "Hey, Mimi," he whispered. "Check out this guy."

I swiveled around and there, in the dead center of my room, my oldest friend was asleep and snoring. Sam's chest rose and fell in a staccato rhythm, just as it had when we'd napped together as children.

"What a little baby." I made a comical grimace for Boris's benefit. Boris didn't laugh back. He gazed right at me, his expression serious and intense, the same one he'd worn in the cab ride back to Dis/Play. "Hey there, cowgirl," he said softly, and motioned for me to come closer. Was this what I thought it was? I got up, moved toward the chair, and perched on the armrest. Boris's breathing quickened as I inched toward him and pressed my lips against his. He returned the pressure and then some, while his hands explored the contours of my body, quick and spazzy. I giggled—the inside of my stomach tickled. At some point I cracked open my eyes and saw that Boris's were open, too, and I was about to shut mine again when I heard a sound from somewhere behind us, a cough. And then Sam's voice: "Dude . . . And I thought the *dream* I was having was weird."

House Arrest

BACK IN SEVENTH-GRADE ENGLISH CLASS, we learned that most stories adhere to a predictable structure: buildup, climax, and resolution. If only real life worked that way.

After the unforgettable events of that Friday—Ms. Singer's defending me, Zora's suspending me, Boris's poking his tongue into my mouth—I braced myself for further drama: a cross-examination in the Baldwin boardroom maybe, a death threat from She-Michael, or a judo match with Nikola Ziff, some serious drama to up the ante. But in the ensuing days not much happened. Saturday night, the girls and I went out for sushi and then to one of Mia's bizarre parties in Prospect Heights, where I saw Harriet's rainbow-afro friend and had my tarot cards read by a burlesque dancer. (Apparently, I have a long life and many voyages ahead of me.) We slept over at Pia's and wasted Sunday watching a *Love Boat* marathon and eating Ciao Bella gelato. But when Monday rolled around and the girls went back to Baldwin, life as I knew it came to a complete standstill. After a semester spent racing in circles, neglecting loved ones, and missing crucial hours of sleep, the tempo all slowed down. Way, way down. My biggest struggle Monday involved tweezing a hairball from the bathtub drain, and by Tuesday morning, I actually missed Baldwin. Obvious drawbacks aside, school did have a way of passing the time. And now, with Quinn committed to a new energy-draining cabbage soup fast and my dad stalking squirrels in Washington Square Park, I had only the cable box to keep me company.

The girls dropped by Tuesday night to bring me boredom-busting gifts: from Viv, a home-burned CD of Israeli hip-hop, and from Pia a Pucci print bathrobe "for lolling about the house in style." Lily contributed a bucket of Margaret Morton's crispy fried chicken, straight from a "picnic" soundstage where they'd shot an episode of *House and Home* that afternoon. The most thoughtful gift of all, though, came from Jess: a DVD of *His Girl Friday*, the 1940s comedy about a kick-ass girl reporter. I loved the gifts, obviously, but I still felt sad and even the tiniest bit resentful when the girls, anxious to resume their lives, left within the hour. Afterward, the evening dragged on even slower. By Day Three of my "provisional suspension," when the thrill of watching back-to-back cop dramas had decisively passed, I gave up showering. Why bother? Boris Potasnik's silence fed my overall inertia—I hadn't heard a syllable from him since that fateful Friday and in the countless hours I'd devoted to figuring out why, I could only conclude that Boris hadn't enjoyed our kiss as much as I had.

Thursday morning, I hit my limit. I woke up, made a pot of hot chocolate, and then moseyed back down to my room to shoot off a round of desperately chatty e-mails to anyone and everyone. Lily. Sam. Rachel. Even Amanda France, the only one who wrote back right away. "Mimi Schulman, daredevil reporter!"

Squashgirl85's message began: "Been meaning to check in on you. I saw your article. Fearless stuff. I hope you're OK—you sound sort of down. I know you're not in school for now, but if ur interested in joining the Baldwin golf club (Courtney and I co-founded it last year), U totally shld! As soon as snow thaws, we go every Sat. 2 driving ranges in Westchester, L.I., etc. I'm sure you're rolling your eyes, but it's so much fun. got 2 go 2 bio now . . . C u soon, I hope! Call me. Oh and P.S. Have a great book of poetry you might want 2 borrow if ur bored. U might like it b/c you're such a gifted writer . . ."

Weird. Amanda certainly won the gold medal for complexity. Her interest in poetry just didn't seem to gibe with her squash-playing self, but somehow she harmonized the two identities like a cashmere twin set. Politely ignoring the golf suggestion, I sent a reply saying I'd be glad to borrow her book.

Then, I clicked on Google and typed in "private schools" and "New York City," to see where I might end up if Baldwin gave me the boot. The first Web site that came up was Swift, an all-girls academy on the Upper East Side, known for its rigorous etiquette seminar. Sam had predicted that a post-rehab Nona Del Nino would be shipped to this institute of lower learning, which he'd characterized as a "juvenile detention holding pen posturing as a Swiss boarding school." He elaborated: "But it's not *Swiss*—it's *Swift*. Also known as Stupid White Idiots Farting Together." As I browsed Swift's incredibly depressing Web site, page after page of girls with perfect hair and empty eyes, I vowed never, ever to stoop so low. However much it had betrayed me (and its own ideals in the process), Baldwin was the epicenter of my New York life. If I couldn't go there, I'd be better off moving back to Texas. Sure, Mom had her issues, bigtime, but at least I had a few friends in Houston—and no criminal record to prevent me from attending class with them. Viv could charter her dad's plane and the girls could even visit occasionally, who knows.

Not that I had a chance in hell of getting into another New York school at this point. I'd landed a spot in Baldwin's sophomore class only because Sam's mother had pulled some strings, but the Geckmans were the extent of my local connections. Besides, what sane person would go out on a limb for a proven troublemaker? As I surveyed the lobotomized blondes at Swift, I finally acknowledged the truth I'd been dodging all week: I was scared. Really, really scared. I'd soon be hearing from Zora, who'd probably forbid me ever to set foot on Baldwin soil again. And though Dad acted confident that everything would work out, he was no Laurence Olivier. It was beyond obvious that he, too, was freaked. Whenever he left the apartment, he'd call at least every hour, claiming that he was "just checking in," and not inquiring about the dreaded update from Zora. Six hours of cable later, I started pondering my future in Texas, and I decided to call Rachel. We'd hardly spoken since I'd canceled our tentative Presidents' Day plans, but I assumed that she had been as busy as I had. "Hey, Rach?" I said, relieved that she'd picked up her cell on the first ring.

"Mimi?" she said, as if straining to recognize my voice. "Oh, hey. I can't really talk right now because I'm kind of driving on the freeway. You know, like, behind the wheel?" Oh, God. Rachel had turned sixteen and I'd totally forgotten all about it. I was the most awful person ever. Has any worse long-distance ex–best friend ever lived? I *knew* how Rachel felt about her birthday. How could I how could I how could I? Somehow, though, I couldn't own up to my sin and apologize. I was just too tired. So instead, I imitated Rachel's sluggish tone when I said, "Whoa, you should get a hands-free device ASAP. My mom got two tickets for that."

"Actually," Rachel said, "I have one and I'm on it. But it still breaks my concentration, so I prefer only to talk on the phone when I really need to, you know?"

"OK, I'll be quick," I said, stung by the implication. "I was just thinking, we haven't seen each other in a while, and maybe you wanted to come up for that all-you-can-eat-see-and-shop New York weekend we talked about? You can get really cheap last-minute tick—"

"Mimi," Rachel interrupted, "I kind of have a lot going on right now, with AP history and Physics. Plus, I'm steering the Camp Longawanga reunion committee. Presidents' Day would've been *perfect,* but rescheduling's not really an option this late in the semester."

Then, relenting a little, Rachel promised to call me when she got home, but we both knew that wasn't going to happen. I went back downstairs and checked my e-mail for the umpteenth time that day. Finding no new messages, I randomly decided to write Harriet. We hadn't spoken since her return from her sister's in Florida, mostly because I had no desire to reveal how the whole Serge exposé had gone down. Taking the tell-all angle had been

Harriet's idea, and I didn't want her to feel responsible for the mess the article had spawned. But Harriet was my friend, and right now I could use one—especially one with a loose daytime schedule. With this in mind, I started to type. I gave Harriet a blow-by-blow of the showdown with Zora, my provisional suspension, my Swift-induced panic. I typed on and on, disposing of my happy-go-lucky pretenses and venting my terror and loneliness. It helped, of course, that Harriet wouldn't see the e-mail until long after the crisis had passed: she logged on once a season at most, and only with the help of a Kinko's staffer. After sending my confession into the void, I roamed the house in my bathrobe, skimmed old magazines, and took two naps. A rustling sound roused me from the second one. I opened my eyes to see Sam slouched against the door frame, with a bottle of red wine half hidden under his parka.

"Wine before lunch?" I was admittedly taken aback.

"It's almost five," Sam said, and then: "You're welcome." He remained in the doorway as if waiting for permission to enter. Last semester, Sam had practically lived on Barrow Street, but these visits had subsided after our hookups. Now, with Viv in the picture, he stopped by only infrequently, and never unannounced. He seemed aware of the difference, too, and it was with some self-consciousness that he walked over to the window and slid it open, probably to ventilate my moldy body odor. "I'm going to get cups. Be right back," I told him. I ran upstairs to retrieve a couple of glasses and a corkscrew, instinctively tucking the equipment under my robe, just in case Dad finished squirrel-shooting early. While up there, I took the opportunity to deodorize myself with Dad's organic air freshener. When I got back to my room, I found Sam settled comfortably in my pistachio green armchair—the selfsame site of my tongue-hockey session with Boris. "How'd you break in?" I asked.

"The Judys," he said. "You didn't answer the door, so I rang their bell. They let me in with the spare key your dad gave them—#2 told me I was an 'enlightened male,' though I have no idea what inspired that." As he talked, Sam opened the bottle and filled the glasses. "Yummy," I said after my first sip of the heavy, warm liquid. "This was really nice of you." I held up the bottle to study the label—a futile pretense, given I knew exactly one fact about wine: that it was either white or red.

"It's quality stuff," Sam told me. "My parents just bought a whole case of it. They're going through this God-awful wine snob phase. Every night at dinner, they stick their noses in their glasses and claim to detect 'undernotes' of cherry or chocolate, and then they barely touch the stuff. I don't get it—wouldn't it be cheaper just to buy cherries and chocolate?"

We agreed that wine was a waste of middle-aged energy and cash. "Gulping techniques are far more important than 'undernotes,'" I said. "The wine gulp can be the new tennis stroke. Fast and powerful. And loud. Very loud." To illustrate, I polished off half my glass in one noisy swig. "Like that." Sam applauded, and I urged him to try, remembering to add, "Just remind me to stick the glasses under my bed so my dad doesn't kill me, OK?"

Sam nodded, then performed a beautifully earsplitting swallow.

I clapped, telling him, "That would score a ten in the Gulp Olympics. You should become a gulp pro. Get it? Like a golf—"

"Oh, hey, I almost forgot," Sam said, cutting me off midwitticism. "I brought you another gift." From his backpack he pulled out the new issue of the *Baldwin Poetry Review* and instructed me to turn to page thirty-two, which featured a poem called "Molten Core."

He comes
to me
jagged cusp.
I ache,
lacerate.
He is there, and
I,
inches away,
universes
away.
With me, with me
inside the molten core of the
Earth. I sit on the station platform,
skirt torn,
heart—
he is there,
everywhere,
with me, with me,
in the engines that smear
the night sky with
ash.

Underneath the arresting composition were three unexpected words: "By Amanda France."

"Whoa," I said, putting down the magazine. I knew Amanda wrote poetry, but I'd imagined her topics to be seagulls and cherry-blossom trees, squash matches and fat-free baked goods, not, well, this. Boy, was I wrong. Or maybe I just sucked at reading first impressions. I was still mulling this shortcoming when my computer bleeped—someone had written me back at last! I trotted over to my computer, clicked on the mouse, and gasped to see Harriet's name in my inbox.

"You don't understand," I told Sam, "Harriet *never* checks her e-mail, and I only wrote her this morning. This makes me want to believe in astrology or something," I said, remembering the burlesque tarot card reader at Mia's party.

Harriet's e-mail was rife with typos and capitalization eccentricities and creative punctuation. "MIMI—have a GOOD IDEA for YOU—Theres A DINNER—TONIGHT—CINQUE—54 E. 66 ST. BE—There—with BellS ON 8OCLOCK!!!!!—xioH." I had to read the message twice before I understood that Harriet was inviting me to dinner at eight. I glanced at the clock on my computer and saw that I had only forty-five minutes to get there.

Interpreting "Bells" as "no sleepwear or athletic shoes," I decided on the kimono-style dress I'd bought at a stoop sale in Brooklyn Heights.

Getting rid of Sam was a more complicated task. "What if I don't want to leave?" he protested when I told him I needed to shower. "I'm comfortable here—can't I just sit here and read my new graphic novel? I promise I won't mess anything up." Though Sam and I were ninety-nine percent back to normal, I wasn't about to let him loose in my bedroom. Last time that had happened, he'd stolen my diary. "Sorry, but my dad might be freaked when he comes back from his shoot," I said, though I knew this was untrue. "Why not just go to Viv's?"

"I could, I guess," Sam said. "The problem is, she has a bio exam next week, and I'm getting a little tired of tutoring."

"Oh, *really?*" While fascinated by this development, I needed to haul ass. I dragged Sam up and gave his shoulders a shove. To avoid falling backward, he caught my hands and didn't let go, even after regaining his balance. He held on tight and looked me straight in the eye.

"Ew, don't be nasty!" I cried. "Seriously, I smell like a can of tuna!"

Sam's cheeks turned the color of his hair and he nearly knocked me over on his way out. When I heard the front door slam shut upstairs, I locked myself in the bathroom, scoured my mildewed skin, and tamed my eyebrows. I cabbed it to Cinque, and when I got there, right on time, I didn't regret the extra effort I'd put into my appearance. The place was over-the-top chi-chi, more like a Las Vegas casino than a restaurant, crowded with gold frescoes and shiny Venus de Milo statuettes and oversize potted palm trees.

"We don't seat incomplete parties," the buxom hostess contemptuously told me, but I'd already spotted the circular table where Harriet was seated with about a dozen immaculately dressed grownups. When Harriet saw me approach her table, however, she started shaking her head with increasing urgency, the closer I got.

Confused, I ducked behind a tree. Why did Harriet seem so

alarmed to see me when she was the one who'd invited me? I looked back at her table, and this time I understood. There, directly opposite Harriet, sat She-Michael, Serge Ziff's fembot assistant, draped in the couture equivalent of a teepee, a white swath of itchy blanket fabric irregularly cut to reveal one angular shoulder. I was plotting my getaway when a handsome waiter joined me under the palm fronds and, without a word, guided me to the ladies room and told me to stay put. "Your friend will be here shortly," he said on his way back to the dining room. In under a minute, Harriet traipsed into the palatial bathroom. "Sorry about that," she said. "I had *no* idea she'd be here, but I guess the New York art world just keeps on shrinking." I didn't reply as Harriet steered me into the handicapped stall. "Now, listen," she said, lowering her voice. "I came here tonight with a man who can help you. His name is Ed Stern, and we used to be quite close. His company, Stern Media Group, just bought a little stake in the *New York Tribune*—you know, that obnoxious weekly paper nobody ever reads?"

I didn't, but I nodded as if I did. "Well, not only is Ed an all-powerful billionaire," she went on, "but he's also a good egg—*and*, as luck would have it, a Baldwin alum. When I told him about your predicament earlier, he was *very* interested. You see—" She broke off as the bathroom door swung open.

A male voice crowed "Hell*ooo?*" whereupon Harriet unlatched the door and let a full-bellied, amiable-looking man into our stall. "Ed Stern," he said, and shook my hand. "What a fantastic place to meet someone—I should start holding board meetings in the company john."

Ed was short and balding, with shiny cheeks and crooked teeth, and he was wearing a hilarious tie patterned with cartoon crocodiles. All in all, he was the least intimidating billionaire I'd ever met in a toilet stall. Ours was massive, with a cupola-shaped sink and towel rack, but three people still exceeded its capacity and the enclosed space soon became stuffy and overheated. Harriet noticed my discomfort, and advised patience. "Some of us are making real sacrifices in here," she said. "Just think—if Ed gets caught in the ladies' room, he'll be all over the tabloids faster than you can say 'cross-dresser.'"

Ed Stern chuckled and removed his blazer, revealing stained armpits, then twisted around me to hang it on the door hook. "Harriet here tells me you've landed in some trouble," he said, swabbing his damp forehead with the crocodile tie. "If there's one thing I enjoy, it's trouble—I was thinking I'd get some of my people at the paper to do some follow-up work. How does that sound?" Ed loosened his tie and unfastened his top button. "With your help, of course."

"Fine, I guess," I said. "But I'm not sure I get it."

"Go on, tell her, Ed," Harriet prodded. But right then the restroom door opened again. Through the crack in the stall door I saw She-Michael at the mirror, rearranging her cleavage. When I mouthed her name to Ed and Harriet, their faces contorted in disgust. To reduce the number of visible feet, Ed leapfrogged onto the toilet while Harriet hoisted her butt into the basin sink. I positioned my feet in the skier's stance, and continued to peer through the door, watching Michael pressing numbers into her cell phone. "It's me," she drawled in that awful accent. "The dinner's mezzo-mezzo, I guess . . . Nah, not much . . . Oh, except, you'll like this. Remember Harriet Yates? Exactly—Miss Postmenopausal Party Girl?" Michael puckered her lips, still scrutinizing her reflection in the mirror. "Roiiight, roiight. . . . She and Ed Stern can't keep their hands off each other. They both left the table before appetizers. . . .Well, yes, roight, *exaaahctly*—when you reach *that* age, you take whatever you can get!" In the stall behind me, Harriet squeezed herself out of the basin and threaded her arm through Ed's Buddha posture to flush the toilet. After she slipped out of the stall, I quickly relatched the door and returned to my observation post. When she discerned Harriet in the mirror, Michael dropped her phone. "Oh, *haaahlo*," she said. "Excuse me, I'm experiencing some mild symptoms of *naaawshuh*." Michael tottered backward, toward the handicapped stall where Ed and I were hiding. "

I wouldn't go in there," Harriet cautioned. "I used the last square of toilet paper, and there's an *awful* stink. If you think sex is a challenge at my advanced age, try shitting." It was a close call, but Harriet's vulgarity saved the day. Michael emitted an inhuman gurgle and fled the restroom.

"Do you have a copy of your article?" Ed asked at the gilt mirrors afterward. I nodded. "Good, good," he said. "Can you come to our office on Monday morning?"

"As luck would have it," I said, "I happen to have that entire day free."

Ziffgate

AT CINQUE, Harriet had said Ed Stern owned a "little stake" in the New York Tribune. The next morning, when I called her for a postmortem, Harriet was more descriptive. Ed's "little stake," it turned out, was actually a ninety-two percent share in the operation. He not only owned the paper but exercised more influence over his staff of young reporters than a feudal lord over his serfs.

Harriet divulged a few more interesting factoids during that conversation, too. First, that she and Ed had dated once, "lifetimes ago," and second, that Ed was currently in the process of redesigning the publication, transforming the *Tribune* from a fusty society rag into a must-read broadsheet that focused on local scandals. Harriet only devoted one sentence to her long-ago relationship with Ed, but she went into great detail about the new and improved *Tribune*, as if somehow I should care more about a publication I'd never heard of than her love life.

Monday morning, when I showed up at the *Tribune*'s Upper East Side offices, the staffers flocked to me, plying me with questions about Serge Ziff. By midday, Ed had laid out his plan. My Serge Ziff exposé, he said, had the potential to grab the city's attention, to reestablish the *Tribune*. With little hesitation, I gave

Ed the green light—what more could I lose? While crediting me for the legwork, Ed had his minions verify the minutiae of my article, to back up every claim with a source. Conveniently enough, the *Tribune* reporter in charge of me, Melinda Robertson, had worked for Serge Ziff right out of college. A decade later, she still looked the part of a Ziff assistant, with her gaunt frame, anemic complexion, and spiked, Corvette-red hair. Cyborg appearance aside, though, Melinda was nothing like Michael. Melinda had a sweet Midwestern accent, a wonderful neighing laugh, and a tendency to get overexcited about botany. She'd decorated her cubicle at the *Tribune* with potted begonias and snapshots from a recent family reunion at Yellowstone National Park. When the time came (and with Harriet's permission), I handed over Ezekiel Allen's phone number and address. Melinda added his "contact details" to her microwave-size Rolodex, which overflowed with the bigtime contacts she'd collected since leaving the art world to become a society reporter.

Early in the week, Melinda and a junior reporter, Edie, trucked out to East New York, where Ezekiel hosted another tea party and corroborated my story, even supplying tax receipts to bear out his claims. Melinda also met with everyone who had accompanied me to Dis/Play that night, excluding Ariel, Decibel, and Big Priz, who were shacked up together in Austin. Of all my accomplices, Mia Steinmann made the strongest impression on Melinda. Though she hadn't actually entered the VIP lounge that night, Mia showed up to her interview in a cardboard shift dress with feathers in her hair, part of her performance piece on the migratory patterns of North American geese. The *Tribune* would be featuring Mia in its next issue. After every interview, Melinda dished out gossip about my high-profile informant friends. "Pia Pazzolini—that's one tough cookie," she said after visiting the Pazzolinis' Trump Tower digs. "I thought those big publishing heirs were all dimwits, but that girl's razor-sharp."

"She sure is," I said, "but she's not a publishing heiress. Pia's parents are these big-deal ambassadors who spend time in every country except this one."

"Come now, Mimi," Melinda said, laughing indulgently, "one doesn't just wake up and crown oneself ambassador. A century ago, Pia's great-grandfather founded the first portable dictionary company in Europe, and the Pazzolinis have been rolling in it ever since."

"Wow," I said. "I had no idea. I thought they were just diplomats."

"Mimi, darling," Melinda said, "fortunes like that do *not* sprout from government salaries."

Melinda could be condescending, but I didn't dislike her for it. The Chelsea art scene could infect even the most earnest Iowan with a terminal case of name-dropping-itis, and besides, I welcomed her insights into my new closest friends' backgrounds. Like, that Lily's mother, Margaret Morton, had been married before, to a wealthy stockbroker, and had used her hefty divorce settlement to open her first catering company. Or that Nona Del Nino's mother, Gayle, had battled a serious coke habit and once overdosed at a New Year's party at Gracie Mansion, losing consciousness at the mayor's feet. Or that, when Viv was in kindergarten, her parents separated after Mrs. Steinmann caught Mr.

Steinmann in bed with Viv's aunt. Though I generally gobbled up these tidbits, I became uncomfortable when Melinda brought up Boris. "I expected the Potasnik kid to be a real spoiled brat," she said, "but he was refreshingly normal. And what a cutie pie—he should get a patent on that hair!" I nodded, waiting for Melinda to move on. Unfortunately, she didn't. "I always used to see his dad, Alexei, at my gym," she said. "He would go at six a.m. and run an hour on the treadmill, without music or even a glance up at the television monitors. Creepy vibe. Boris, though, he seemed a bit snugglier. Have you known him long?"

"Not really," I said quickly. "Well," Melinda said, "he had extremely nice things to say about you." Yeah, right. The guy kisses me and then doesn't even Instant Message me afterward—I'm sure he had nothing but high praise. First Max Roth, then Boris Potasnik—how had I not yet learned that all crushes end in disappointment? The only people I knew who'd found eternal happiness were the Judys.

Melinda could probably read the anguish on my face, and though she was a good reporter she was also a decent person. Instead of pressuring me, she launched into a long anecdote about the party she was organizing for her grandmother's eighty-ninth birthday: "We're serving all of Nana's absolutes: ribs, coffee cakes, and Manhattans . . ." While Melinda's duty was quizzing my friends, her colleague Edie Fastow was investigating my allegations about Dis/Play. Because Edie resembled a coked-out supermodel, she fit right in at the club's VIP lounge, where she flirted with Serge's male staffers and scored a few phone numbers. "Easy," she'd said, when I told her how impressed I was. But catching Serge red-handed was a more difficult matter. On the first night, Edie saw the Neanderthal peddling his merchandise, but no Serge Ziff. On the second night, she saw Serge and the Neanderthal but never together, and found it impossible to link their activities. A frustrated Edie called me after her third trip. "It's fishy in there," she said, "but I need it to *stink* of fish." I suggested enlisting an out-of-work actor to copy Officer Padin's movements and see what happened. As luck would have it, I had the perfect candidate for the job.

Over the course of my suspension, I'd thought on several occasions about Ricky Marino, Orzo Scott's sidekick and Bravura Island's resident depressive, particularly when Quinn bemoaned the impossibility of finding a "non-psychotic guy in this city." Now, at last, I had an excuse to reconnect. That night, Ricky Marino swaggered into Dis/Play's VIP lounge in a tight NYPD uniform, black hair slicked over his elephant ears. To throw off Serge, Ricky added a pair of wraparound sunglasses to his ensemble, which only enhanced his fearsome *Terminator* presence. Before Ricky had completed his first lap around the lounge, the walkie-talkies came out and the Neanderthal stamped behind that swinging door. "Officer Marino" hightailed it out of there, and Edie stayed behind to watch Serge issue the all-clear. The morning after the "bust," Edie called her new club-employee friends and met with them one on one at different Starbucks locations all over the neighborhood. Despite having signed a confidentiality agreement when hired by Serge, one discontented bartender, unable to resist Edie, spilled the sordid workings of the undercover drug trade at Dis/Play. When the article came out in the *Tribune* the following Monday, the local media went wild. Serge Ziff had made many enemies over the years, and they all savored his downfall. By lunchtime, Serge Ziff was officially under investigation by the Manhattan district attorney's office, and *le tout* Manhattan knew it. For me, though, the most sensational item in that *Tribune* appeared on page three, under the headline THE HIGH SCHOOL GUMSHOE WHO ZAPPED ZIFF. Melinda, Edie, and a few other *Tribune* bloodhounds had collaborated on an opinion piece that depicted me as the coolest tenth-grader ever. I hardly recognized myself as I read the insanely flattering article." Most people live their whole lives and never get this kind of tribute," a teary Dad said that morning at breakfast, after reading it for the twentieth time. "You should be very proud of yourself. I know I am."

"Dad—!" I loved the man, but sometimes he overdid the cheesiness. Quinn walked into the kitchen then, flapping his copy of the *Tribune* at me. "Just one complaint, Mimi dearest— where's your glossy? I mean, honestly! What kind of publication runs a picture of that platinum platypus Ziff and not of you?"

"Hear, hear!" Dad trumpeted, getting up to grab his digital camera off the counter. "You deserve to be in the National Portrait Gallery," he said, looking through the viewfinder. "Now tilt your head up . . . good . . . that's it."

When he saw the picture, Quinn decided the *au natural* pose was too, well, natural, so he handed me Dad's green glasses and made me pretend to write in a notepad while assuming an expression of great seriousness and introspection. Over my half-hearted cries of protest, Dad took about twenty pictures before he and Quinn agreed on a winner. He then scanned the "High School Gumshoe" article onto his computer, attached the glamour shot, and forwarded it to every address in his book. Except for Mom's, that is. There was no such thing as halfway disclosures in my family—because we still hadn't told her about the provisional suspension, I couldn't tell her about the triumph just yet. And besides, it was too perfect a morning to tamper with.

White Lies, Whiter Teeth

LATER THAT DAY, Ed Stern took the Tribune staff, Harriet, and me to lunch at Rio, a Brazilian restaurant in Midtown.

"Serge Ziff is toast!" Harriet whooped, clinking her caipirinha against my Coke. "How's that for a toast?" We were seated in a plush banquette with Ed Stern and Wilson Moynihan, the *Tribune*'s beachball–proportioned lifestyles editor. The sidewalk outside the restaurant teemed with gossip reporters and local newscasters. I watched Melinda and Edie through the window as they juggled questions from five news teams simultaneously. Ed bit into his flank steak sandwich and laughed. "It's incredible," he said, swatting a crumb off his beaver-print tie, "absolutely incredible. You're a genius, Mimi, a goddamned genius!"

"So, when are you offering her a job?" inquired Harriet.

"Sorry," I told them, "but I think I should secure my diploma first."

"You never know," Ed said. "A self-starter like you might not need a diploma."

Rio's front door whooshed open as he spoke, and Melinda shoved inside the restaurant. "Those TV reporters are absolute *vultures*," she said after strutting to our table. As soon as she slid into the booth, she snapped open a mirror compact and began de-shining her nose. Then, just as swiftly, Melinda jumped back up, promising to return in a second.

She'd only gone a few steps when she whirled back around. "Oh, Mimi, before I forget . . . . You had a secret admirer swing by the office an hour ago. Asked me to pass this along."

Melinda extracted a folded triangle of paper from her skintight jeans and dropped it on the table. I waited for her to dive back into the fray outside before opening the note:

> I MISS MY COWGIRL
> IT'S LONELY ON THE RANGE
> WITHOUT MIMI SCHULMAN
> LIFE CAN BE SO STRANGE

Sam is such a wonderful freak, I thought, smiling as I smoothed out the note. How like him to deliver an unsigned poem when he could so easily pick up the phone and call me— he was obviously over our awkward little interlude in my bedroom the other night. And then I remembered something—but no, I was a delusional freak. It was just that Boris had called me cowgirl twice, the night of the dance and again on the day of my suspension, and—no, no, enough. I wasn't going to sit there thinking about Boris. He hadn't even had the decency to call me and see how I was doing. There was no use hoping he was spending his free time writing me poems.

Soon after the platter of fresh fruit was put on the table for dessert, Ed tapped his glass and stood up to congratulate his staff on their great work "reinventing this little paper." I was still stuffing myself with papaya, mango, and blueberries when Ed and Harriet got up to leave (together, I noted giddily). I stayed another hour, leaving the restaurant around three-thirty, after the media circus had relocated. Oh, well, so much for my fifteen minutes of fame. I untangled my iPod headphones and decided to walk home, however long it took. First, though, I had to find Seventh Avenue, which always eluded me in the Theater District. I stuck my headphones into my ears and walked half a block to the left, then backtracked when I realized I was headed in the wrong direction. I turned around, and the man behind me did the same thing. Noticing this, I quickened my pace, now more concerned with losing him than with finding the right street. After half a block, I looked over my shoulder, and the man seemed to be calling my name. I paused the Talking Heads track to verify.

"Excuse me?" he was saying. "Are you Mimi Schulman?" He smiled, exposing a preposterously white set of teeth.

"Why?" I asked warily. The man introduced himself as Trey Pearson, a reporter for the six o'clock news. He'd read the *Tribune* story, he said, and now he wanted to ask me a few questions. Even though Ed Stern had discouraged me from granting interviews, I found myself nodding my consent. What can I say—I'm not a natural wallflower.

Trey lifted his arm and a camera crew poured out of a white

van down the street. After the equipment was set up, Trey lobbed a lot of softball questions at me—about my background, my interest in journalism, my experiences working with a real grown-up newspaper staff. Then, just as I was lowering my guard, Trey asked about Baldwin. "We hear you've been taking some heat from the school's administration. Care to give us a few details on that?"

How had a member of the six o'clock news team learned about my suspension? The *Tribune* certainly hadn't included that detail—not even Ed Stern knew about it. "You must be confusing me with someone else," I said. "It's Wednesday afternoon," Trey pursued. "What were you doing in a churrascaria all day? Don't you have classes?"

Maybe this was my big chance, I thought, inhaling deeply. Maybe I could expose Baldwin's hypocrisy just as I'd exposed Serge Ziff.

Or maybe not. Whistle-blowing was an exhausting business, and I'd had my share of it for the time being. Besides, cataloguing Baldwin's flaws on television probably wasn't the best way to get readmitted to the school, which I still missed desperately. But is *was* a great opportunity to lay it on thick.

"I'm glad you asked," I said. "Baldwin is an amazing place, and ranks among the most progressive schools in the nation. They've been incredibly supportive of the work I've done. Sure, it was a mistake taking Serge Ziff's money, but once I brought that to their attention, the administration has been nothing but grateful."

And as I spoke, I understood that even though I was lying, I was also telling the truth. Baldwin *was* an amazing place, and I couldn't imagine my future away from it. Trey hurriedly tried to reframe his question, but I was done. I wagged my head and, like so many celebrity lawyers I'd seen do the same, I said: "Thank you. I will be taking no further questions."

Community Fabric

"It doesn't get better than that," Dad said as the end credits of *The Third Man* scrolled down the screen. "Does the trick every time." He shook out his long legs to get his blood flowing again before rising to his feet and announcing that he should get moving. He had an evening rendezvous with Fenella, to see one of her favorite world-music acts, Mnbgatu Nmekka. She had purchased the tickets before Dad had imposed the cool-down period, and they'd decided to keep the date and go as friends.

Me, I stayed on the couch, wondering if I was the only person with nothing to do on a Friday night but watch DVDs and pick through takeout containers in the fridge. After the head rush when the *Tribune* came out, I could no longer handle Zora's silence. Earlier that evening, Lily had invited me to a Baldwin party, but I wasn't in the mood to feel conspicuous. No, I preferred rotting into that couch and, in fact, heaved myself off it on just two occasions—once to pry a tub of chocolate chip cookie dough ice cream from the freezer, and once to evacuate the remote control from beneath a cluster of Fenella's floor pillows. *Strangers on the Train* had just started on Channel 40, so I prepared for another long evening.

The next day I woke up on the couch to the sight of a melted half-tub of ice cream and the sound of birds celebrating the first taste of spring. Why hadn't Fenella made herself useful and bought soundproof curtains instead of all these pillows?

Dad was sitting on the reading chair in a ridiculously huge tie-dyed Mnbgatu Nmekka T-shirt, wringing his hands. When he saw me stir, he breathed a loud sigh of relief. "I was just about to wake you. Zora Blanchard just called. She wants us to meet her at her office in forty-five minutes, so we'd better get moving."

"She called now?" I asked, already on my way downstairs to get dressed. "On a Saturday morning? Whatever happened to business hours?"

A few minutes later, Dad and I took a cab to my former stomping ground. We spent the ride gazing out our respective windows, neither of us talking much. Dad had changed from his tie-dyed Mnbgatu Nmekka souvenir and now looked almost respectable in an unironed button-down. Only I could tell that the creases on his forehead were deeper than those on his shirt.

I stopped myself from making any consoling remarks. How could I soothe Dad's fears when I shared them? I was quite possibly ten minutes from being forbidden ever to set foot on Baldwin property again, a prospect that made me extremely ill. Who would keep Dad company if I left New York—and who would keep *me* company?

Dad followed me into the Baldwin lobby, where some theater kids, who must have come in for play rehearsal, eyed me curiously. I took Dad's hand and we walked on in silence. Zora was waiting for us in her office, pacing back and forth, slurping coffee.

As on my last visit to her office, I marveled at the quantity of coffee stains everywhere—on her calendar, old napkins, students' midyear reports.

"Welcome," she said, in a tone I wouldn't exactly call welcoming. "Thanks for coming in on a weekend. I've called you here today, Mimi . . ." Zora paused for a fortifying glug. "The Board of Trustees was here until very late last night discussing your situation, and they've decided . . ." Again, Zora broke off, as if reluctant to impart bad news. "Well, in short, Mimi, it's my pleasure to invite you to reintegrate into the fabric of the Baldwin community."

Zora's voice might have said "pleasure," but her face said "Chinese water torture." She was twitching so severely that I almost didn't process the content of her statement, which was that Zora Blanchard was letting me back into Baldwin.

I wanted to laugh, to shout, to climb the wall, to kiss the tips of her purple clogs, but instead I just took Dad's hand again and squeezed it hard. He was grinning big as Zora insincerely commended my "courage and perseverance" and detailed the arrangements she'd be making with my teachers to catch me up.

Zora was so obliging, in fact, that I momentarily wondered if someone had put her up to the whole performance, but I dismissed this thought as Dad stood to shake her hand, saying, "We can never thank you enough. You'll never regret your generosity, *that* I can promise you."

"It was the least we could do. Now, Mimi, we'll see you back here Monday morning, and we're"—a brief spasm of pain passed over Zora's face—"looking forward to it."

So I didn't have to move back to Houston after all, and when Mom called on Sunday and asked, "What's up, sea urchin?" I could say in all honesty, "Not much."

Monday morning, Zora's behavior made a little more sense. Dad rushed into my room just as I was putting the final touches on my back-to-school outfit (a chunky white cardigan over a blue and white polka-dot dress). He was waving the Metro section of the *New York Times* and shouting, "You're not going to *believe* this!"

I took the paper from him and there, in the lower-right corner of page B5, was a short paragraph on the media tycoon Ed Stern's donation to his alma mater, the Baldwin School. Ed had more than doubled the pledge that the Ziff Foundation had withdrawn, making it the largest donation in the history of New York independent schools.

The article went on to say that the school would be building a new gym, a "math-kinetics" lab, a roof garden, and even an ambient-lighted yoga studio. Best of all, Ed had instituted an "endowed" chair for the faculty advisor of the *Baldwin Bugle*, effectively doubling Ms. Singer's salary overnight.

"We're just thrilled beyond words," the Metro reporter quoted Baldwin's high school headmaster as saying. "This really puts our school in a whole new league of progressivism."

A-ha! Was Ed Stern behind Zora's sudden change of heart? Had his cash somehow secured my place in the "fabric" of the sophomore class? Although it wasn't yet eight in the morning, I dialed Harriet's number. She answered on the seventh ring, her voice thick with sleep. "Yuuuuu-es?"

"Harriet, get your coffee ready," I said. I told her what I

knew—and what I suspected. "Did Ed bribe them or something?" I asked her. "Did he make them take me back?"

"Mimi, I have no idea what you're talking about," Harriet said, and giggled coquettishly. "If you really want to know, why don't you ask Ed yourself?"

"But Harriet, I need to know *now* and it's seven-forty-six in the morning."

"Hold on," Harriet said, and there were muffled noises on the other end of the line. And then Ed Stern came onto the phone.

"How's my favorite gumshoe reporter this morning?" he asked, jovial even when half awake.

Good thing I was sitting down. Ed Stern was in Harriet's *bed*? If I were a character in a cartoon, my head would have rotated around my neck ten times and my eyes would have boinged out of their sockets.

"Ed, listen," I said, and told him how uncomfortable I'd feel going back to Baldwin if he'd bought my place. I didn't want to be like Jess's icky ex-boyfriend Preston, whose admission to Dartmouth was entirely contingent on his father's alumni fund contributions.

"Mimi," Ed said, "I respect what you're saying. And I understand where you're coming from, really, so let me assure you that you have no reason to worry. I'd *never* blackmail Baldwin into inviting you back—I'm an above-the-table businessman, unlike *some* donors. All I told Zora was what she already knew: that it'd be a damn shame to let go of Baldwin's finest student reporter out of wounded pride." He paused. "That's it."

"You promise? Cross your heart?"

"Absolutely. End of story."

I hung up the phone ecstatic and amused. So Michael had been right about Ed and Harriet—good for Harriet! If anyone deserved a fun-loving billionaire, she was my top choice.

In the halls of Baldwin that morning, my classmates stopped and whispered as I passed. They couldn't have seemed more astonished to see me walking among them if I had risen from the dead. For once, I actually enjoyed being the center of attention. By Friday, though, my celebrity had faded, and the sophomore class had turned its attention to that night's blowout party at Jasmine Lowenstein's, held in celebration of her acceptance letter from Princeton. Over lunch at the same Mafia spot on Court Street where Nikola had gone with Ulla, Sam brought me up to speed on the Jasmine situation. She'd received a rejection letter earlier that week, but some insinuating phone calls from her father had secured the shoe princess a spot in the freshman class. Jasmine's proud papa had ordered champagne, hired a DJ from Hot 97's afternoon lineup, and commissioned the pastry chef from Bouley to fashion petits fours into tigers, a nod to Princeton's mascot. In assembly that Wednesday, Jasmine had invited the entire Baldwin upper school to her party, and my friends were about the only ones who turned her down. Given that Preston and Jasmine had recently taken their romance public, most people assumed that we were ditching the festivities out of loyalty to Jess, but they were wrong. Since Trevor, the investment-banking intern, had entered the picture, Jess no longer pined over Preston. In fact, she probably would have attended Jasmine's bash if not for an even better conflicting invitation.

Dad was a born entertainer, and didn't need to shell out for a celebrity chef or event planner. He could deliver the special touches all on his own, like blowing up the photo of me in his green glasses and taping copies of it everywhere—inside the freezer, underneath the toilet paper roll, on every cushion—with a different heartwarming message ("#1 Cowgirl," "Ace Sleuth," "You Go, Girl!") superimposed over each picture. It was a little embarrassing, but also very sweet. "For your next journalistic triumph," Quinn said, "you get your own Times Square billboard."

The food was a smorgasbord of old favorites: Doritos, mini-cheeseburgers, thin-crust pizza, hummus, quiches, baked ziti, ice cream, chicken quesadillas, Rotel queso with blue corn chips. An unorthodox combination, I'll admit, but a delicious one. The real showstopper, though, was the company. All but one of the ten people I know and love in New York showed, everyone except Boris, whom Dad, oblivious to all romantic distress, had invited without consulting me. Not that I cared—huffiness had pretty much replaced the initial hurt.

Harriet and Ed arrived together, she in an expensive-looking skirt suit with an hourglass cut, and he in a tan suit and a tie spotted with cartoon otters. The pair was soon entrenched in the Judys' debate over the merits of organic toothpaste.

"I don't see what the rainforest canopy has to do with gingivitis," #1 was saying.

"I'm with you," Ed said. "Aloe vera belongs *outside* my mouth."

"Believe what you want," #2 ranted, "but my daughter will *never* brush her teeth with nuclear waste!"

"By the way," #1 said, inspecting Ed's tie up close, "those wouldn't happen to be the endangered hairy-nosed otters of Thailand, would they?"

At this, I wandered over to where Ms. Singer and Lily were murmuring conspiratorially. Ms. Singer looked softer than usual in blue jeans and a fuzzy white sweater. Without the tortoiseshell combs, her hair flowed down to her shoulders. "We have some news for you," Ms. Singer told me. "It's big, so you'd better have a seat." She patted the couch next to her and I sat between her and Lily. Ms. Singer smiled and said to me, "You're sitting next to the new deputy editor of the *Bugle*." I grabbed Lily and hugged her. "You rock star! Does your mom know?"

Lily's eyes glistened. "She's—she's *proud* of me. I didn't think she knew that word, but she said it."

"But wait," I said, "what about Ulla? I thought she'd *never* share her power."

"That's the strange thing," Lily said. "She's the one who suggested it. She's graduating soon, but in the meantime she wanted one last chance to work on the *Poetry Review*. Apparently her heart hasn't really been with the *Bugle* lately and she's been concentrating on her sonnets."

"Maybe I should've invited her," I said, picturing Ulla Lippmann tangoing with Quinn. "Pia could give her some fashion tips." And speaking of which—I glanced across the room and realized I hadn't seen our glamorous Italian associate for a while. "Where'd Pia go?" I asked Lily.

When Lily only shrugged, I got up and repeated the question to Jess and Viv, both of whom responded with noncommittal shrugs. I knew Pia could be impetuous, but would she really just get up and leave my party without even saying goodbye?

"She'll be back," Jess said. "It's just . . ."

"You'll see," Viv added, raising her eyebrows devilishly. Several minutes later, Dad opened the door to let in Pia, who had changed into a black cocktail dress, with Isaac at her side. Was that why the girls had been so cagey—because Pia was bringing a date? What a ridiculous misunderstanding.

"Welcome back!" I exclaimed, to make sure Isaac felt wanted.

"Listen, Mimi," Pia said curtly, "you know how Nona was getting out of that farm school soon?" I nodded apprehensively. How could I not know? Nona's homecoming—and the social stresses it would bring—was never far from my mind.

"Right," Pia said, "so here's the thing. She's out, and this is her first weekend back in the city, and her mom's in L.A. for divorce proceedings. And well, Nona doesn't have that many friends in New York, and it's really hard for her to be alone at this point—her therapist said she needs a 'support network' and, well . . ."

So Nona Del Nino was back, and instead of stealing my friends away from me, she was trying to steal her way into my party. I laughed out loud. "You mean can she come over tonight?" I asked, and when Pia nodded, I said, "Sure, of course."

"You sure?"

"Absolutely. Call her up."

"Oh, I don't need to call her, actually," Pia said. "She's, um, waiting in a cab outside."

As Pia rushed to the window to signal Nona, I thought about

how strange it was: one semester later, and Nona was the one raiding my party instead of the other way around. The only difference was, I was terrified of Nona, whereas she couldn't have cared less about who I was when I'd shown up to her party at the beginning of last semester. She was still intimidatingly gorgeous and dour, but seemed less out-of-it and detached. Her trademark black dreadlocks had been replaced by a cropped haircut that drew attention to her huge eyes. They looked fierce, less cloudy than last semester.

Only after hugging all the girls hello did Nona acknowledge me. "So," she said at last, in an ambiguous tone of voice. "I hear you've been taking care of my girls for me." She pursed her lips and looked at me expectantly, her brow darkening.

I didn't know how to respond. Last semester, Nona had been scary, but scary from afar. But here, up close, now that I'd essentially taken her place in the group, she was much, much scarier, and all I could do was stand there, frozen and dumb. I was relieved when the doorbell rang, giving me an excuse to dart past Nona into the hall.

But when I opened the door, the paralysis returned, for there stood Boris Potasnik, his hair longer than before, but still vertical and electroshocked. He waved out his hand, slowly, shyly, and every emotion I'd supposedly flushed out of my system since our kiss came flooding back. Once I started breathing again, I wanted to bawl him out for dropping off the face of the earth, but no, I'd better leave reconciliation up to him. With exaggerated nonchalance, I brought him inside and then immediately floated over to Pia and Isaac. As Isaac detailed his adventures scouring a warehouse in the Bronx for a perfect mouse tank, I scanned the room. Ed and Harriet were slow-dancing to a Big Priz song. Sam and Boris were engaged in what looked to be a serious conversation, while Viv stood by the food table shoveling mini-quiches into her mouth. I'd never seen her eat that much or that fast. When my eyes passed over him, Boris signaled at me and screwed up his face, as if trying to communicate a message. I shrugged—why did I care?—and looked over to Nona in the corner, who was murmuring into a cell phone with her hand cupped over the mouthpiece. Boris was a jerk, a world-class jerk, just like his infamous father.

"Mimi? Earth to Mimi?" Isaac was waving his hand in front of my face.

"Sorry," I said. "What were you saying again?"

"I wanted to know if there are any good pet stores around here that carry—"

"Sorry. I need to borrow this girl for a second," Boris said from behind, and before I could defend myself, he took my shoulders and piloted me out of the living room, then down the stairs into my bedroom, where, without a simple apology, he pushed me against my Dolly Parton poster and planted his lips on mine, skipping the trancelike prekiss faces he'd made a few weeks ago. He was frantically moving his tongue around inside my mouth, and it felt warm and wet and more dribbly than the last time.

"Stop! What are you *doing*?" I twisted away from him and wiped the slobber off my mouth. "You can't just *do* that."

"What?"

"You can't just ditch me during the biggest crisis of my life, and then show up for a party, interrupt my conversation, and try to hook up with me! Could you *possibly* be any sleazier?"

"Mimi, I'm not trying to hook—"

"Maybe you want to visit Jasmine Ho-enstein." I walked over to my desk and hurled the Baldwin directory at him. "It's actually Lowenstein. With an L."

"What are you *doing?*" Boris cried as the phone book cascaded to his feet.

"Or, I know," I raged on, "why not call Nikola Ziff? You have a lot in common morally, you two." Nikola hadn't resurfaced since the paper-shredding incident. Rumor had it her father's defamation had affected her so deeply that she'd had to flee to Gstaad to complete her Baldwin course work. "What do you two do for kicks, hang out swapping stories about all the people you use?"

"Mimi," Boris said very quietly, "will you please listen to me for a second?" I had nothing more to say, so I just stood there and glared. "I was going to call you," he began, "but I walked home with Sam the night we . . . the night we all hung out here. Sam and I were just shooting the shit, as we tend to do, until I made the mistake of bringing you up. I said how cool you were, and Sam just went mute. I tried to talk to him about Vivian, but he was totally shut off." Boris looked at me imploringly. "Don't you get it, Mimi?" he asked. "Viv doesn't mean anything to Sam— he's hung up on *you*. What was I supposed to do? I tried to lay off, but I couldn't stop thinking about you." Boris took a few steps toward me, and I didn't move, not even when he reached out and placed his palms on my shoulders. "Didn't you get the message I gave Melinda?"

"The mess—?" Of course! I'd instinctively known that Boris had written the "Lonely on the Range" ditty but had managed to convince myself otherwise. So that was it, then: Sam had a thing for me, a *real* thing, and I was the last one to figure it out. I felt both sick to my stomach and extremely excited. "So Sam actually told you to back off?"

"Not in so many words," Boris said. "He pretended he was being protective, like a big brother."

"But he's *not* my brother. And he's going out with one of my friends—how does he get off telling you what to do?"

"He didn't tell me what to do. I just didn't want to piss him off. I tried to be a gentleman. Don't want to disrespect your homeboy." Boris made a fist and thumped it against his chest. "It was just very clear that he didn't want me to molest you."

"But he saw us the other night. You already *had* molested me."

"What would you do," Boris said, and he tilted his face to look at me. "What would you do if I molested you again?"

"I'll save you the trouble," I said, laughing as I wrapped my arms around his neck and leaned in to kiss him. This kiss lasted longer, and I'd soon lost track of whose mouth was whose. "I hate to admit it," Boris said when we finally disengaged. "But I kind of like pissing Sam off."

I mussed his hair. "Me, too." I nuzzled into Boris's neck before kissing him again. He smelled amazing, like detergent or croissants or both.

Fifteen minutes later, the two of us were back upstairs, in separate corners of the room behaving as if nothing at all had happened. I sat at the edge of the couch, collecting my thoughts, and, as far as I could tell, the only one who may have noticed my flushed face or matted hair or inability to stop grinning was Sam, who was standing alone in the corner of the room and grinning weirdly at me. Considering the time—not even nine o'clock yet—the party was most impressive. Even Nona, who was still whispering into her phone, didn't seem to be suffering that intensely. Quinn and Ms. Singer were lambadaing, and the girls were dancing in a semicircle with Harriet, Ed, and the Judys. I'm not saying my life was one hundred percent perfect, but things were certainly looking up. So what if I had Nona and Sam to worry about, or a summer with Mom and Maurice to look forward to? On the whole, life was pretty decent. I'd survived a very long game of cat and mouse, and hadn't lost a single friend in the process—or not yet, at least. Best of all, perhaps, I had the number one coolest dad in all of Manhattan.

"C'mere, Dad," I called out when he walked into the room.

"Just who I've been looking for," Dad said, stooping down to kiss my forehead. I grinned up at him, and just couldn't stop. Two smooches in five minutes, I thought: not too shabby. I was feeling a lot of things right then, but lonely on the range wasn't one of them.